PRAISE FOR A SONG FOR I

"Vincent B. "Chip" LoCoco transports readers to small town Italy in his stunning new book, A Song for Bellafortuna. The book is one part tribute to the beauty of Sicilian rural lands and one part suspenseful drama . . . an outstanding achievement by an Italian American with a passion for Sicily. The intriguing plot not only entertains readers but serves as a conduit to better understand rural life in Sicily."

   -Primo Magazine

"I absolutely adored this book from cover to cover. Everything about it evoked small village Italy. The characters and events were completely believable, as well as memorable, and the book managed to provide me with a strong education in opera . . ."

   -Historical Novel Society

"Vincent B. LoCoco writes a heartwarming piece of historical fiction . . . The reader can see the colors, smell and taste the food and wine, and hear the music throughout the narrative . . . The ending was moving and I was left with a shiver and goosebumps. A Song for Bellafortuna is a beautiful tale of antiquity."

   -Reader's Favorite 5 Star Review

"We are overtaken by these characters and their village 'glistening in its golden glow from the setting sun.' Within these well-crafted pages we find beautiful descriptions of Sicily and its people LoCoco clearly loves, and the seeds of hope available to all."

-John Keahey: Author of *Seeking Sicily and Hidden Tuscany*

"The author paints a picture of the era before motorcars, when agriculture provided the most employment. One gets the feeling of the slower pace of life. Journeys take longer. Distances feel greater . . .The author has a stylized voice, giving the book a fairytale feeling."

-Italophile Book Reviews

"Vincent B. "Chip" LoCoco again takes the reader on a figurative and literal journey through Italy in a spellbinding, historical fiction novel of a young man's desire to free his Sicilian village from the domination of one family's long reign . . . If you are interested in all things Italian; if you are interested in human relationships; if you are intrigued by the states of the human dimension; if music or opera are your loves, A Song for Bellafortuna is a must-read."

-Italian American Digest

BOOKS BY VINCENT LOCOCO

Tempesta's Dream:
A Story of Love, Friendship and Opera

BELLAFORTUNA SERIES

A Song for Bellafortuna - Book 1

Saving the Music - Book 2

A SONG FOR BELLAFORTUNA

VINCENT B. "CHIP" LOCOCO

Cefalutana Press

A Song for Bellafortuna
An Italian Historical Fiction Novel
Copyright 2015 © by Vincent B. "Chip" LoCoco
All rights reserved.
Revised January 2020

Book 1 of the Bellafortuna Series

Published in the United States by Cefalutana Press
Cover Design by Ana Grigoriu

ISBN - 9780972882446 (Paperback)
ISBN -9780972882460 (Hardcover)
ISBN- 9780972882453 (Ebook)

LIBRARY OF CONGRESS CONTROL NUMBER: 2015901748

Opera lyrics and translations used in the book:
"Va, pensiero" from Verdi's *Nabucco*
"Vesti la giubba" from Leoncavallo's *Pagliacci*
Both selections are in the Public Domain

Print Font: Palatino

To Matthew and Ellie:

I hope this book helps you to see that to be fully human is to live for other people, no matter what you are facing personally. This message, after Hurricane Katrina took our home and our possessions, shines even brighter for it is the measure of our true worth.

Dad
New Orleans, Louisiana

CONTENTS

"To have seen Italy without having seen Sicily is not to have seen Italy at all, for Sicily is the clue to everything."

— GOETHE, GERMAN POET

A SONG FOR BELLAFORTUNA

ANTONIO AND GIUSEPPE
SANGUINETTI

There is an ironic paradox in that courage requires fear. Fear provides the opportunity for courage. However, one must be willing to face the hard demands of courage, confront that fear, and ultimately triumph over it.

For the villagers of Bellafortuna, there was fear, but little courage. No one dared to fully take on the Vasaios, the controlling family of the village of Bellafortuna. The villagers came to believe that change would never come - neither now nor ever.

Bellafortuna, Sicily 1898

ON A BEAUTIFUL SEPTEMBER EVENING, Antonio Sanguinetti closed his wine store a little early and then, along with his nine-year-old son, Giuseppe, climbed aboard a horse-drawn cart. Just as the sun began its slow descent, sinking below the Sicilian hills far off in the distance, father and son began making their way out of the hilltop, secluded village of Bellafortuna headed toward the fertile valley below.

Antonio Sanguinetti was a wine merchant in the small village of Bellafortuna. His wine store was known as *Il Paradiso*, an homage to Sicily being referred to as the "Paradise of the Grape."

As Antonio and his son descended the hill, they passed a few of their fellow villagers who were on their way back to the village after a hard day's work in the vineyards and olive groves in the valley. Antonio greeted them all with a wave and a smile as they yelled their greetings to him and his son in return.

In his haste to leave the store that evening, Antonio had forgotten to remove the white apron he always wore while working, which was tied tightly around his waist. The elder Sanguinetti was tall and slim, with salt and pepper hair that gave him a distinguished look. He had a kind face, hazel eyes, and a pencil thin mustache that made him look slightly older than his forty-two years.

Unlike his father, Giuseppe had milk-chocolate colored brown eyes and raven black hair. But there was no denying that he was a Sanguinetti. He always enjoyed taking the trips down to the valley with his father.

Near the bottom of the hill, Giuseppe asked his father, "Papa, where are we going?"

"Vito Occipinti's vineyard. Your grandmother made dinner for the family. Vito's poor wife has been very ill."

As the cart continued down the *Via Valle*, a steep, narrow dirt road leading to the valley, Antonio held his horse's reins loosely in his hands. His horse knew the route just as well as he did.

When Antonio and Giuseppe reached the valley, Antonio slowed the cart and raised a finger upward, saying to his son resolutely, "This is how you know there is a God. Look at the valley, Giuseppe. It is stunning at this time of the day."

Even though Giuseppe had lived in Bellafortuna his whole life, the views offered by the valley still revealed to him new vistas every time he traveled there. Giuseppe scanned the entire valley, taking it all in.

Mulberry trees, with their gnarled branches, shimmered in the light of the setting sun alongside the grapevines, olive trees, and wheat fields. Patches of clouds floating in the blue sky cast long shadows that danced along the valley floor. The sound of the church bell from Bellafortuna echoed across the entire valley, letting the workers know that the workday was coming to a welcome end. Small farmhouses, with a wisp of smoke coming from the chimneys as the wives readied dinner, sat close to the road. Behind most of the homes were the vineyards, laid out perfectly, row upon row. A gentle breeze carried the smells of oleander, rosemary, and lavender from the nearby yards.

Giuseppe whispered to his father, "*È bello.*" (*It's beautiful.*)

Antonio replied pointedly, "*Bella ma triste.*" (*Beautiful, but sad.*)

After traveling a short distance, Antonio turned to the right off of the *Via Valle* and onto an older, even narrower, dirt road, the *Via Boccale*, which passed the crumbled remnants of the Boccale Winery, which at one time produced *Vino di Bellafortuna*, a wonderful, focused wine with precise scents, aromas and flavors that were produced and known all over

Sicily and Southern Italy. Now the ruins of the winery, partly protruding from high grass and weeds, were a painful reminder of the past.

Giuseppe, peering intently at the old remains, asked his father, "Papa, will you tell me again what the winery looked like?"

Giuseppe loved how his father would become animated as he related to his young son the stories of the past, which he usually did when passing through this area of the valley. Antonio's stories would always tell how life once was in the village of Bellafortuna, back when Bellafortuna was a great producer of wine and olive oil, and all of the inhabitants prospered and thrived.

However, that all changed when the Vasaios moved into the village. The Vasaios, who had made a fortune in land speculation in eastern Sicily, set up shop in Bellafortuna in 1832, loaning money to any of the villagers whose harvests were poor due to droughts or other natural disasters. The large loans were laden with heavy interest charges and were made with the condition that the loans could be called at any time. Over time, the Vasaios' power became virtually absolute, allowing them to fully control the agricultural life of the inhabitants of Bellafortuna, and which now continued under the "tutelage" of Vittelio Vasaio.

To make matters worse for the villagers, Vittelio, in the very same year that he had come to power, had his first child, a son named Santo. Like all of the Vasaios before him, Santo, at a very young age, would be sent to boarding school in Taormina. It would be expected that when the time came for Vittelio to step down, Santo would be fully prepared to take control of Bellafortuna, thus assuring that the Vasaios' rule would continue over the entire village.

Perhaps due to Giuseppe's young age or because of his father's own financial wealth, he did not fully comprehend the crushing impact that the Vasaios had on his village. While Antonio had instilled in Giuseppe the importance of living life with compassion, humility, and a willingness to help the villagers of Bellafortuna, Giuseppe's empathy remained unstirred, as he lived a carefree life in the village, sheltered from the plight of his fellow villagers.

The Sanguinettis finally reached their destination in the valley, a small home on the *Via Boccale*, surrounded by recently picked grapevines. Antonio stopped the cart and handed the reins to Giuseppe, advising his son to stay put. Antonio then climbed out of the cart and made his way to the front door. In his hands, he carried a large platter covered with a kitchen towel. At his gentle knock, a young boy answered the door.

Antonio smiled at the child and said, *"Buona sera, Vincenzo.* Where's your Papa?"

"He's still working in the fields, *Signor* Sanguinetti," the boy replied. "He's been working so hard with Mamma being sick. It's his harvest time."

"Si. I know. How is your Mamma?"

"Still not well, *Signor. Sta dormendo."* (*She's asleep.*)

"Well, Mamma Lucia made your family a nice platter of her lasagna. She asked me to bring it to you."

The young boy's eyes grew wide. Everyone knew what a great cook Antonio's mother was, especially when it came to her lasagna. *"Grazie, Signor Sanguinetti,"* said Vincenzo. He then waved to Giuseppe sitting in the cart and said to

Antonio, "Please thank Mamma Lucia for me." He grabbed the platter and went inside the home toward a small, very old looking wooden dining table.

As Giuseppe sat quietly in the cart, he suddenly became aware of the sound of horses coming at a fast gallop on the road. He turned in his seat and soon spotted three *Scagnozzi dei Vasaios* (*Bloodhounds of the Vasaios*), riding toward the Occipinti home. At the sight of them, fear gripped Giuseppe's very soul, and his heart started to pound in his chest. Just as he was about to jump from the cart and run to the comfort and protection of his father, he saw his father already walking toward him. With a forceful yet reassuring tone, Antonio said, "*Aspetta, Giuseppe.* Stay where you are."

The *Scagnozzi* passed Giuseppe, stopped their horses, and slid out of their saddles. Antonio approached them while Giuseppe sat motionless in the cart, nervously staring at the three riders.

They were wearing their normal all-black outfits, which were dark as night. Each rider wore knee-high black leather riding boots with a riding crop stuck in the outer portion of their right boot. Short black capes were wrapped tightly around each of them. Above their right breast on their capes was the Vasaio family crest: two black leopards on a gold shield. The appearance of the *Scagnozzi* always put dread in the hearts of the villagers of Bellafortuna.

The taller of the *Scagnozzi* spoke first. Giuseppe recognized the man from his visits to the store to purchase wine for the Vasaio family. He seemed to be the leader of this band of men.

In a commanding voice, the taller man asked Antonio,

"*Signor* Sanguinetti, what brings you down to the valley this evening?"

"To see a friend," Antonio said curtly. "What brings you here, Italo?"

"We are here to see Vito Occipinti. Do you know where he is?"

"Out in the fields," replied Antonio, "making a living for his family."

Italo chuckled out loud, "If that is what you call it."

By this time, Vincenzo had returned, and at the sight of the *Scagnozzi* was frozen with fear in the doorway. Italo looked past Antonio and yelled, "Hey, boy, go get your father."

The young boy only trembled in place. Antonio stepped in the line of sight between Italo and Vincenzo. He said, "Leave the boy alone. As I said before, his father is out in the fields."

Italo turned to the other *Scagnozzi* and began barking out orders to them. Suddenly, from around the back of the home, Vito Occipinti appeared.

He was covered in sweat and dirt. He walked slowly as if every step took all the energy he could muster. However, when he saw Antonio, a smile broke out across his face, and, removing his gloves, walked up to Antonio to shake hands, completely ignoring the *Scagnozzo*. He then turned toward Italo and said, "I understand you are looking for me."

Italo stood very erect, which made him look even taller than before and said, "I am here in the name of Vittelio Vasaio. Your harvest this year was very poor. You cannot meet your obligations to the Vasaio family. You are foreclosed upon. You and your family have one hour to vacate the premises."

Vito replied, "*Signor,* my wife has been very ill. I promise I will do what I can to get current on my loan. Please tell Vittelio that for me."

Italo stood stoically and replied, "*Avete un'ora.*" (*You have one hour.*)

Vito pleaded, "Once my wife gets better, I will have a fruitful harvest. *Prometto.*" (*I promise.*)

Italo repeated again, but slower this time, "*Avete un'ora.*"

"My wife is too ill to be moved."

"That is your problem, not ours."

"Have a heart, *Signor,*" replied Vito.

"In one hour, the rest of the *Scagnozzi* will be here to assist you in your . . . packing," replied Italo, with a wry smile.

Vito, fighting back tears, fell to the ground. His son ran over to him, also in tears, and collapsed on the ground in his father's arms.

Giuseppe sat in the cart with his entire focus on young Vincenzo, a boy close to his own age, holding tightly to Vito Occipinti. As Giuseppe watched the intense drama being played out, a single tear tracked down his cheek.

Vito, trying to get control over his own emotions, rose to his knees and said, "*Signor,* my family has worked these same fields for generations. Vittelio's father, Carlo, provided me with loans years ago. I cannot make the payments this year. Yes, as of late, I have been on hard times. Please. I beg you. I will make it better. My wife..." he stopped, overwhelmed by tears before crumpling to the ground with his son.

The *Scagnozzo,* unmoved, shrugged his shoulders and said, "Vittelio's orders. It is out of my hands. *Avete un'ora.*"

As the scene unfolded in front of Giuseppe, something stirred deep inside of him, an unknown, powerful feeling so intense that it frightened him, yet at the same time, reached down to the very depth of his being and strengthened him. He quietly climbed out of the cart and walked over to his own father, who had been standing nearby in silence. In almost a whisper, Giuseppe said, *"Papà, farà qualcosa."* (*Father, do something.*)

His son's voice startled Antonio. He looked down at his son, whose steely gaze was fixated on him, and whose very eyes were pleading with him to act. But Antonio had never before crossed the Vasaios or their *Scagnozzi*. Yet the way his son was looking at him, made him realize that he had to do something. Antonio patted his son on the head and then walked over and grabbed Italo by the shoulder and led him away from everyone. Giuseppe could see the two men talking animatedly for some time. He finally saw Italo nod his head in agreement.

When the men returned, Italo said to Vito, "Let this be a warning to you. Next year, if you cannot meet your obligations, you will lose your home. For now, your loan is current." The other two *Scagnozzi* looked surprised by the comment.

Italo snapped his fingers and instructed the other *Scagnozzi* to get back on their horses. From atop his horse, he said to Antonio, *"Domani.* I will be by the wine store first thing in the morning."

Antonio nodded his head in agreement.

The *Scagnozzi* quickly left the area and headed back toward Bellafortuna.

Vito, holding onto his son, stood up, and wiping the tears away, said, "Antonio, what did you do?"

"I met your obligations, Vito, for the year."

A smile broke across the face of young Giuseppe Sanguinetti, as he looked at his father. It was a look filled with pride.

"I can't let you do that," replied Vito, shaking his head.

"Yes, you can, Vito. And, yes, you will."

Shaking hands with Antonio, Vito replied, "God bless you and your family. Someway, I will pay you back."

Antonio replied, "Just get Caterina better."

"Antonio, this village is truly blessed to have you."

"No, Vito. It is blessed because of its hard-working people like you. One day, perhaps the Vasaios will leave, and then life will be good - the way it used to be for our ancestors."

Vito replied, "I dream of that day, *amico*. We all do. What a wonderful day it would be."

Antonio said, "Mamma Lucia sent her lasagna for your family."

"It will be good for little Vincenzo to have a fine meal."

"Well, go eat with your family, Vito. *Buona sera.*"

With that, Antonio told Giuseppe to get in the cart. As Antonio climbed back into the cart, Vito came over and shook hands with Giuseppe. "Take care of your Papa, Giuseppe."

"I'll try, *Signor* Occipinti. Mamma Lucia and I will do our best."

Vito chuckled and then quickly grew serious and said to Antonio, "*Grazie.* I don't know how to thank you."

"Don't tell anyone, that is all I ask," replied Antonio.

"I will respect your wishes. *Addio Sanguinettis. Addio.*"

———

IT WAS dark by the time Antonio and Giuseppe began making

their way back to their home in the village of Bellafortuna. Antonio spoke very little, as he reflected deeply on the events of the evening and how he had been persuaded by his own son to act. He was certain that Vittelio Vasaio was already made aware by the *Scagnozzi* of what had occurred down in the valley. Vittelio would not be happy that Italo had given into Antonio, and that Antonio had gotten involved.

Giuseppe interrupted the thoughts of Antonio when he asked, "Papa, will they be all right?"

"The Occipintis? They will be fine."

Giuseppe took a deep breath and then asked, "Papa, one day, will the *Scagnozzi dei Vasaios* come in their black outfits and kick us out of the wine store and our home?"

Antonio immediately noticed the concern in Giuseppe's voice. He tried to relieve the child's anxiety. He smiled at his son and said, "No, Giuseppe. Don't be concerned. We do not live in debt to them."

"But why are we different?"

His father was quiet for a few moments. He then replied, "It is the way life turned out for us, Giuseppe."

"I was so scared when the *Scagnozzi* rode up."

"You showed courage. I am very proud of you. Remember, God wants us to always stand up to powerful people who are treating others unfairly. With your nudge tonight, that is what I did. That is what you made me do."

"You did a good thing back there."

"His wife is so sick. I feel just terrible for them. They're under such constant pressure because of the Vasaios."

"You did the right thing."

"*Si*. But don't tell anyone, ok."

"Ok, Papa. I won't tell anyone. Can I tell Mamma Lucia?"

Antonio laughed and replied, "*Si*. She will be a nervous wreck all night. When we get home, I want you to go straight to bed. You have a big day tomorrow. Your first day as an acolyte."

Giuseppe nodded his head in agreement, as the little cart made its way along the winding road back to the village of Bellafortuna.

LATER THAT NIGHT, Antonio thought about Vito's words from earlier. Indeed, it would be a wonderful day if the Vasaios could be forced out. All of the villagers of Bellafortuna shared that same dream.

Every now and then, there were rumblings among the villagers that the time had come to remove the Vasaios; that it was time to stand together and bring freedom to the village. Eventually, however, such feelings would quietly die out, as the villagers had no idea how to bring their dream to fruition.

They believed it would take a miracle. But, miracles never happened anymore, at least not in Bellafortuna. The idea of freedom became just a hope, an idealistic dream. So, they, along with Antonio, went on with their simple lives in the village, all the while praying for that miracle.

2

BIAGGIO SPATALANATA AND THE SANGUINETTI SLAP

*T*he next morning, Giuseppe jumped out of bed before sunrise, excited about his first day as an acolyte at the *Chiesa della Madonna*, the Baroque house of worship located on the southern side of the *Piazza Santa Croce*, the main square in the village. Giuseppe got dressed and kissed his father goodbye.

The Sanguinettis lived above their wine store, *Il Paradiso*, which sat directly on the opposite side of the Piazza from the Church. Giuseppe quickly made his way across the Piazza.

The *Chiesa della Madonna* was the focal point of the entire village; well, at least until the palatial *Palazzo Vasaio* was built on the Eastern side of the Piazza. The Church was now dwarfed in size by the home of the Vasaios. But, it was still a beautiful structure and was an integral part of the life of the village. The exterior was a pale yellow limestone that, on cloudless days, glistened under the Mediterranean sunlight.

On the right-hand side, there was a two-story rectory. The entire complex was landscaped with beautiful gardens.

A tall bell tower stood on the left-hand side of the Church. At the top of the tower were rounded-archways around the four sides. The single bell was mounted at the top, directly in the middle.

The church bell was interwoven into the fabric of the life of the village. It provided serenity and order to the lives of the villagers. It called the villagers to work, let them know the time of the day and told them when work was over. It also called the faithful to mass, and it announced the death of a villager whenever it tolled. But more than that, it reminded the villagers daily that God was with them. During the day, when the sound of the bell echoed all across the valley, it offered solace to the villagers hard at work in the fields. It provided a gentle reminder that, although life was difficult under the Vasaios, they were not alone.

Almost the entire village of Bellafortuna was Catholic. Even those not Catholic were respected because of the way life was lived in the village. Live a good life, put up with the Vasaios, and God would welcome you to Paradise when your time was up, was the way an inhabitant of Bellafortuna lived his/her life.

Monsignor Carlo Montarsolo was the pastor of the Church. A very young priest, Padre Pietro Mancini, aided him. Their status established them as the voices of reason in the village, the people with a direct connection to God. When they came to Bellafortuna, the villagers hoped that they would lead the effort to rid the village of the Vasaios. However, neither Monsignor Montarsolo nor Padre Mancini ever said anything derogatory or insulting about Vittelio

Vasaio and his family. The inhabitants of Bellafortuna never heard from the pulpit on Sunday that the Church was ready to stand with them and support any effort to end their oppression.

For years, even before the present priests came to serve Bellafortuna, the religious leaders remained silent. Some people believed it was because of monetary deals that were worked out years ago by the Vasaios, perhaps even with the Vatican itself. But those may have been merely rumors by believers trying to figure out how their religious leaders could remain so silent. Be that as it may, the villagers liked both priests, and the priests did perform their duties well around the village.

Giuseppe had spent a whole week learning what was expected of him as an acolyte. After that week of training, he was assigned to the daily 6:00 a.m. weekday Mass. This was the typical assignment for new altar servers.

Giuseppe arrived at the Church at 5:45 a.m. and entered the sacristy to prepare for Mass. Monsignor Carlo Montarsolo was saying Mass that morning. Padre Pietro Mancini had been in charge of Giuseppe's training. He was very kind to Giuseppe and showed him exactly what to do during the Mass. Monsignor Montarsolo, on the other hand, was not kind to the acolytes.

The parishioners respected Monsignor Montarsolo, and he was thought to be a kindhearted person. The acolytes would disagree with that description. Giuseppe had been warned during his week of training by the other acolytes that Monsignor Montarsolo was known to snap his fingers on the altar to get the attention of the acolytes, shout at them during and after Mass, and even to slap them.

While Giuseppe was getting dressed that morning in the sacristy, Monsignor Montarsolo came up to him. The Monsignor was dressed in a beautiful vestment, blood red, laced with gold trim. Large gold cuff links on the Monsignor's shirt under the vestments protruded out. He asked in a very authoritative manner, "Young man, who is the other acolyte who is supposed to serve with you today?"

"I don't know, Monsignor."

"Where the hell is he? Mass is about to begin. *Gran Dio! Bel rispetto!*" he mumbled as he stormed off, adjusting his French cuffs and cuff links under his alb.

Giuseppe finished getting dressed, grabbed the crucifix, and waited for Monsignor Montarsolo to walk to the front of the Church for the procession. Just at that moment, a small, frail-looking boy came running into the sacristy.

The boy ran up to Monsignor Montarsolo and apologized to him for being late. Before he finished, Monsignor Montarsolo let his right-hand fly. It struck the young boy right across his left cheek.

With tears in his eyes, the young boy went to get dressed. Giuseppe looked at Monsignor Montarsolo and thought to himself that Jesus would not have done that. God would be offended by the Monsignor's action.

The young boy quickly got dressed and grabbed a candlestick, and then the trio walked outside the Church to the front to start the procession up the aisle. As they did so, Giuseppe extended his hand to the young boy and said, "My name is Giuseppe Sanguinetti. This is my first day."

The young boy, still with tears in his eyes, shook Giuseppe's hand and said, "My name is Biaggio Spatalanata. This is my second month. I have seen you before. We are in school together, but my birthday is in March, so you are a year ahead of me in classes."

Monsignor Montarsolo snapped his fingers and said very sternly, "*Taci!*" *(Quiet!)*

As they reached the front of the Church, the 6 a.m. Angelus sounded from the bell tower. When the bell stopped ringing, the voice of a villager, Turiddu Monachino, bounced off the buildings in the Piazza, as it did each day at this time, as he yelled his usual question to the Vasaio home: "*Vittelio, sei morto la notte scorsa?*" *(Vittelio, did you die last night?)* Then, after yelling his question, he would urinate on the wall of the *Palazzo Vasaio*, loudly cursing the whole time, before returning to his establishment.

Turiddu was the owner of a small *trattoria*, Bellini's, named after the famous bel canto opera composer, Vincenzo Bellini, from Catania, Sicily. His entire family (wife, son and daughter) worked in the small *trattoria*. The *trattoria* was located on the same side of the Piazza as Antonio's wine shop and very close to the *Palazzo Vasaio*. Turiddu Monachino hated the Vasaios. Having a fiery and passionate personality, he could not understand why the inhabitants of Bellafortuna never rose up as one to throw the bastards out.

As Giuseppe and Biaggio started to walk up the aisle of the Church, they tried to keep from laughing as they thought of Turiddu, shouting at the Vasaios' home and relieving himself on the wall of their home.

At the front of the Church, Giuseppe noticed the pew reserved for Vittelio Vasaio. It was unoccupied, as usual for a weekday Mass. However, Vittelio was the first of all the Vasaios to actually attend Sunday Mass. Ada, his wife, and his retired father, Carlo, never attended Mass with him. His son, Santo, was already away at school. Vittelio always sat alone at that Mass and left without speaking to anyone, except for congratulations to the Monsignor or Padre Mancini on their sermons.

Giuseppe and Biaggio made their way to the altar, and the Mass began. Monsignor Montarsolo's homily that day concerned the second part of God's most important commandment, "Love your neighbor as thyself." He explained that this was to be done by following the Church's teachings concerning moral obligations.

Giuseppe leaned over to Biaggio and whispered, "He sure did not show love to you."

Biaggio smiled and nodded his head in agreement.

At the offertory part of the Mass, Monsignor Montarsolo went to pour wine into the chalice. However, the flask that held the wine was empty. The Monsignor shot a glance filled with anger over to Biaggio.

Biaggio walked up to the altar to retrieve the flask so that he could quickly fill it. Giuseppe was just a few steps behind. The Monsignor's hand was shaking with anger. As Biaggio reached for the flask, Monsignor Montarsolo raised his right arm, and for the second time that morning, let it fly.

The light reflecting off of the Monsignor's cuff link caught Giuseppe's eye. Just as the Monsignor cocked his arm back, Giuseppe reacted. He leaned over and pushed Biaggio out of the way. The Monsignor's hand made full impact with Giuseppe's face instead, with his chin being scrapped by the cuff link. Giuseppe grabbed and wrapped both of his arms around the Monsignor's right arm, held it, and would not let go. The parishioners gasped. Two male parishioners, Tomaso Gianfala and Nicolo Bonura, who were the village barbers, quickly rushed onto the altar, grabbed Giuseppe from behind, and pried his arms loose to release his hold on the Monsignor's arm.

The two men brought Giuseppe to the sacristy. They could not believe *Signor* Sanguinetti's son had attacked the Monsignor. Giuseppe tried to defend himself, but they would not listen. They told him to disrobe, and they would take him home and would speak with his father.

After Giuseppe had left the sacristy, Monsignor Montarsolo tried to begin the Mass again after taking some moments to compose himself. He turned to Biaggio and snapped his fingers. Biaggio, in awe at what Giuseppe had done for him, walked off the altar and went to the sacristy to disrobe. He then left the Church.

Antonio Sanguinetti, who was in the wine shop preparing for the workday, was indeed mortified when he was informed by Tomaso and Nicolo what happened at Mass that morning. He assured them that appropriate action would be taken.

When the two men left, Antonio berated his young son. Giuseppe tried to explain what happened, but Antonio would not listen. Antonio said, "The Monsignor is the symbol of the Church. He represents God Himself. What is the matter with you? Are you a heathen? I thought I raised you better than that." Antonio then said with emphasis, "Giuseppe, we have to be very careful what we do in the village."

Giuseppe stammered back, "Papa, at dinner, when we discuss religion, you always say the Church is not the pope and the priests. The Church is the people. The Monsignor is a mean man. Look at my chin; he cut it with his cuff link."

"Giuseppe, you attacked the Monsignor. You were wrong.

There can be no argument. Go to your room. *Lasciami. Va! Va!*"

Shortly after Giuseppe had left the wine store and went upstairs to his bedroom, there was a knock at the wine store door. Being early in the morning, the curtains were pulled shut over the large window that faced the Piazza, not allowing Antonio to see who was at the door. When Antonio opened the door, he noticed a young boy. The boy said, "*Signor* Sanguinetti, my name is Biaggio Spatalanata. May I come in for a second?" Biaggio had seen the two men exiting the wine shop and had waited for them to cross and leave the Piazza before approaching the Sanguinetti wine store.

Antonio asked, "You're Dondo's boy, aren't you?"

"*Si.*"

Antonio let him in, and Biaggio explained to Antonio all that had transpired that morning and how Giuseppe had protected him. When he finished speaking, Antonio had tears in his eyes as he realized that Giuseppe was just trying to help the young boy. Antonio called Giuseppe down to the wine store and told him that Biaggio had explained everything and that perhaps Giuseppe was correct in what he did.

Antonio told them, "There are men in this world who will do anything at all costs for control. Power has that influence. Vittelio Vasaio, at one time in his life, was a good person. But the power ruined him. Even some of our religious leaders act with such temerity. They are corrupted by power and influence. They forget that Jesus never wore French cuffs."

Giuseppe and Biaggio both grinned broadly, thinking of the Monsignor and his own pair of gold cuff links.

Antonio continued, "Never be afraid to stand up to the

powerful. The alternative is fear and degradation. I am proud of what you did, Giuseppe."

Giuseppe said, "Papa, I don't want to be an acolyte anymore."

"Giuseppe, I don't think you or Biaggio have to worry about that. I don't think the Monsignor wants you to be one either."

Both Giuseppe and Biaggio showed relief in their faces. Antonio then told the two boys to come get a bite to eat before they walked to school together.

As they left for school a short while later, Antonio slowly closed the door after them. He had raised his son well, he thought. Giuseppe had stood up for what he believed in and had done so to a powerful person to make his point. His deceased wife, Giuseppina, would be proud.

Unbeknownst to all, a friendship that would last a lifetime had been born between Biaggio and Giuseppe.

3

LUIGI TAVELO

*A*fter Giuseppe and Biaggio left for school that morning, Antonio began sorting through his wine inventory at *Il Paradiso*. It was understood by all that Antonio would groom his son to take over *Il Paradiso* one day. It would offer Giuseppe the opportunity for a comfortable life in Bellafortuna, and hopefully, like his father, the ability to avoid ever going into debt to the Vasaios.

For generations, the Sanguinetti family had owned the wine store. Antonio had inherited it from his father, Salvatore Sanguinetti, who, in turn, had inherited it from his father, Gianni Sanguinetti.

Il Paradiso was a large-sized store, with numerous wine bottles laid row upon row on wooden wine racks. A large window next to the front door looked out toward the *Piazza Santa Croce*. A small table was set up inside by the window where villagers and visitors alike could sit and have a glass of wine and watch time pass by out in the Piazza.

Antonio always had the best stock in his store, even better than the wine stores in the much larger nearby cities of Palermo and Monreale. Bellafortuna was situated only four miles northwest off the *Corsa Calatafimi*, the main road that ran between the two larger cities. Even though the village of Bellafortuna was easily accessible by a well-maintained narrow road, it remained secluded because of its hilltop location. However, because of its excellent inventory, *Il Paradiso* had a good reputation along the northern coast of Sicily. Antonio's store profited from sales of wine to local *Palermitani* or tourists who, on their return trip to Palermo after seeing the famous *Duomo (Cathedral)* in Monreale, made the trip to the hilltop village of Bellafortuna.

Antonio made two trips a year to the mainland of Italy to visit Rome, Florence and Milan to purchase wines from producers and distributors whom his father, Salvatore, and he had grown to know well over the years. The trips were regularly taken in July and November. On those trips to the mainland, Antonio would take the opportunity to indulge in his other passion.

He loved opera and never missed an opportunity to see a performance at the glorious opera houses located throughout Italy. He also would travel the seven miles to nearby Palermo with his neighbors to see operas at the *Teatro Massimo*, the largest opera theater in all of Sicily.

Antonio became a major sponsor of the *Opera Orchestra di Bellafortuna,* which had been in continuous existence in the village since the late 1700s. The small orchestra performed opera concerts on the last Sunday evening of each month, usually to a large audience sitting out in the *Piazza Santa Croce.* The vocal part of the music was provided by a few selected villagers, none professionally trained, but at least in fine voice. Usually, before the end of the concert, the audience would sing along, not always in key or in tandem.

On that September morning, Luigi Tavelo came into the store. He was a very kind, friendly man and a confirmed bachelor. He was also the owner of a bakery, *Primavera*, which was located next door to the Sanguinetti wine store on the Piazza. For the past ten years, he was the conductor of the *Opera Orchestra di Bellafortuna*, having succeeded his own father. Although Luigi had no professional training, he excelled at playing music, and with many passing years of experience and serious dedication, he became an accomplished conductor. The present twenty-five members of the orchestra had great respect for him.

Luigi had come into *Il Paradiso* to get a bottle of wine for a special dinner he had planned that night. Antonio, neatly dressed with his white apron tied tightly around his waist, was working behind the counter at the back of the store

Luigi said, "*Buon giorno, Antonio.*"

"*Buon giorno, Luigi.* How's the bread?"

Laughing, Luigi said, "It's rising. How's the wine?"

"*Bene. Molto bene.* Drink too much of it, and you won't rise."

Luigi laughed heartily and said, "I heard your son made quite a first impression as an acolyte this morning."

"Oh, he most certainly did. I guess he must be the talk of the village by now. I hope Mamma Lucia doesn't find out about it."

Luigi responded, "Yes, probably a good idea to keep that from her. She is such a nice lady and has done such a wonderful job helping you raise that boy."

"When Giuseppina died, I did not know what I would do. I try my best to raise Giuseppe. But it's hard. Mamma Lucia has saved me. There is not a day that goes by that I don't think about my wife. I miss her so much."

"You have a good boy, Antonio. She would be proud. Even if he attacks priests."

Antonio rolled his eyes and laughed hard.

Luigi said, "It's a glorious day in Bellafortuna. Not a cloud in the sky. The Piazza will be filled at siesta time today. All of the vineyard workers will be relaxing after their morning toil in the fields. And they have very little to show for it. Damn the Vasaios."

Antonio replied, "*Vero.*"

Luigi asked, "Have you heard about the Occipintis?"

"What about them?"

Luigi said, "Vito's harvest was poor this year. I am hearing that the *Scagnozzi dei Vasaios* are preparing to foreclose on the Occipintis' home and vineyard. They say Ada Vasaio is directing this one. Supposedly, Vittelio is reluctant to act, but he can't stand up to that wife of his from Taormina. *La donna dall'inferno.*" (*That woman from hell.*)

"Actually, the *Scagnozzi* showed up at Vito's vineyard last night. Giuseppe and I were there."

Surprised, Luigi responded, "You were. What happened?"

Antonio said, "Those poor people. It was a terrible sight. I committed to the Vasaios to get current on the loan for the Occipintis."

How did you get them to agree?"

"Italo was there. *Gli piace il mio vino.*" (*He likes my wine.*)

"Vittelio Vasaio will not be happy with you getting involved. As you know, after a foreclosure, he always lets a

Scagnozzo and his family take over the land until he can sell it to another villager."

"I know, Luigi. My son asked me to step in. I could not say no. I had to do something."

"Thank God Vito's vineyard is saved. But I am worried for you. The Vasaios are very powerful, with even more powerful friends all over Sicily and Italy."

"I am more concerned that eventually, with none of the villagers willing to purchase property on credit from the Vasaios, Vittelio may own all of the vineyards and olive groves in the valley. Then we will have to live with a tenant farmer economy. That is probably what he wants."

Luigi said, "He must be furious that you helped a villager."

"Oh, I am sure he is. I had never witnessed an actual foreclosure by the Vasaios before. I just had to do something. I wish financially there was a way I could assist all of our villagers. But that is not realistic. I couldn't sleep at all last night after Giuseppe and I returned. I kept replaying the scene at Vito's vineyard over and over again. All of our villagers live under the control of the Vasaios."

Antonio grew silent and slowly walked to the window that overlooked the *Piazza Santa Croce*. Luigi quietly watched Antonio, who was looking out of the window toward the eastern side of the Piazza. Antonio was staring directly at the *Palazzo Vasaio*, which served as both the residence and office for Vittelio Vasaio and his henchmen. Antonio was certain Vittelio was sitting in his first-floor study, pouring over account books, making sure he was getting every overcharged penny owed to him from the villagers. He then thought of Giuseppe's actions this morning, defending Biaggio from the Monsignor.

Antonio took a deep breath and then turned toward Luigi and, while pointing to the *Palazzo Vasaio,* said with conviction, "I have come to the absolute belief that we have to find a way to destroy the control of the Vasaios over our people."

"But how, Antonio? How can we overcome their domination?"

"I don't know. We have to try. Thanks to Giuseppe, what occurred last night at Vito's vineyard was just the opening volley of a much larger war. Vittelio and his *Scagnozzi* will be watching me now."

"And for that, I am very worried for you and for all of our villagers."

Antonio walked over to Luigi and putting his hand on his shoulder, said, "Storm clouds are gathering, Luigi. I can feel it. We need to come up with a plan to rid us once and for all of the Vasaios. How? I don't know. Perhaps it will take a miracle, and so be it. We will seek a miracle if need be."

Luigi laughed, saying, *"Un miracolo.* It may take more than a miracle. It would certainly require a great deal of courage by our fellow villagers."

"Ah, *mio amico,* you are at the very heart of the matter. Nothing will happen without the coming together of all of our neighbors. It may be a long time away, but there will come a day when we will all rise as one and remove the Vasaios from power. The key is keeping our people together, waiting for that day when we will act. That is what kept me up last night. I tried to think of ways to bring our villagers together, preparing them for the day when we can act and rid ourselves of the Vasaios. Little steps for now, while we wait. Which brings me to a proposition for you; I have been wondering if you would do something for me?"

"Anything, Antonio. For all that you do for this village, all you have to do is ask."

"These people of Bellafortuna are special people. They work hard every day, they work for their families, they work for their village, but in reality, all they are working for is to line the pockets of the Vasaios. I want to give them back something, even if it's just an hour's worth of enjoyment once a week."

"They deserve it, Antonio. We all do. What do you have in mind?"

With passion in his voice, Antonio said, "*Musica.*"

Luigi asked quizzically, "*Musica*? What do you mean?"

"Music, and especially opera, can touch a person's soul in a way that nothing else can. The music allows one to inhabit another world. To feel the pulse of the orchestra as it plays a beautiful line of music combined with the passionate sound of the human voice stirs the heart. It can bind the listening audience together.

"You know that on the one evening of the month when the orchestra plays out in the Piazza, these people, if only for a short time, are able to forget about their lot in life, under the rule of the Vasaios. They can get lost in the music; it is a peace that only music can provide. And that is what I want to give them, Luigi. *Pace.*" (Peace.)

"Antonio, I would love to give them that, but exactly what are you proposing?"

"Instead of a monthly concert, I want the *Opera Orchestra di Bellafortuna* to perform in the Piazza every Saturday afternoon during the last hour of siesta. Our villagers with good voices will continue to sing the arias at those concerts. Giuseppe and I will provide wine and cheese at little cost. Perhaps, through music, our dual-purpose can be achieved. The villagers will get peace from a hard week's work, and at the same time, they will grow closer with each other. Our villagers will be biding their time, as we all prepare a plan to one day take down the bastards."

With a chuckle, Luigi responded, "Antonio, you are a dreamer, beloved by us all, but a dreamer none the less. Let's give it a try and see how it works."

"*Grazie, amico.*"

4

ANTICA CAMPANÈLLA

*I*n Bellafortuna, siesta occurred every day from 12:00 p.m. to 2:00 p.m., with all work ceasing in Bellafortuna, the valley, the groves and the vineyards. Siesta was a time for the villagers to renew their energy for the rest of the day. The Vasaios always believed that siesta made the villagers more productive, so they were willing to allow it to continue. Most of the locals, a majority of whom had been working in the vineyards and in the olive groves, would all congregate during this time in the Piazza.

The *Piazza Santa Croce* was a beautiful centerpiece for a small village like Bellafortuna. In the middle of the Piazza, sat a large statue of the revered Enzo Boccale, the founder of the Boccale Winery centuries before. During siesta, under the shadow of the Boccale statue, the villagers would eat light lunches, and discuss different aspects of life; in particular, just as earlier generations had done, their dislike of the Vasaio family.

Antonio's Saturday concerts began immediately. Young Giuseppe would help his father at a table set up in front of *Il Paradiso* where the wine and cheese were sold to the villagers.

As Antonio had hoped, for one hour every Saturday during siesta, the residents of Bellafortuna, who came to love the weekly concerts, were able to have a peaceful respite from work and get lost in the music while drinking wine provided by the Sanguinettis. All the while, young Giuseppe listened to the beautiful music and voices resounding throughout the Piazza.

From an early age, music affected Giuseppe, and it had to be a direct result of his upbringing. While the orchestra played, his father would relate to Giuseppe the story of the opera from which the music was being played.

Without a doubt, Giuseppe's favorite story and favorite aria was the recently premiered opera, *Pagliacci*, by Leoncavallo and its great tenor aria, "Vesti la giubba." Tears would well up in his eyes whenever it was played, as Giuseppe would think of the poor clown in the opera, broken-hearted over his lost love.

Giuseppe's early years were filled with music, love and happiness. He enjoyed a carefree life living in Bellafortuna raised by a loving family: his father, Antonio and his grandmother, Mamma Lucia. He also began to spend hours on end with Biaggio, and their friendship grew closer and closer.

BIAGGIO WAS the youngest of three children and the only son. His father and mother, Dondo and Victoria Spatalanata, lived down in the valley, where they grew grapes at their small vineyard, located very near to the ruins of the old Boccale Winery. The Spatalanata family had worked these same fields and lived in the valley for generations. It was hard work from which, thanks to the Vasaios, they reaped few rewards.

Biaggio was a small boy for his age. He had been very ill as a baby. As a child, he was somewhat frail-looking. Because of his sickly condition, he could not work in the fields for long periods of time with his family. Instead, he handled all of the household chores for the family.

Giuseppe towered over the much smaller boy. Biaggio, like Giuseppe, had dark hair and dark eyes. He was very thin, and his hair was always unruly. He was a quiet child with few friends. As the weeks since their meeting passed, Biaggio began to feel most comfortable with Giuseppe. The two friends enjoyed spending as much time as possible together.

The two of them worked at the outside table in front of Antonio's wine store during the concerts on Saturday afternoons. Every now and then, Giuseppe and Biaggio would also partake of a swig or two of Antonio's wonderful wines.

After working the first time at the table, Antonio told Biaggio, "For your hard work today, here is some money for you."

"*Signor* Antonio, I can't take that. I just like spending time with you and your son."

"Yes, you can take it, and you will."

"*Grazie, Signor* Antonio. I will give it to my family to help."

Working the table also introduced Biaggio to the magic of

opera. Before each aria was performed out in the Piazza during the concerts, Giuseppe would tell Biaggio the story behind the aria. Thanks to Giuseppe, Biaggio grew to love the arias.

In turn, Biaggio introduced Giuseppe to fishing, his favorite hobby, as the two dear friends began to enjoy together all that Bellafortuna had to offer.

Every weekend, the two friends would go to the *Stagno Azzurro*, a pond located in the valley, and fish, sitting among the ruins of the *Cappella di Campanèlla*, an abandoned chapel located at the water's edge.

The two friends also loved spending time together, exploring the earthquake destroyed village of Campanèlla down in the valley. All of the residents of Bellafortuna had a strong connection to the valley, and the remnants of the old village of Campanèlla now referred to by the locals as *Antica Campanèlla*. Before Bellafortuna was built on the hilltop, Campanèlla, centuries before, had been established in the valley.

DATING BACK TO ANCIENT TIMES, this valley had always been inhabited. Over many centuries, the Greeks, the Romans, the Byzantines, the Arabs, the Normans, the French, the Austrians, and the Spanish Bourbons all ruled the area. By the 16th century, the village of Campanèlla was established in this green, fertile valley. It was named *Campanèlla (small Church bell)* after its chapel, the *Cappella di Campanèlla*, located along the banks of the *Stagno Azzurro*.

Those early villagers were well aware that Campanèlla

was blessed with a beautiful location and fertile soil. Over time, they gave their village the nickname, *Bellafortuna.* *(Beautiful fortune.)* Unfortunately, its location did not always prove to be so fortunate.

In 1752, an earthquake destroyed the entire village of Campanèlla. Under the leadership of Enzo Boccale, the owner of the Boccale Winery and the producer of *Vino e Olio Bellafortuna*, the villagers immediately set out to rebuild the village they loved so much. In order to avoid the destruction of their village again, the decision was made to move the village two miles from its original location in the valley, up a large hill containing many olive groves and vineyards. It was built perched dramatically high upon a hilltop. The views offered by the new location were indeed spectacular. To the North, in the far distance, was the deep blue expanse of the Tyrrhenian Sea. To the South, beyond the green valley, one could see the heartland of Sicily.

With its new location, and almost as if to tempt fate, the name of the village was officially changed to Bellafortuna. Its inhabitants hoped that by changing the name, so too their fortune and destiny would improve as well. Of course, because of the arrival of the Vasaios, that was not to be.

GIUSEPPE AND BIAGGIO crawled all around *Antica Campanèlla*, pretending to be the old inhabitants of the village. Often, they would wander around the ruins of an ancient, outdoor Greek amphitheater where once the early inhabitants of the valley had seen live drama and which now only provided to the villagers of Bellafortuna another glimpse of the valley's ancient past. The amphitheater was located by the *Stagno Azzurro,* near the ruins of the *Cappella di Campanèlla.* Giuseppe would stand on the stage of the amphitheater and sing arias from operas to Biaggio and the birds down in the valley. "Vesti la giubba" was his specialty, at least in the fact that he knew the words. The quality of his voice, on the other hand, was not something to brag about.

During Giuseppe's peregrinations with Biaggio, together roaming all over Bellafortuna, the valley and its surrounding areas, Giuseppe was afforded a close view of the controlling hand the Vasaios had over his fellow villagers. However, because of his youthful and happy outlook on life, as well as his family's financial position, he never realized the full extent of the suffering caused by poverty.

When Giuseppe was not in school or spending time with Biaggio, he spent a large portion of his time at *Il Paradiso.* Antonio taught young Giuseppe everything there was to know about running the store. And most importantly, he taught Giuseppe how to get the best wine at the best prices to stock *Il Paradiso.* But to fully learn the trade, Antonio knew it was imperative that Giuseppe travel with him to the mainland of Italy to see how Antonio got such low prices and good wines from the different producers and distributors.

Arrangements were made with Giuseppe's teacher to have him bring his schoolbooks and work assignments to keep up with his studies.

For the young boy, that trip would alter the history of his life and the village where he lived forever.

5

THE PREMIER OF GIORDANO'S
FEDORA

*I*n November of 1898, father and son carried their luggage to the stables located behind *Il Paradiso*. Onofrio Pandolfini, the brother of Antonio's late wife, Giuseppina Pandolfini Sanguinetti, was the stable master. Onofrio was a caring, simple man, who, after the loss of his small olive grove to the Vasaios many years ago, was offered the job of stable master by Antonio. To aid Onofrio in attaining some feeling of self-worth, Antonio always referred to the stables as the Pandolfini Stables. Antonio kept his own horse and cart at the stables, and visitors to the store and other establishments in the Piazza were directed to park their own horses and carts there as well.

Antonio and Gualtiero del Monaco jointly owned the stables. Gualtiero del Monaco was the proprietor of a large restaurant, Del Monaco's, located on the Piazza next to Antonio's wine store.

Antonio and Giuseppe loaded their luggage into the cart

that Onofrio had prepared for their journey, and they traveled to Palermo. As Antonio always did on his trips, he left the horse and cart with Giorgio Bertocchi, one of his wine distributor friends who lived in Palermo, and then traveled by train – crossing by ferry to *Reggio di Calabria* - all the way to Milan. Giuseppe was mesmerized by the entire train trip, as the landscape of Italy rolled by the window. It was all so beautiful. As they passed the different wine-producing areas of Italy, Antonio explained to Giuseppe which wines came from those regions, who were the main producers and distributors, and what wines were the better wines to sell back in Bellafortuna. Particular mention was made of which wines sold well to the different clientele who came to the store from Palermo and Monreale, since they provided such a huge profit to the store.

The majority of the wines stocked by Antonio were Sicilian wines, particularly Regaleali, both Nozze d'Oro and Rosso del Conte. But, as a result of his trips to the mainland, he carried wines from the Tuscany region, especially Chianti; as well as the Valtellina wines of Northern Italy; wines from the Pavia region; Frascati from the region around Rome; Lacryma Christi wines from Campania; and Orvieto wine from Umbria.

Antonio's knowledge of wine amazed Giuseppe. He wondered if he would ever have such a vast knowledge of wine as his father did.

When Giuseppe and Antonio finally arrived in Milan, they walked out of the train station and into the commercial powerhouse of Italy. Giuseppe was immediately in awe of the size of Milan and how fast everything moved in comparison to his hometown.

Antonio and Giuseppe walked the streets to their hotel, carrying their luggage with them. As they walked, Giuseppe looked around at the sights of the big city. The buildings were huge, and the streets were filled with people.

For a southern Italian or a Sicilian, Milan was the best place to seek employment. Most of Italy's industry was located here. There were great restaurants, unbelievable fashion stores and three opera houses.

Once their bags had been placed at the hotel, *La Piccola Casa*, located a few short blocks from La Scala, the great opera house, Antonio took Giuseppe for a brief tour of the city.

One of their stops was to view the painting by Leonardo Da Vinci of The Last Supper located in the convent next to the *Santa Maria delle Grazie* Church. Giuseppe had never seen anything so beautiful before in his life.

After viewing a few more sights around the city, including the *Duomo (Milan's cathedral)* and La Scala, father and son made their way back to the hotel. A sign near their hotel caught the attention of Antonio. It read:

Premiere of Fedora by Giordano
Tonight at the Teatro Lirico

Antonio excitedly said, "We must get tickets. Imagine the chance to see the premiere of an opera."

Of course, the performance was sold out, but for triple the price and minus one pocket watch, Antonio and Giuseppe had their tickets. Antonio thought the cast seemed promising, except for the tenor, whom he had never heard of before. This would be the first opera young Giuseppe would attend.

In 1898, the world of opera was at its height of glory with new operas written regularly and the cities of Italy packing the theaters to see the new works. Verdi had crowned his illustrious career with *Falstaff*. Puccini had set the world on fire with *La Bohème* and was working on the music for *Tosca*.

The opera composer, Umberto Giordano, was coming off of a huge success with his opera, *Andrea Chènier*. It had brought him fame and financial benefits as his opera made the rounds of opera houses all over the globe.

His publisher, Edoardo Sonzogno, urged him to begin work on a new opera. Giordano's choice for a subject was a play by the French playwright, Victorien Sardou. The play was called *Fedora*. After repeated attempts by Giordano, Sardou finally agreed to permit the composer to turn his play into an opera. At once, Giordano engaged Arturo Colautti to prepare the libretto for *Fedora*.

Colautti finished the libretto quickly. Throughout the rest of 1898, Giordano worked on the score. He wrote the two main roles specifically for the voices of two close friends, a husband and wife. Roberto Stagno was to be the tenor, and the wonderful soprano, Gemma Bellincioni, was to sing the lead. While Giordano was completing the orchestration for *Fedora*, the tenor died suddenly of a heart attack.

Giordano and Sonzogno immediately set about trying to find a replacement. The lyric tenor, Fernando de Lucia, was the first choice, but he had been fighting with the management of the *Teatro Lirico*, so he was out of the question.

They searched all over Italy to find a suitable replacement.

During their quest, Sonzogno was told about a young Neapolitan singer.

Sonzogno heard about the reviews and asked the soprano, Bellincioni, to travel from her nearby villa to the opera house in Livorno to hear this young singer.

When she attended the performance, Bellincioni was at first unimpressed with the young singer. That was until the tenor reached the climax of "Vesti la giubba". At once, she was bowled over. Never before had she heard such a sound come from the throat of a human being. The hair on her arms stood up as the young singer let loose with his vocal volley.

After the performance, she went backstage and met the young singer and was immediately captivated by him. Upon leaving the theater that night, she telegraphed Sonzogno, advising him of the young singer's magnificent voice and urged that he should be signed immediately for the part of Loris in Giordano's opera. Sonzogno agreed.

Opening night for *Fedora* was set for November 17, 1898. Many *Milanisi* turned out for the premiere, as well as a father and son from the small village of Bellafortuna, Sicily.

ANTONIO AND GIUSEPPE arrived at the Teatro Lirico just a few minutes before the start of the opera. As they made their way into the theater, young Giuseppe was very impressed with the well-dressed ladies and gentlemen. Father and son took their seats in the theater just as the conductor walked toward the podium. The composer himself, Giordano, conducted the opera.

From the start, for whatever reason, it seemed the opera

was doomed for failure. The crowd sat quietly throughout the entire first act, which ended in hushed silence. Antonio, not impressed with the opera, kept thinking that he had given up a perfectly good watch for nothing.

Giordano was beside himself with grief during the intermission, afraid that he had a flop on his hands. Sonzogno paced nervously backstage, counting the losses he would suffer as a result of this failure.

And then, the second act began.

In the second act, the tenor made his first appearance in the opera. The young, virtually unknown singer walked on the stage and immediately sang the aria, "Amor ti vieta". The crowd sat quietly throughout the aria, but this time in enraptured silence.

At the conclusion, pandemonium erupted in the theater. Bravos rang throughout the house. The entire opera came to a stop. The young singer, with a gleam of confidence, bowed to accept the applause. The audience demanded an encore. The young singer obliged. A star was born that very night. The opera was saved.

For the rest of the performance, Giuseppe sat mesmerized while his father had tears in his eyes. At the end of the opera, the young tenor was met with bravos ringing down on him from throughout the theater. Giuseppe joined the crowd in giving the singer a standing ovation, clapping spiritedly for the tenor. Giuseppe leaned over to his father and said, "Imagine that voice singing 'Vesti la giubba'."

Antonio said, "I already am, and it's magnificent."

From that night on, Giuseppe could never get the unbelievable sound and passion of the young singer's voice out of his head. He would never forget the absolute majesty and beauty of that voice. It was a deep, rich and powerful tenor voice.

The young singer's name was Enrico Caruso.

AFTER A LONG OVATION and many curtain calls at the end of the performance, Antonio and Giuseppe went to get supper at a Milan restaurant.

A lady sitting next to them at the opera had recommended Angelo's, which was located close to La Scala and very near their hotel. The restaurant was packed with operagoers from the *Teatro Lirico*. They were electrified by the performance of Caruso.

The restaurant had a few photos of singers on the walls as well as posters of operas. The tables in the restaurant were decorated with Valtellina wine bottles with a candle stuck in each bottle.

After they placed their order, Antonio and Giuseppe spoke about their experience that night. At one point, Giuseppe asked his father, "Papa, why doesn't Bellafortuna have its own opera company?"

"We are too small, Giuseppe, and too poor."

"Not if we had singers like Caruso. One day, I want to bring opera to Bellafortuna. I want to convert the old Greek amphitheater in *Antica Campanèlla* into a venue for opera."

Antonio chuckled and said, "Giuseppe, what do you think? Caruso would sing in Bellafortuna for Mamma Lucia's spizatedda? No! God wants you to be a wine merchant. Stick with that. *Capisce*?"

Their conversation came to a halt when Enrico Caruso and

some friends walked into the restaurant. The group sat at a table very close to where the Sanguinettis were sitting. Antonio said, "Giuseppe, I believe that may become the greatest voice in the world. He is terrific."

"I agree, Papa. This was my first opera, but that voice moved me like I never knew I could be moved. It definitely is better than the voices of the villagers in Bellafortuna during our concerts."

The Sanguinettis spoke about the performance for the rest of their meal. As they were leaving Angelo's a little while later, Giuseppe walked by the table where Caruso was sitting. The singer was enjoying a very large portion of spaghetti and meatballs.

Moved by both the emotion of seeing his first opera, as well as by the effect of Caruso's voice, Giuseppe stopped by the tenor's table and said, "*Signor* Caruso, I am Giuseppe Sanguinetti from Bellafortuna, Sicily. You will be the greatest of the greatest."

Caruso's friends looked at one another, amused that this young boy was saying such a thing. Giuseppe continued, "Your signature song should be 'Vesti la giubba' from *Pagliacci*. After hearing you sing tonight, I can't wait to hear you sing it one day. Your voice would fit it beautifully."

Caruso put his fork down on his plate and stared in amazement at the young boy. He finally said, "*Grazie, amico.* I hope you are right about my career. And I will listen to your idea and will think of you whenever I sing 'Vesti la giubba'."

With that Caruso shook hands with the young boy. As Giuseppe started to walk away, Caruso said, "*Aspetta. Un momento.*" Caruso reached into his pocket and pulled out a pen. On a napkin from Angelo's, he quickly started to draw a picture. Not only was Caruso a fantastic singer, but he was also a truly gifted artist, a great caricaturist.

After a few moments, he handed the napkin to Giuseppe. On it, Caruso had drawn a caricature of himself, in full clown costume from the opera *Pagliacci*, with his mouth wide open, belting out an aria. Across the top of the drawing, he wrote the words, "To Giuseppe Sanguinetti, Vesti la giubba. November 17, 1898, Angelo's *Milano*, Enrico Caruso."

Giuseppe smiled appreciatively when he saw it, and he thanked Caruso. Caruso pulled Giuseppe close and whispered into his ear, "You are an admirable young man. If you ever need me, please feel free to call upon me." Giuseppe nodded his head in agreement and then turned and ran to his father to show him the drawing.

As they walked through the door, Antonio looked back toward Caruso's table and mouthed the word, "*Grazie.*"

The young Caruso winked back with a smile.

6

PADRE PIETRO MANCINI

When Antonio and Giuseppe returned from their trip to the mainland, Antonio placed a frame containing the drawing by Caruso on the sidewall near the front entrance of the wine store. As Caruso's fame grew and grew, villagers and visitors alike who came into the store were told about the meeting Antonio and Giuseppe had with Caruso and how young Giuseppe told the great tenor that "Vesti la giubba" would be his song. Antonio took great pride in telling the story.

After seeing his first opera on the stage in Milan, opera became Giuseppe's passion. He started going to see operas in Palermo, the feared bastion of the Mafia, with his father and Biaggio.

At least twice a year during the opera season in Palermo, the entire village of Bellafortuna would shut down. Many of the villagers would climb into wagons and carts and make the seven-mile journey to Palermo to see the emblazoned love stories and tragedies of opera at the newly built *Teatro Massimo*, located in the heart of Palermo. Being too poor to purchase anything better, the villagers would buy a large number of the cheap seats in the balcony in the *Teatro*.

The residents of Bellafortuna were despised by some of the big city folk of Palermo. The *Palermitani* would make insulting remarks to the villagers on their way into the Teatro. Thankfully, during the performance, the villagers were seated in the balcony and were isolated from the local audience.

After the opera, the close-knit community of Bellafortuna inhabitants would return to their carts and wagons and head back home, usually trying to dodge the tomatoes being thrown at them by a few of the *Palermitani*.

Once they cleared the city and were on the road back to Bellafortuna, the villagers, some whose clothes were discolored with tomato stains, would begin to sing the arias from the opera they had just attended and, as any good Italian would do, argue about their reviews of the evening's performance. The love of opera kept the inhabitants of Bellafortuna willing to put up with the journey to Palermo. It provided a momentary respite from the daily pressure of living in debt to the Vasaios. Giuseppe hated the way his fellow villagers were treated by some residents of Palermo, but he loved seeing the operas there with his father and his friend.

Over the next few years, while attending grammar school, traveling with his father, working at the wine store, spending time with Biaggio, and living life in the village, Giuseppe was afforded a wonderful opportunity for growth - personally, intellectually, and spiritually.

As Giuseppe made his way into his teens, he grew into a

very handsome boy. He was tall for his age. He had a gleam in his eyes and the aura and presence of a person who would grow up to be someone special. He almost always had a smile on his face, and that smile would brighten up an entire room. He was very well-liked by his fellow villagers, who enjoyed his good-natured personality.

Twice a year, he took trips with his father to the mainland of Italy, which provided them with the opportunity to attend operas together. During those trips, Giuseppe saw and heard the greatest singers, performing the greatest roles in the greatest opera houses in Italy. His knowledge of opera grew.

However, Giuseppe never had another opportunity to see Caruso again. The tenor's career had taken off and, after his debut at the Metropolitan Opera House in New York City in November 1903, the tenor stopped singing in Italy and became a fixture at the Met every year.

One July day in 1903, Antonio and Giuseppe returned from one of their trips from the mainland, as always, just in time for the Festival Boccale, the annual festival held in honor of the founding father of the village. Antonio had with him a Victrola that he had purchased on the trip. He and Giuseppe set it up near the entranceway of the wine store, below the frame containing Caruso's drawing. As they did so, some villagers began to inquire, "Sanguinetti, what the hell is that contraption? It looks like a tulip."

Antonio laughed as he pulled out a record and put it on the machine. He had purchased only one record for the Victrola - Caruso's 1902 recording of "Vesti la giubba". When Caruso's voice leaped out of the horn of the Victrola, the villagers in the store stood in awe. This was the greatest voice they had ever heard. Sanguinetti's contraption was wonderful. As the voice of Caruso sailed out of the open door and echoed off the buildings in the Piazza, numerous other villagers sitting out in the Piazza shook their heads in disbelief. They were amazed at the power and the beauty of that voice. They all gathered around the Victrola. When the aria was finished, they demanded that Antonio and Giuseppe relate once again the story of hearing Caruso live and their meeting with the great tenor at the Milan restaurant after the performance.

GIUSEPPE'S TRIPS with his father to the mainland of Italy were not only taken up with opera and wine. Antonio took him to see the famous historical sites of Milan, Florence and Rome. He saw the great pieces of artwork, the magnificent architecture and the beautiful land of Italy. No one of Giuseppe's age in Bellafortuna had this type of education.

Rome became his most beloved destination with the Coliseum in Rome, perhaps his favorite of all the ruins. Giuseppe tried to imagine the gladiator fights that had once occurred on the very spot. Giuseppe spent long hours walking among the ancient ruins of the Roman Empire. On these walks, he would think about the great Roman leaders and people who had walked on these same streets.

Whenever he was in Rome, Giuseppe always had to go to the top of the *Castel Sant'Angelo*, which is the building in Rome from which Tosca takes her fatal leap in Puccini's opera of the same name. From the ramparts of the building, one was afforded a panoramic view of all of Rome and its surrounding seven hills. Giuseppe loved taking in the view. The dome of St. Peter's Basilica loomed off in the distance.

Antonio was an excellent tour guide. He was an astute student of history, particularly of his Italian and Sicilian homeland and the stories of peoples' striving for freedom and liberty throughout the world. He put all of his learning in the form of a story for Giuseppe. When the trip was over, father and son would make their way back home to Sicily. Giuseppe would be filled with the sites and sounds of Italy and his father's wisdom, and Antonio's wine store filled with the purchases he made while away.

IN THE MEANTIME, Giuseppe's love of music grew. One day, shortly after his 14th birthday in 1903, and while on his way back to *Il Paradiso* after school, he walked in front of the *Chiesa della Madonna*. A few people were mingling outside the Church. Giuseppe noticed Signora Fiorenza D'Arcangelo.

She was the owner of a clothing store, *Meridiana*, located on the Piazza. A woman running a business was unheard of at this time, yet Fiorenza D'Arcangelo was a different type of woman. A fifty-year-old widow without children, she threw herself into her business. She took great pride in her shop. Her prices were moderate for the poor villagers. She made most of the clothes herself.

She was stunningly beautiful, and all the men sitting out in the Piazza would always sit up straight when she passed by, wishing her a good day.

Giuseppe thought she looked as gorgeous as ever as he approached her and said hello.

"Ahh, Giuseppe. How is your father?"

"*Bene, Signora.*"

"Please tell him hello for me. I need to go see him and get some of his wonderful wine."

"He would like that, *Signora*. Why is everyone standing around outside the Church?"

"We were having chorus practice when a *Scagnozzo* came in and demanded to see Alfredo Cocuzzo. The *Scagnozzo* demanded that we leave, so we did of course, while poor Alfredo was berated and threatened in Church to get current on his loan. He just left in tears."

As Giuseppe was speaking with her, the sound of an organ and a singing voice from inside the Church caught his attention. He recognized the song as Handel's "Ombra mai fu" from the opera, *Xerxes*, which aria the *Opera Orchestra di Bellafortuna* played often at the concerts.

He asked, "Who is playing the organ and singing?"

"That's Padre Mancini. He is our Chorus Director. I think he hid himself up in the choir loft while the *Scognozzo* yelled at Alfredo."

"I love that song he is singing."

"Well, with the arrival of the *Scagnozzo* our rehearsal is over. Go in and listen. Padre Mancini won't mind."

"It was nice speaking with you, *Signora*."

Giuseppe entered the Church and looked up to the choir loft located directly above the front door. Padre Mancini was playing the organ and singing. Giuseppe made his way to a pew and sat down. There was no one else in the Church. The young priest had a beautiful voice that must have been professionally trained.

At the end of the aria, Giuseppe stood up and clapped.

The man peered down over the ledge of the choir loft and said, "*Grazie, amico.* I didn't think anyone was in here."

Giuseppe responded, "Padre, it is Giuseppe Sanguinetti. I heard the organ and singing from outside and felt compelled to come inside. That was beautiful."

"*Gran Dio.* Giuseppe Sanguinetti. It's been a long time since we have spoken. I see you at Church, but you leave before I ever have the chance to speak to you. I know you're out in the Piazza every Saturday helping your father with those concerts, but Monsignor Montarsolo thinks it's not proper for us priests to be out in the Piazza during the concerts. I disagree, but I have to listen to the Monsignor. Some of us don't know how to stand up to the powerful." The priest said the last words of that sentence with a smile on his face. He then told Giuseppe to stay right there, and he would make his way down from the choir loft.

When he had come down, he came over to Giuseppe and shook his hand. "How is your Papa? He is a good man."

"He's doing fine. He's fighting a touch of the gout. Mamma Lucia's food got the best of him."

The priest laughed and said, "From what I hear about her cooking, it's a chance one is willing to take. Just put your health in God's hands and Mamma Lucia's spoon."

Giuseppe knew Padre Pietro Mancini was a nice man, dating back to that first day Giuseppe served as an acolyte. He wished he had had the opportunity to get to know him better. He asked the priest, "Padre, where did you learn to sing like that? Your voice is truly wonderful. And to think, that aria you just played and sang is about how beautiful are the branches of a tree, and yet, you made it into a religious experience."

The priest looked curiously at Giuseppe and asked, "How in God's name do you know what that aria is about?"

"My father taught me everything I know about opera. For years now, as the *Opera Orchestra di Bellafortuna* plays out in the Piazza, my father tells me the story behind the opera being played and what the aria being performed is about. I have also seen many operas across Italy and, of course, in Palermo."

"I had no idea you had that much knowledge. Do you sing or play music?"

"Unfortunately, my father does not have a musical bone in his body. He loves music, but he can't play and has never had training. I suffer the same fate."

"Giuseppe, as Saint Augustine always said, 'to sing is to pray twice'. I learned how to sing and play instruments in the seminary. As a seminarian, we were expected to learn Gregorian chant, which music I came to love. When I entered the seminary in Rome, I soon discovered the joys of opera at the Rome Opera House. That music affected me, and I was hooked. I don't get to see much of it anymore. But you can bet that when the orchestra plays out in the Piazza, my window in the rectory is kept open. What your father has brought to this village is truly wonderful. I am in charge of the choir here at the *Chiesa della Madonna*. I also teach music. If you are interested, I can take you on as a pupil and teach you the fundamentals of music."

"You would do that for me?"

"*Si.*"

"I would love to learn how to play an instrument or even how to sing like you."

"*Bene*. We can start tomorrow. Can you come after the 6

a.m. Mass? That will give us an hour to work before you have to report to school."

"I will be here. I can't wait to start. But Padre, why are you willing to teach me?"

The priest smiled and said, "Maybe in so doing, you can teach me how to stand up to the powerful."

7

SALVATORE SANGUINETTI

*A*fter Giuseppe's run-in with Monsignor Montarsolo years ago, he thought he would never be able to have respect for a religious leader again. Padre Mancini changed all of that. Next to his father, Padre Mancini became Giuseppe's closest older friend.

Giuseppe practiced hard with Padre Mancini and learned how to sing, play the violin and read music. Padre Mancini was an excellent teacher, both patient and kind. Giuseppe excelled at violin training. His vocal training, however, did not go nearly as well. Singing was not his forte.

The summer after he graduated from grammar school, he spent most of his free time away from the wine store split between practices with Padre Mancini and fishing with Biaggio. By the end of the summer, when Giuseppe was turning fifteen, the time had come for Giuseppe to attend high school.

Bellafortuna was too small of a village to have a high

school of its own. Most of the children who completed grammar school would never attend high school anyway. They were usually required to help their family by working in the fields down in the valley or on the slope of the hill.

Antonio was adamant that his son would have the opportunity to attend high school. Less than eight miles away, in the city of Monreale, was *St. Ignatio*, an all-boys high school run by the Jesuits. Antonio had attended school there and it was where he wanted Giuseppe to go.

That fall, in 1904, Giuseppe started school at *St. Ignatio*. His father bought Giuseppe a small pony for him to ride to and from Monreale every school day. Giuseppe named him Caruso.

The saddest person in the entire village on the day Giuseppe started school was Biaggio. He walked with Giuseppe, who was holding Caruso by the reins, from the stable all the way to the road in the valley leading away from Bellafortuna.

As Giuseppe climbed onto Caruso, Biaggio said, "I'm going to miss you, Giuseppe."

"Biaggio, I'll be home tonight. I'll come see you. Are you ready to start your last year of school tomorrow?"

"What's the point of going back to school? I'm stupid, poor and will never go to high school. Why continue on with schooling? My life is down in the valley with my family, but even there, I'm always too tired and weak to help."

"Biaggio, God will choose your destiny. Just be ready for his call."

"I'm not sure God knows where I live."

Giuseppe laughed and said, "*Amico*, he knows. You're just upset because I'm leaving."

"That's not it, Giuseppe. I really mean it when I tell you I don't want to go to school anymore."

"And what are you going to do, sleep all day?"

"I want to take your place at *Il Paradiso* and help your father with the store. That is what I really want to do."

"Your father will never agree to your quitting school."

"Giuseppe, if you would talk to him, I think he would support me."

"I'll talk to you about it tonight. Agreed?"

"*Sì.*"

Giuseppe nudged Caruso slightly in the ribs, and the pony began making its way down the *Via Valle*. When Giuseppe had traveled some distance, he turned around and looked back at Bellafortuna. As usual, the view was stunning.

When the village of Bellafortuna was built after the earthquake of 1752, almost all of the buildings and homes in the new village were made with colored brick, which over time, mellowed into a golden hue. In the morning and especially at sunset, the entire village glistened in the light of the sun, making the buildings shine like gold. As a result of the care that had been taken in planning and rebuilding the village, it resembled a scene one might find in a storybook.

Giuseppe then turned his gaze away from the village and back toward the road in the valley leading to it. Biaggio, still standing in the middle of the road, was watching Giuseppe make his way away from the village.

Giuseppe had come to love Biaggio like a brother. He looked out for him and hoped that one day his friend could find happiness. If Biaggio's working with his father could achieve that, then Giuseppe would make sure that it would be done.

MONREALE IS LOCATED on the slopes and the hilltop of the *Monte Caputo*, at the edge of the *Conca d'Oro*, the golden fertile plain of Sicily, which begins at Palermo and is covered with lemon and orange groves.

King William II, Sicily's Norman King, built a Benedictine monastery and a cathedral in Monreale in 1174. A medieval village soon grew up around the two buildings. The city's name means royal hill *(mons reule)*. The views from the city are spectacular, stretching across the *Conca d'Oro* to Palermo and the far off sea.

Like Bellafortuna, Monreale's history was one of conquests. The last conqueror of the city was the Mafia, which many believed still controlled the city.

The architecture of the city is a mixture of the different cultures that ruled the land over the centuries. It's most famous building is the *Duomo di Monreale*. Great artisans, under the direction of King William II, decorated its interior with shimmering mosaics in a Byzantine style, depicting scenes from the Bible.

When Giuseppe started school in Monreale, he felt like an outcast in the much larger city. Not being from Monreale and being the only boy in his class from Bellafortuna made it very difficult for him. While in school, he couldn't wait for the day to end or for the weekend to begin.

Giuseppe had tried to talk Biaggio out of leaving school, but finally gave his approval and stood up for his friend when Biaggio spoke to his father, Dondo. After many arguments put forth by Biaggio, Dondo spoke to Antonio and finally acquiesced into allowing Biaggio to quit school.

Biaggio went to work full-time for Antonio. He made neighborhood deliveries, cared for the wine inventory, and was in charge of serving the wine and cheese with Giuseppe during the Saturday concerts.

The real money Biaggio now made helped his family's situation. For years, he always felt that he had not helped his family enough. Now he was actually producing for his family.

THE YEARS PASSED QUICKLY while Giuseppe attended school in Monreale. He studied hard, with history becoming his favorite subject.

He became a very good violinist through his studies with Padre Mancini. Sometimes, while fishing with Biaggio at the *Stagno Azzuro*, Giuseppe would bring his violin and play on the shore. Biaggio complained that, with the racket, there was no way the fish would bite. Biaggio's complaints would only make Giuseppe play louder.

Even while attending high school in Monreale, Giuseppe remained close to the villagers of Bellafortuna. Being one of the few villagers ever to attend high school, he became respected by the older villagers. The villagers looked to Giuseppe as one day becoming a leader in the village, like his father. After all, they were aware of the story of the "Sanguinetti slap". They viewed young Giuseppe as a special person.

ONE SUMMER DAY, in 1907, Giuseppe and Biaggio went to get a light lunch at Bellini's. The small *trattoria* was not crowded, as most of the villagers were still working in the fields.

Giorgio Monachino, Turridu's strapping young son, made his way over to the table to take their order. Giorgio was a few years older than Giuseppe and Biaggio and ran with a different group of boys in the village.

Giorgio was a hot-tempered person like his father. He could be very sarcastic, particularly when having a bad day. Today, unfortunately, was such a day; he was in a foul mood.

As he approached the two boys, Giorgio said, "What brings the two of you in here today? You're not playing down in the valley today?"

Giuseppe immediately picked up on the mocking tone, but ignored it and placed their order. Before leaving the table, Giorgio turned to Giuseppe and said, "I take it, you will be picking up the bill?"

Biaggio quickly replied, "No. I'm paying for my food."

Giorgio leaned across the table and said to Biaggio, "Why don't you get a real job and help your family around their vineyard instead of working at the wine store as Antonio's errand boy. I'm sure your father could use your help."

Biaggio was stunned by the remark. Giuseppe quickly stood up from the table and said, *"Vai indietro, Giorgio."* (Back off, Giorgio.)

Giorgio responded, "Oh, the fair-haired boy of Bellafortuna is getting mad. Be careful, Giuseppe, I'm not an old priest."

Giuseppe grabbed Giorgio by the shirt. Biaggio quickly pulled him away, begging Giuseppe to leave. As they began to depart, Giorgio said to Giuseppe, "There they go. One who is a nothing and one who thinks he and his family are very important. Giuseppe, how does one think so much of himself without answering for the actions of his grandfather?"

Giuseppe replied, "What are you talking about?"

"*Nulla*, just that your grandfather was a *traditore*." (*Traitor*.)

At that very moment, Turridu, who overheard the comment, walked out of the kitchen. He yelled to Giorgio to shut up and ordered him to come clean some plates.

Giuseppe and Biaggio left the *trattoria*. Once outside, Biaggio asked Giuseppe, "What was he saying about your grandfather?"

"I have no idea," replied Giuseppe.

LATER THAT NIGHT, Giuseppe told his father and Mamma Lucia about the incident at Bellini's. Mamma Lucia bowed her head, got up from the table, and went silently into the kitchen.

Giuseppe said, "Papa, I didn't mean to upset her. Why would Giorgio call your father a traitor?"

Antonio shook his head and said, "Giorgio has a fiery, passionate personality just like his father. Still, I don't know why he would say that."

"But it was as if he knew something that I didn't about my own grandfather."

Antonio was quiet for a few moments. He took a deep breath and said, "Giuseppe, I loved my father. I know you hear me speak of him fondly all the time; however, there is one aspect of his life that I never speak about. It is in the past. There is no need to discuss it."

"I have to know. He was called a traitor to my face, and I have no idea why."

"Giuseppe, I have made a supreme effort to live a good life, dedicated to these people of Bellafortuna, and I have tried to earn their respect. What your grandfather did is in the past. We live in the present, living our lives in such a way to repay these people for his actions."

Frustrated, Giuseppe said loudly, "But what did he do?"

"He worked for the Vasaios."

Giuseppe was stunned to silence, before finally asking, "He did what?"

"He worked with the Vasios. Years before, Alessandro Vasaio had moved into Bellafortuna and established a foothold here in the village loaning money to the villagers. When he died, his son, Aldo Vasaio, succeeded in power. He broke with the tradition of not hiring local villagers and hired your grandfather as his personal accountant. After a few years, in consideration of Salvatore's very successful accounting work, Aldo offered to assist Salvatore in stocking our store with excellent wines from all over Sicily and Italy. He helped Salvatore set up a very small, yet lucrative export business for his Sicilian wines to the mainland of Italy."

Giuseppe asked, "He accepted their offer?"

"*Si*. I think he thought he had no choice. You see, when Aldo was in power, and after the death of Enzo Boccale, the Boccale Winery, now run by Enzo's family, was hurting, which meant the production of *Vino di Bellafortuna* was slowed."

"Why were they hurting?" asked Giuseppe.

"A large number of the villagers of Bellafortuna were in deep debt to the Vasaios. This, in turn, allowed the Vasaios to acquire more and more of the villagers' harvests as payment on the loans, which meant the Boccale family received fewer and fewer grapes and olives into their facilities. Eventually, they too went into debt to the Vasaios.

"By the mid-1800s, the beloved Boccale Winery and olive presses were foreclosed upon, seized, and then closed down by Aldo Vasaio. The Boccale family left Bellafortuna never to return, and *Vino e Olio di Bellafortuna* and the Boccale Winery became nothing more than a memory.

"Since your grandfather no longer had *Vino di Bellafortuna* to sell, the Vasaios' offer couldn't have come at a better time. *Il Paradiso*, because of the Vasaios, eventually acquired a good reputation because of its excellent wine inventory, which allowed Salvatore to profit from a regional cliental.

"For years, your grandfather performed his accounting duties for the Vasaios. He continued working for the Vasaios even after Aldo retired and was succeeded by Carlo, Vittelio's father.

"Soon, due to Carlo Vasaio's continuously expanding control over the villagers' economy, Salvatore was compelled to hire two people to help him with the books. Unable to find locals willing to work for him in his arrangement with the Vasaios, he hired two men from Palermo. With the additional help, Salvatore perfected the collection process for the Vasaios, making Carlo Vasaio very happy."

"Papa, how could he do that? How could he work for them?"

"As time passed, Giuseppe, Salvatore asked himself those very same questions. He began to realize the misery that the

Vasaios had brought to the village of Bellafortuna. He began to believe that he had betrayed his friends and neighbors. But what could he do? He was just one individual in the village. He couldn't stand up to the powerful Vasaio family. So instead, in 1876, he walked away from it, washed his hands of the Vasaios, and returned full time to selling his wine and managing his store.

"After the end of the business relationship with the Vasaios, our wine store no longer had the backing of Carlo Vasaio. That didn't matter now because of the wealth that your grandfather had gained over the years working for the Vasaios and the store's reputation. Salvatore began to travel to the mainland to purchase the inventory from the very same producers and distributors whom we go to see now. Salvatore had been introduced to them by the Vasaios. This allowed *Il Paradiso* to continue with its reputation as a fine wine store with a large inventory of both Sicilian and Italian wines and a local and, more importantly, regional clientele."

"Papa, what did the villagers think about him? About what he did?"

"I can't explain why the villagers never turned against your grandfather. They still shopped at his store, bought his wine, and, when he died in 1885, they attended his funeral. Not attending a Sicilian's funeral is regarded as the highest insult. Even if you killed a man in a duel, you were obligated to show your respect to the family by going to the funeral.

"When I took over *Il Paradiso* after my father's death, I never suffered any want as a result of his former dealings with the Vasaios. But inside, I always knew how my father provided this comfortable life for us. He gave assistance to the powerful by participating in the financial burdens visited upon our fellow villagers."

Giuseppe found himself at a loss for words. He finally responded, "That means our family assisted the Vasaios in taking control of the village."

"In a way, Giuseppe, but it would have happened without him."

"But it didn't happen without him, Papa. It didn't. He helped."

"That is so. And that is what I have lived with my entire life. I have still been able to gain the people's respect. That is why I have always told you that we must be careful how we live our lives in the village. We owe these people a debt. So we continue with the wine store, providing them with good wine at cheap prices. Is that enough to pay back the debt? No. But at least it is something."

"Why wasn't I told this before?"

"Your grandfather loved his family. I loved him. To tell you earlier would have made you think badly of him. Perhaps, being older now, one day you will understand and forgive him. After all, his fellow villagers did."

"Did my mother know about your father?"

"Of course, Giuseppe. She knew all about it. She knew your grandfather before he died and loved him, even though he had aided the very people who hurt her own family financially. Is it too much to ask for you to forgive him?"

"I don't know. You should have told me sooner."

"You are probably right."

Giuseppe slept not a wink that night. First thing that next morning, he went to speak to Biaggio about his conversation with his father. Biaggio assured Giuseppe that his father, Dondo, had never mentioned to him anything about that part of the Sanguinetti family history. So perhaps Antonio was correct that it was something forgotten.

As for Giuseppe, he couldn't get the revelation out of his mind.

8

DONDO SPATALANATA

*A*s the rest of the summer progressed, Giuseppe continued to speak with his father about his grandfather's past. Since Giuseppe was in high school now, he could only make the trip in July with his father to the mainland of Italy. The summer before Giuseppe was set to begin his senior year of high school, he traveled to Italy with his father. That trip affected Giuseppe like no other trip before had. His increased maturity opened his eyes to the crushing hand that the Vasaios had over his village.

As he and his father traveled to Milan by train, they passed the smaller Tuscan cities of Montepulciano, Cortona, and Fiesole as well as numerous other smaller villages. He had passed these same cities and villages on other trips with his father. But on this trip, he viewed them in a completely different light.

Out of the window of the train, Giuseppe noticed how well kept the vineyard owners' homes were that dotted the vast countryside of Tuscany. It was evident that these people thrived on the profits from their grape harvests. The vineyard fields, however, did not appear to be as fertile or as large as the fields in Bellafortuna. Still, these people seemed to prosper. Their prosperity was reflected in the beauty of their homes, gardens and yards.

WEEKS AFTER GIUSEPPE returned to Bellafortuna, he was unable to get the visions of the other communities out of his head. He sat for hours a day on the slope of the hill behind the *Chiesa della Madonna*, looking out over the vast valley below, meditating on what he had seen on his trip. He watched as the villagers worked tirelessly among the olive groves and the vineyards below. Men, women and children scrambled up and down ladders that leaned against the olive trees. Men, driving ox carts, made their way down the long rows of grapevines, stopping to prune.

The fear of foreclosure kept the villagers working every day. In contrast, Giuseppe lived a carefree life in the village.

He was compelled to do something to help his fellow villagers. After all, his grandfather had betrayed these people. He began to wonder why the villagers did not treat his family harshly. His fellow villagers respected his father and treated Mamma Lucia with affection.

As the weeks and months passed since his trip to Italy, Giuseppe began to feel more and more ashamed of what his grandfather had done. He also began to think that his father should have done more for the villagers; to repay them for the actions of Salvatore. And still, the question of why the villagers accepted his family burned in Giuseppe's breast.

One evening in early October, after he had eaten supper at the home of the Spatalanatas down in the valley, he stepped outside with Dondo to help light some of the barrels to heat the vines on the unseasonably cool night.

As they walked along the rows, Giuseppe told Dondo, "Your vineyard is beautiful. You take great care of it."

Dondo, a small man with eyes full of life and wisdom, touched with hardship, said in reply, "I work the fields the same way my ancestors did back when the village of Campanèlla was still in existence. All of us in the valley work the fields by the tradition passed down to us through the centuries. We spend our days caring for our vines. We prune them daily and check them for disease. We know each vine like it is one of our children. Our lives are dedicated and tied to these vines. But our times are changing, Giuseppe.

"Before the Vasaios came to our village, harvest time was a truly wonderful time for our ancestors. All of the grapes were handpicked and loaded into carts. The carts were all decorated with wildflowers from the valley. Once loaded, the carts made their way to the Boccale Winery, where the priest would bless the harvest. Then the grapes were unloaded into large tubs and crushed by the bare feet of the villagers, bringing forth the juice, which would, over time, create wine.

"Harvest time was a joyous and sacred time. Those days are now over. It is no longer a time for celebration. We grow our grapes and harvest them to send to other wineries. We do not get to see the fruit of our labor."

Giuseppe looked across the vineyard and said to Dondo,

"And yet, all of the fields are so well kept down here in the valley."

Dondo agreed and said, "These people are still proud. This is their life. They care for the vines in anticipation of the day when the Boccale Winery of Bellafortuna will be rebuilt, and *Vino di Bellafortuna* produced once again." Dondo pointed up to the village of Bellafortuna and said to Giuseppe, "To do that, we must rid ourselves of the Vasaios once and for all. Our people are slowly losing faith that such a blessing will ever occur."

Giuseppe cleared his throat and asked Dondo, "Did you know my grandfather?"

"Salvatore? I knew him. I was a much younger man when he died. But sure, I knew him. My father knew him better than I did."

"Dondo, what do you think about what he did?"

"What he did about what?"

"I mean with respect to his working with the Vasaios. I feel as though my family is partly to blame."

Dondo smiled at the teenager and said, "For the past few months, Biaggio has been asking me questions about your grandfather. Why the sudden interest?"

"It was something that was said by someone in the village."

"Who?"

"Giorgio Monachino."

Dondo laughed and said, "He's a hothead like his father."

"My father recently told me what my grandfather did. I feel like he betrayed all of you. I know my father feels he owes so much to the village because of what Salvatore did."

"*Amico*, don't worry about that now; that was a long time

ago. I think I can speak for everyone in the village that your grandfather is respected because he realized the wrong he was doing and walked away from the Vasaios. He moved on, and we moved on. He was merely looking out for his family's interests. Ultimately, he saw the pain caused by the Vasaios and walked away. For that, he was respected and welcomed back into the community. We all make mistakes, Giuseppe, but it is what we do to correct those mistakes that make them. . ." Dondo tried to think of the right word and finally said, "forgivable."

Dondo put his arm around Giuseppe's shoulder and said, "Your father is an honest, good man, just like his father. Pay no attention to comments made by people. Live a good life and help others. In that way, you will have the respect of everyone, as your father does now."

Giuseppe shook his head affirmatively.

LATER THAT NIGHT, as Giuseppe made his way back up the hill to his home, the words of Dondo Spatalanata echoed in his heart. He now believed, the same as his father, that he owed something to the village.

Somehow, someway, Bellafortuna would have to rid itself of the Vasaios to become free from the strangulation hold they held. Giuseppe began to think that he owed it to the villagers to do anything and everything in his power to achieve that goal.

Less then two weeks later, a trip to Palermo to see a performance of Verdi's *Nabucco* started the wheels in motion.

9

VERDI'S NABUCCO

*T*he *Teatro Massimo* in Palermo had scheduled Verdi's opera, *Nabucco*, to open the opera season that year. It was the first time the opera had ever been performed in the city. The inhabitants of Bellafortuna quickly purchased the available tickets for opening night.

As the night of the performance drew near, Bellafortuna was alight with excitement. To be able to see an opera that they had never seen before, especially one by the greatest opera composer Italy had ever produced, raised their excitement to another level.

When the day finally arrived, the residents of Bellafortuna flocked to Del Monaco's to have lunch before making their journey to Palermo. By noon, most of the businesses in the Piazza were closed. Soon, the workers in the vineyards and the olive groves made their way to the restaurant as well.

A little after noon, Antonio, Giuseppe and Biaggio made

their way to the restaurant. The trio entered Del Monaco's and immediately noticed the excitement in the air. The tables were loaded with patrons, eating their lunch, and drinking wine. Antonio, Giuseppe and Biaggio found a table and ordered their food. All three ordered the same item, *pici con funghi e salsiccie*, large rolled pasta mixed with local herbs, wild mushrooms and grilled sausage made from the finest pigs in the area; and of course, simmered in olive oil. It was delicious.

A short while later, the time came for everyone to climb into their carts and wagons and begin the journey to Palermo. The wagon Antonio was in was filled with people. His wagon was always loaded with people because of his knowledge of opera. On the return trip, his review of the opera seen that night was always a highlight of the trip.

Most of the wagons were loaded with wines from the Sanguinetti store for the return trip. Once everyone had packed into the carts and wagons, they pulled out of Bellafortuna and made the trip to Palermo to see *Nabucco*. Little did they know the effect that seeing this opera would have on their village.

IF ONE WOULD KNOW the events surrounding Verdi's writing of *Nabucco* as well as what occurred at its premier, one would understand that what happened that night in Palermo to the villagers of Bellafortuna was history repeating itself.

In the 1830s, Giuseppe Verdi was at the very beginning of his career. Tragically, within the span of a mere two months, his son, daughter, and then his wife all died as a result of an infectious disease. At the same time, his just finished opera was not well received.

Verdi immediately went into seclusion, swearing that his days of being an opera composer were finished.

A few months later, by chance, Verdi ran into Bartolomeo Merelli, the Impresario of La Scala. Merelli asked Verdi if he would read the libretto of a new opera, *Nabucco*, to see if it was worthy for some composer to tackle.

Verdi, only out of respect for Merelli, finally agreed and took the libretto with him, even though he was certain he would never look at it. When he arrived home, he disgustedly threw the libretto on his desk in his study, and it fell open. The wind from an open window blew a few pages over, catching Verdi's attention. The composer stood over the pages, and his eyes caught one line of text in the libretto, *"Va, pensiero, sull'ali dorate."* (*Go, thoughts, on wings of gold.*)

Jewish slaves who are being held captive in Babylon sing of their homeland and the hope to rid themselves of oppression. Verdi picked up the libretto and read the entire text for the song. Upon completing it, Verdi couldn't put the libretto down. The opera's theme of freedom borne of oppression resonated with Verdi.

At that time, the Austrians ruled Milan. They controlled the lives of the Milanese, both socially and economically. It was Verdi's hope that one-day, Milan and all of Italy could be freed and unified.

Verdi brought the libretto back to Merelli and told him it would make a great opera. Merelli offered the job to Verdi. He returned home with the libretto and began to work on it. The entire opera was completed within three months.

On March 9, 1842, *Nabucco* had its premiere at La Scala. At the beginning of the third act, the chorus of slaves sang "Va, pensiero", the words which had moved Verdi to write the opera in the first place.

The audience went wild when the chorus was completed. It didn't take much of a leap for the Milanese to put themselves into the role of the Hebrew slaves. Here was music that shouted to them to rise up and bring freedom to the land. They found in Verdi's hymn their rallying cry.

For the people of Italy, it became their secret anthem of freedom from the Austrian yoke. The voices of Italians up and down the peninsula echoed its refrain until liberty was finally achieved.

WHEN THE OPERA BEGAN, the inhabitants of Bellafortuna were immediately captivated by the opera. The singing and staging were well done, and the music of Verdi moved them.

In the third act, after a brief orchestral interlude, the chorus of Hebrew slaves started to sing. The chorus at the *Teatro Massimo* was always large. However, the stage director for this performance really went big. Over one hundred voices thundered out across the *Teatro*.

Va, pensiero, sull'ali dorate;
Go, thoughts, on wings of gold;

va, ti posa sui clivi, sui colli,
go, and settle upon the mountains and hills,

ove olezzano tepide e molli
where you feel and smell the

l'aure dolci del suolo natal!
sweet breezes of our native soil!

Del Giordano le rive salute,
Greet the banks of the river Jordan,

di Sionne le torri atterrate.
and the destroyed towers of Zion.

Right at this point, Verdi wrote the music to hit a crescendo and proceed directly into the next two lines, which words are to be sung with great emotion.

Oh, mia patria sì bella e perduta!
Oh, my country so beautiful and lost!

Oh, membranza sì cara e fatal!
Oh, memory so dear and fatal!

At these lines in the chorus, way up in the balcony section in the *Teatro*, tears began to flow down the faces of most of the residents of Bellafortuna. This chorus was about them; an oppressed people hoping to rise up from oppression and find freedom and the return of their land.

Arpa d'oro dei fatidici vati,
Golden harp of our ancestors,

perché muta dal salice pendi?
why do you hang mute upon the willow?

Le memorie nel petto raccendi,
Rekindle the memories in our heart,

ci favella del tempo che fu!
and speak to us of times gone by!

O simile di Solima ai fati,
Mindful of the fate of Jerusalem,

traggi un suono di crudo lamento,
either sound a cruel lament,

o t'ispiri il Signore un concentoto
or else allow God inspire with a sound

che ne infonda al patire virtu!
that will give strength to bear our suffering!

At its conclusion, every single resident of Bellafortuna, who had made the trip to Palermo that night, stood up in unison and screamed with an excitement never heard before at the *Teatro Massimo*. The villagers drowned out the cheers and bravos coming from the rest of the house. Turiddu Monachino shouted at the top of his lungs, *"Bis! Bis! Da Capo!"* (Encore! Encore! From the beginning!) The conductor agreed, and the chorus was sung again.

Pandemonium erupted again in the balcony at the

conclusion of the song. Giuseppe looked at his father, who was crying uncontrollably. He asked his father, *"Come va?"* *(Are you all right?)*

His father turned to his son and said, "I have never been moved like that before by a piece of music. Verdi understood what it meant to be oppressed. And through music, he tried to raise his people out of the depths of oppression."

Giuseppe thought for a moment and finally told his father, "Papa, this music can lead our village to freedom."

"Figlio, you have a worthy thought there. Look at the reaction around us. Have you ever seen that look in the eyes of our neighbors before? For the first time, you can see a glimmer of hope, a realization that life could be better. We need to find the music and the words to the chorus. When we drive back to Bellafortuna tonight, we can discuss how we may be able to get our hands on a musical score."

As Antonio finished speaking, the crowd finally settled down, and the opera continued. Giuseppe sat in his seat, but his mind was no longer on the action on the stage. His father was right. For the first time, there was a look of resolve in the villagers' eyes.

Later that night, at the beginning of the fourth act of the opera, the conductor walked to the podium, accepted the applause of the audience, and as he turned to conduct, he noticed that his softbound musical score of the opera was missing from the podium. The opera was delayed as the conductor had to retreat to his dressing room to get another score.

As the theatergoers waited for his return, Giuseppe was sitting in his seat with a huge grin across his face. Without anyone else being aware of it, wrapped within Giuseppe's winter coat was the conductor's musical score. Unnoticed, Giuseppe had reached over the guardrail and grabbed it from the pit during the intermission. The village of Bellafortuna had the words and music to "Va, pensiero".

10

VA, PENSIERO

*A*s the wagons and carts left the city of Palermo on the return trip to Bellafortuna, tomatoes in a very heavy barrage pounded the villagers. Unlike previous nights, the villagers of Bellafortuna struck back. They began to pick up the pieces of tomato that had been splattered on them and throw those pieces back at the *Palermitani*. A near-riot broke out in the streets of Palermo that night. The *Palermitani* were shocked that these upstart villagers were actually fighting back.

Finally, the wagons and carts made their way out of the city and onto the *Corsa Calatafimi*. Antonio was seated in a wagon, his clothes splattered with tomato juice. He said to Giuseppe, "I never thought I would see this day. I'm so proud of these people. Look at them, they are chatting like school children. They know that what occurred tonight was special."

Biaggio asked, "What has got into all of them?"

Antonio put his hand on Biaggio's back, saying, "Music. Verdi, in particular."

As the wagons and carts reached the *Via Valle*, under a bright full moon, the faint sound of people trying to hum the chorus from *Nabucco* could be heard.

Antonio continued speaking to Giuseppe and Biaggio. He said, "Verdi understood oppression. People who are oppressed need the belief that their cause for freedom is just. Then they will act. Look at the Americans. With the Declaration of Independence, the colonists knew their cause was right. As for us Italians, we're not much for legal proverbs. What we need is music. I believe that is what happened tonight. For the first time, we all came together. That's why I want to find the music and words to the chorus of 'Va, pensiero'."

Giuseppe opened his coat, resting on his lap and pulled out the softbound book. It had a cloth cover with the word "*Nabucco*" embossed in gold. He handed it to his father.

Antonio asked, "What is this?" He opened the book and immediately received an answer to his question. "You have the score of *Nabucco*? How did you get it?"

"Let's just say that's why there was a delay in starting the opera after the intermission."

"*Figlio, mio Figlio. Ascolta.* Listen to this."

Antonio quickly paged through the score until he came upon the chorus, "Va, pensiero". With great emotion, he read the words.

Tears began to flow down his face.

Oh, mia patria sì bella e perduta!
Oh, my country so beautiful and lost!

Oh, membranza sì cara e fatal!
Oh, memory so dear and fatal!

When he finished, Biaggio and Giuseppe clapped. Others in the wagon with them inquired why they were clapping. Biaggio told them that Giuseppe had gotten the score and that Antonio was reading it. They made Antonio recite it again and again.

Word spread quickly among the villagers in the other carts that Antonio had the words and music to the chorus. Slowly, the wagons and carts pulled to the side of the road and awaited the arrival of the wagon with Antonio.

"Give us the words," they shouted as Antonio drew near.

Antonio's wagon came to a halt. He stood up and addressed the crowd. "It is true. My son, Giuseppe, has gotten us the words and music to that wonderful chorus we heard tonight. Before I read the words to you, I want Luigi to give you the tune."

Luigi, who was in another cart, climbed into the wagon with Antonio, and then he began to hum the tune for the chorus. The villagers tried to hum along with him. When Luigi finished, Antonio stood up and began to recite the words.

When the wagons and carts started rolling again on the way back to Bellafortuna, the wine began to flow, and "Va, pensiero" was sung the entire way.

WHEN THEY FINALLY ARRIVED BACK IN Bellafortuna, the loud singing awakened the villagers who had not made the trip.

As the line of wagons and carts pulled into the Piazza, people came out of their homes to see what the raucous noise was about. Giuseppe jumped from the wagon and ran into his home. He returned back to the Piazza with his violin and a lantern.

He got the music from his father and began to play the melody. The returning villagers of Bellafortuna stood in the middle of the Piazza, in the dead of night, and proceeded to sing the chorus in full voice. The villagers who had not made the trip that night thought the returning villagers all must have had too much Sanguinetti wine on the way home, but soon, they too were taken over by the emotion of the words of the chorus.

The door to the rectory flew open, and the Monsignor, followed by Padre Mancini, came out into the Piazza. The Monsignor bit his lip, shaking his head at the unruly behavior. Padre Mancini listened intently to the words and smiled when he saw Giuseppe leading the people with his violin.

In the open window of the *Palazzo Vasaio*, one could see a single lamp being held by Vittelio Vasaio, as he, with a look of disgust, peered down on the Piazza. After listening to just a few words of the chorus, Vittelio Vasaio quickly slammed the window shut and returned to bed.

When the chorus was completed, the villagers cheered throughout the Piazza. *"Viva Verdi. Viva Sanguinetti,"* were being yelled. The villagers were hugging each other and having a good time.

Finally, the celebration broke up as people made their way home. Before Giuseppe walked into the wine store to make his way to his bedroom on the second floor, he looked across the Piazza to the *Palazzo Vasaio*. Their reign would come to an end if Giuseppe had anything to say about it.

11

SOCIETÀ DELLA LIBERTÀ PER BELLAFORTUNA

*L*uigi Tavelo, at the request of Antonio, spent all of Friday and Saturday morning transcribing the music for "Va, pensiero" into manuscript form for the members of the *Opera Orchestra di Bellafortuna* to use.

By the time of the concert on Saturday afternoon, Luigi had completed about ten transcriptions. He handed them to a few members of the orchestra, telling them to share the music with the other members.

The Piazza began to fill for siesta. The concerts on Saturdays had now become a part of the life of the villagers of Bellafortuna. As usual, among the first people milling around the Piazza was the Terranova family. Giacomo Terranova was the owner of *Cimbrone*, a cobbler shop on the Piazza. He married his childhood sweetheart, Nannetta. They had four children, all girls, who greatly resembled their father. *Signor* Terranova was not a good-looking man. However, the villagers considered the four daughters to be among the most pleasant and intelligent young ladies in the village. The two oldest were teachers in the village's grammar school.

Every Saturday afternoon, during the opera concerts in the Piazza, Giacomo would have his daughters get dressed in their finest clothes and walk all over the Piazza. He hoped that one day they could find husbands. So far, there had been no takers.

Signor Terranova was deeply devoted to his family. He would do anything for them. That is exactly how he was in his dealings with the villagers. If you ever needed anything, you could always count on *Signor* Terranova to help. He provided shoes, at little cost, to all children of school age. He always would say, "It's the least I could do. When I went to school, I never had shoes." Then he would shake his head, point to his feet, and say, *"Non si può studiare con i piedi sporchi." (You cannot study with dirty feet.)*

At precisely 1:00 p.m., the *Opera Orchestra di Bellafortuna* began the concert for the day. Its first selection was the Overture to Verdi's *La Forza del Destino*. This was followed by all Verdi selections, both arias as well as preludes.

The crowd in the Piazza was enjoying the concert immensely. The orchestra played very well. As usual, Vittelio Vasaio could be seen sitting at his desk on the first floor of the *Palazzo*, with his window open, enjoying the music. Vittelio, unlike his wife, was not an opera lover. Three members of the *Scagnozzi dei Vasaios* were sitting on a bench outside the *Palazzo Vasaio*, also enjoying the music and goings-on in the Piazza.

Seated off in a far corner of the Piazza, Giacinto Bordelli was hard at work behind a canvas. Giacinto was the owner of Bordelli's, a tailor's shop on the Piazza. He was a great tailor who could sew with the best. He was a devoted husband and father, with a beautiful wife and three young sons. His hobby was painting. He would sit out in the Piazza or go throughout the village and the valley when time permitted, capturing slices of life on his canvas. Many homes in Bellafortuna were adorned with at least one Bordelli painting.

As the concert drew to a close, and the strains of "La donna mobile" faded away, Luigi turned away from the orchestra and faced everyone out in the Piazza, who were all clapping very spiritedly.

"*Grazie, mille grazie,*" he said. Luigi turned to the orchestra and asked them to rise and accept the applause. After they settled back in their seats, Luigi put his hand up in the air and begged the crowd's indulgence. "At the request of Antonio Sanguinetti, it is my pleasure to offer this next and last selection of the day for you."

Antonio, from behind the table with the wine and cheese, bowed to the crowd, who had turned around to look at him.

Luigi turned to conduct the orchestra. He was startled when every member of the orchestra stood up to play. With his baton, Luigi brought his hand up swiftly, and the initial notes of Verdi's "Va, pensiero" echoed throughout the Piazza. The crowd rose as one. The orchestra played with a passion not heard in the Piazza before.

One by one, the villagers in the crowd grabbed hands and began to sing. If they didn't know the words, they hummed the chorus.

When they reached the line, *Oh, mia patria sì bella e perduta! (Oh, my country so beautiful and lost!),* the crowd instinctively turned and sang the line directly toward the *Palazzo Vasaio.* Vittelio Vasaio quickly stood up from his desk and slammed his window shut. The *Scagnozzi dei Vasaios* stood up from the bench and went inside the *Palazzo*. At the conclusion of the chorus, there were cheers up and down the Piazza.

A short time later, the crowd finally dispersed and went back to work. Antonio made his way over to Luigi, who was helping the orchestra pick up their chairs.

Antonio said, *"Luigi, grazie.* That was wonderful."

"No, amico, this one was all your idea and what an idea you had. Hopefully, soon, I will have the music for everyone in the orchestra. What a way to end each concert."

"I know Vittelio Vasaio loved it."

Luigi laughed and said, "Maybe we can get him to guest conduct it one day?"

"Si. That's a great idea. Luigi, are you on for our meeting at Del Monaco's tonight?"

"I'll be there. Let's see what happens, if anything."

Antonio said, "Perhaps something will. There is a fire in these people's eyes I have never seen before."

"Antonio, all flames eventually extinguish."

"Not true, Luigi. God's flame is the light of the world. It never goes out. These people have motivation now; hopefully, that motivation will turn to action."

Luigi said, "I know, but I hoped for this so many times in the past, all with the same result."

"Have faith, Luigi. It will be different. *Stasera. (Until tonight.) Addio."*

LATER THAT NIGHT, in the back, secluded dining area at Del Monaco's, ten men got together to eat dinner and have a meeting. The ten men were: Antonio and Giuseppe Sanguinetti; Dondo and Biaggio Spatalanata; Luigi Tavelo; Giacomo Terranova; Salvatore Licindoro; Giacinto Bordelli; Gualtiero del Monaco; and Turiddu Monachino. After the meal, Luigi called the meeting to order.

"*Scusate*. Everyone, please find a seat. *Signori*, it is my honor to turn this meeting over to its leader, Antonio Sanguinetti."

The men sitting at the tables banged wine bottles on the table in honor of Antonio. Antonio stood before them, smiling. He replied, "I am not the leader here. We all are."

Luigi said, "You are wrong, Antonio. The events of the last two days are all of your doing. This meeting was your idea, and you are our leader."

"*Grazie. Bene. Mio amico*, Luigi. I asked for this meeting to begin discussions of our life here in the village. A life that I know should and eventually will be better."

The men at the tables cheered as Antonio continued, "Never before have we had the opportunity which has presented itself like this. I have never seen a fire in the eyes of our neighbors like they had Thursday night in Palermo. I believe our people are ready for action."

Salvatore Licindoro, the owner of a carpenter shop on the Piazza named *Palladio*, said, "We have all been waiting a long time for this day, the day we can finally break free from the Vasaios." Salvatore was a real renaissance man. Not only was he an expert craftsman, but he had fought in Sicily's war for unification in the 1860s. He took great pride in telling everyone in the village that he had ridden with Garibaldi. He was also a talented musician, being the Church organist and a violinist with the opera orchestra.

The men shouted their agreement, all of them except for Turiddu. He sat at his table with his hand under his chin. He finally stood up and replied, "I agree with Salvatore that we have all waited for that day. But it is my bet that we will continue to wait. How many times in the past have we thought the whole village would come together and do something, only to have nothing happen?" He then turned toward Salvatore Licindoro and said to him, "Salvatore, you rode with Garibaldi, you strove to free Sicily, where have you been? Why haven't you acted before?"

Angrily, Salvatore stood up and tried to defend himself. "What would you have me do? I'm just a single person. I never saw you do anything either, other than scream and pee on a wall every morning."

Before Turiddu could answer, Antonio put his hand up and said, "Our object here is not to beat each other up. It's to come up with solutions to our problem."

Luigi replied, "Antonio is correct. What has happened or hasn't happened before is all in the past. I agree with Antonio; never before have our people been ripe for action. Let's not lose this opportunity because of useless bickering among ourselves."

Turiddu mumbled to himself as he settled down into his seat.

Giacinto Bordelli inquired, "What is our ultimate goal?"

Antonio, without missing a beat, replied, "Libertà, Giacinto. Freedom for all of us. I want the villagers to live free of debt, free of the Vasaios' control."

Dondo Spatalanata asked, "And how can that be achieved? I look around this room and notice that all of you work here around the Piazza in your stores. The Vasaios have limited control over your lives. You don't live and work down in the valley where our whole way of life is controlled by the Vasaios."

Giuseppe spoke up for the first time and said, "*Signor* Spatalanata, I must disagree with you. The Vasaios' control is far-reaching. What affects someone in the valley directly affects every villager in Bellafortuna."

Giacomo Terranova asked, "What options do we have?"

Antonio said in reply, "That is the purpose of our meeting, to begin discussions of what options we do have."

Turiddu stood up at once and said, "Kill them. Kill every Vasaio, from Carlo to Vittelio to that son of his, Santo, along with the *Scagnozzi dei Vasaios*. With one night, we could be free."

There was a general moan from everyone. Luigi said, "We are not the Mafia, Turiddu. Violence is not an option."

"Besides," replied Antonio, "what we must do has to assure us that the Mafia does not come in and take the place of the Vasaios. As you all know, we have long suspected that the Vasaios cut a deal with the Mafia to keep them out. We don't want to go from bad to much worse. We do not want to invite the *Manu Niura*." (*The Black Hand.*)

Salvatore stood up, and with a shrug of his shoulders, asked, "How do we take action then?"

Antonio, with great emotion, said, "Little did I know the effect my son would have on this village by the simple stealing . . . *perdoni me*, Giuseppe . . . taking of the musical score to *Nabucco*. Since Thursday night, I've been trying to think in my own mind how our dream of ridding ourselves of the Vasaios can be achieved. Some way, this village once again has to have its own winery and olive presses. *Vino di*

Bellafortuna e Olio di Bellafortuna would once again be produced, barreled, bottled, labeled, sold and shipped from here. By doing this, the commercial life of the village will begin to thrive, like it once did for our ancestors."

Turiddu countered, "And how do you expect that to occur?"

Antonio said, "Giuseppe and I have enough funds to rebuild the Boccale Winery and olive presses."

Dondo chimed in, "But without the Vasaios relinquishing the debt on the villagers' harvests, there will never be enough product to produce the quantities needed so that the villagers could continue to pay off their debts and still have excess product from their harvests to send to the winery or olive presses. You would suffer the same fate as the Boccales."

Antonio looked toward Dondo and replied, "Therein lies our dilemma. We must find a way to get rid of the debt. To be honest, I don't know how that can be achieved."

Giuseppe stood up and said, "I may have an idea. Music brought us here in the first place. If not for the music of Verdi, we wouldn't even be here discussing the chance of something happening in the village. I have always dreamed of being able to see operas at our own venue, perhaps at the Greek amphitheater down in *Antica Campanèlla*. If we could find a way to do that now, then the revenue it would bring in would allow us to pay off the debt."

Luigi, shaking his head, replied, "Giuseppe, freedom from debt must come first. The village would never be able to put on a production. Even if we could, who would come? If all we had were villagers attending, then the revenue would be coming directly from them, creating more debt. No, the debt must go first."

Antonio laughed, saying, "My son and his pipe dream of an opera company."

Meanwhile, Turiddu quickly stood up again from his seat, saying emphatically, "Let the Vasaios eat bone." Everyone laughed and cheered. When it quieted down, Turiddu continued, "I have listened to each person who has spoken. But I haven't heard a solution. Is there one?"

Gualtiero del Monaco said, "One thing we should do is continue to play Verdi's chorus of freedom at the weekly concert."

Luigi replied, "I promise it will end every concert."

Turiddu said, "I think it's wise to keep the people together through the use of that chorus, but we need to come up with an idea of how we can change the condition of the villagers."

Antonio replied, "I think there can be one. But it will take time. The Vasaios did not come to rule the village in a day. It took time. So, it will take time for us to free ourselves from their grip. I think the first step has to be to assure ourselves that we have the support of a large number of our fellow villagers. If we act as a group, we can never fail. So we should spend our free time around the village speaking to our neighbors. See if they are willing to join our little group. Perhaps, as we grow in number, the opportunity may present itself that would show us the best route to take to achieve liberation from the Vasaios."

Luigi said, "I agree, Antonio. That is the best first step."

Turiddu chuckled out loud. Antonio asked, "Is that a problem?"

Turiddu replied, "How soon we all forget those great Sicilian proverbs which have been passed down generation after generation; 'Fidarsi è bene, ma non fidarsi è meglio'. (To *trust is good; to not trust is better.)* These people have never done anything to help themselves. It will never work if we rely on them to help us."

Luigi sternly said to Turiddu, "You are wrong, *amico*. Without them, we cannot prevail. To achieve freedom, we must all work together. All of us must act as one and bring freedom to all. Now, I am not naïve. I know it will take time to convince others to join us. Some have been controlled their entire lives, and asking them to stand up now will take courage. But I have faith that over time, our little group will grow. As I said, I agree with Antonio's first step. Each of us should go out and get a feel for people's reactions. If at our next meeting we can get ten more people, we will be on our way. All in favor."

Everyone raised their hands in agreement, with Turiddu slowly putting his hand up last.

Luigi said, *"Bene.* We are all in agreement. Let's have another meeting in a week. Bring anyone you can with you. Make sure they're on board with us."

Giacinto asked, "What are we going to call our little group? You know so that when I discuss this with someone, I can give it a name."

Luigi looked at Antonio and shrugged his shoulders. "I never thought about that, did you?"

Antonio said no. Just then, Biaggio stood up. Luigi said, "Biaggio Spatalanata, the quietest person in the group has waited till the end to speak. Do you have a question?"

Biaggio shook his head no and replied, "The name of our group should be the *Società della Libertà per Bellafortuna."*

There was a moment of silence, and then clapping broke out across the room. Antonio said, "Biaggio, that's perfect.

Gentleman, today, the *Società della Libertà per Bellafortuna* is officially formed. May it one day lead our village to freedom."

Everyone replied, *"Così sia!"* (Amen), before retiring for the night.

———

DURING THE NEXT WEEK, the members of the *Società della Libertà per Bellafortuna* began to promote their group to some of their fellow villagers. Whoever was interested was invited to attend the next meeting to be held that Friday night.

To the amazement of the ten founding members, thirty-five people showed up for the meeting at Del Monaco's on Friday night. The founding members checked everyone in. The little room at Del Monaco's was too small to hold everyone, so the meeting was moved to Antonio's wine store, where everyone could stand amongst the shelves or sit on the floor. Turiddu's son, Giorgio, who had come to the meeting with his father, had the job of standing out front, making sure the Vasaios or their *Scagnozzi* didn't happen upon the meeting.

Once everyone had squeezed into the wine store, Luigi welcomed them all and said how excited the *Società della Libertà per Bellafortuna* was to have so much interest in their cause.

After concluding his remarks, he turned the floor over to Antonio. *"Buona sera* to all of you. Tonight we welcome you into our organization. In our wildest dreams, we never envisioned such a turnout. Thank you for coming. Particular mention must be made of our society's first female member,

Signora Fiorenza D'Arcangelo, who, after hearing about us from my son, immediately wanted to join and has brought with her four other ladies."

Cheers echoed around the room, with many of the men straining their necks to get a look at Fiorenza, the stunning beauty.

Antonio continued, "We know that to achieve our freedom, it will take time. We must act at the right moment. When that moment occurs is unknown, but we must be prepared. That will be the purpose of our meetings in the future. A plan must be developed so that all of us can live free of the Vasaios' controlling hand."

A round of applause broke out across the room at the words spoken by Antonio. He said, "You may have heard in the past that your oppression may be coming to an end, only to have your dreams crushed. Well, I say tonight, we are in this together to the end. Some way, the Vasaios' control will end."

The people in the wine store stood up in unison and clapped, chanting, "*Viva la libertà.*"

Antonio leaned over to Luigi and said, "The fire is still in their eyes. We have a chance."

"I agree, Antonio."

Once things calmed down, Antonio said to everyone, "It is the mission of the *Società della Libertà per Bellafortuna* to bring freedom to our village. But, we must act prudently. Therefore, our meetings will have to take place outside of the village. *Signor* Renato Silveri has agreed to allow us to use his barn in the valley to hold all of our future meetings.

"Also, other than those here tonight, the *Società* is now closed to new membership. Luigi and I have already discussed it, and we believe the key to our success is to remain low key until it is time to act. If we are too large, we will never get anything done. Unbelievably, our quota has been met in just one week."

When the meeting did come to an end, Antonio got a rousing round of applause. Giuseppe made his way to his father and told him what a wonderful job he had done. There was no question that his father was the leader of the *Società della Libertà per Bellafortuna*, the organization that one-day could hopefully bring freedom to the village.

12

MARIA AND RODOLFO GIULINI

*O*n the Sunday following the meeting, Giuseppe and Padre Pietro Mancini made a trip to the *Duomo* in Monreale to hear an afternoon concert. Biaggio was to go with them, but could not because he was not feeling well.

The concert was being given by the wonderful choir at the Cathedral, a polyphonic group that specialized in the music of Palestrina as well as Gregorian chant.

As Giuseppe and Padre Mancini traveled along the road to Monreale, they had a casual conversation about topics ranging from music, school and wine. Giuseppe dared not tell Padre Mancini anything about the little group his father had formed in the village. He liked the priest, but the priest was still under the control of the Monsignor, which in turn meant the Vasaios probably controlled him.

After they rolled into the city, they made their way to the *Duomo di Monreale*. As Giuseppe and Padre Mancini walked up the aisle to find a seat in one of the pews, Giuseppe looked toward the altar. Since he had attended high school in the city, he had been to the Cathedral many times in the past. And yet, each time he entered the Cathedral, it affected him as though he was seeing it for the first time.

The choir was seated at the very front of the altar, awaiting the start of the concert. Above them in the sanctuary was the largest mosaic in the Church, a huge shimmering mosaic of Christ giving his blessing, with outstretched arms.

The Church was very crowded. When the concert began, Giuseppe found the music very moving and wonderfully sung by the choir. What the music lacked in passion, when compared to opera, was made up by the spirituality of the pieces. God was speaking through this music.

At one point, in a piece of music by Palestrina, a male choir member moved away from the rest of the choir and sang a tenor solo. The male looked to be in his thirties, but it would not have surprised Giuseppe to find out he was actually younger than that. He was somewhat chubby, with black hair. As the tenor began to sing, Giuseppe thought that the voice was glorious. It was a lyrical voice but with a dark quality to it, almost baritonal. Giuseppe also found that the singer had a commanding presence. But what really made Giuseppe take notice was that the singer had a passing resemblance to Enrico Caruso. His voice was not close to that of the great tenor, but it was uncanny how much he looked like the Neapolitan.

Later, when the concert ended, and while the crowd was applauding, Padre Mancini asked Giuseppe, "Well, what did you think?"

"I thought it was wonderful. That tenor who sang solo in some of the pieces was remarkable."

"Oh, you mean Rodolfo Giulini. I think he possesses the best voice in all of Sicily. He wants to become an opera tenor one day, but he has never had the break needed. He is a candle maker here in the city with his father. Would you like to meet him?"

"I would love to meet him. I really want to congratulate him."

Padre Mancini and Giuseppe made their way toward the altar. Rodolfo Giulini was speaking to a man and woman. On Rodolfo's arm was the most beautiful creature Giuseppe had ever seen. She must have been sixteen or seventeen - too young for Rodolfo thought Giuseppe - with blonde hair that came cascading down to her shoulders.

Giuseppe and Padre Mancini walked up to the singer who turned to welcome them. "Ah, my good friend, Padre Pietro, has come to the concert. *Come va?*"

"*Bene*, Rodolfo. I'm very well. What a fantastic performance. Every time I hear you, I'm amazed at how your voice is getting better and better."

"*Grazie, Padre.* You remember my sister, Maria?"

The young girl on his arm extended her hand to the priest.

Padre Mancini said, "Sure I do. Maria, it's nice to see you again."

"*Grazie, Padre.* It's been a while."

"*Si*, too long. Maria and Rodolfo, I would like to introduce you to my friend, Giuseppe Sanguinetti."

Rodolfo extended his hand to Giuseppe. Giuseppe said, "You have an extraordinary voice."

"*Grazie.*"

Giuseppe turned to Rodolfo's sister, saying, "You must be very proud of him?"

She smiled at her brother and, turning back to Giuseppe, said, "Absolutely. I keep telling him one day he will have a career like the great Caruso."

Padre Mancini said, "My friend here actually met Caruso a few years ago when Caruso was just starting out his career."

"Did you really?" Rodolfo asked. "I would give anything to hear him sing one time."

"It was the greatest voice I have ever heard in person."

Maria told her brother, "Rodolfo, I'll meet up with you outside when you are done."

He replied, "*Si.* I am going to take Padre Mancini with me to meet our new choral director. I'll see you outside. *Ciao.*"

Maria turned to Padre Mancini and said, "Nice to see you again. Don't be such a stranger." She then turned to Giuseppe and extended her hand to him and said, "It was very nice meeting you."

"Likewise," Giuseppe responded. He watched with interest as Maria walked away from them, making her way to a set of stairs in the vestibule of the Cathedral.

Rodolfo asked, "Giuseppe, would you like to come with us to meet the director?"

"No thank you, I'm going to look around this beautiful Cathedral."

While Rodolfo and Padre Mancini went to the sacristy of the Cathedral to meet the new choral director, Giuseppe quickly followed the path to the stairs that Maria had taken.

GIUSEPPE TOOK the stairs and came out upon the lovely terrace of the Cathedral. He walked along the terrace until he came upon Maria, who was standing at the railing at the northeast corner of the Cathedral.

He was astonished by the views from the terrace. To the North, one could see across the entire *Conca d'Oro,* all the way to Palermo. It was a spectacular sight.

He came to where she was standing and stood next to her. Immediately upon seeing him, Maria said, "Well, hello!"

"And hello to you, Maria. This is a wonderful spot. I've never been up here before."

"This is my most favorite spot in the world. What do you think of the view?"

Giuseppe stared right into her crystal blue eyes and said very slowly, "*Bello.*"

The way he was looking at her made her blush. Pointing to the east side of the Cathedral, she said, "Look down here. See the *Chiostro.* Those are the Arab style cloisters down below with a lovely fountain in the middle. They were built at the same time as the Cathedral. Supposedly, the monks who once lived there used the beautiful fountain as their bathroom."

Giuseppe made a face of disgust and then replied, "Have you always lived in Monreale?"

"*Si.* My father is a candle maker and owns a candle shop right in the *Piazza Guglielmo,* across from the Cathedral. I come up here all the time. It's so peaceful and beautiful. Where do you live?"

Giuseppe pointed to the Northwest and said, "I'm from the village of Bellafortuna."

"Of course, Padre Mancini works there. I've never been to your village. But I do know of it. I have an uncle who loves wine, a little too much his wife thinks. He says the best wine in all of Sicily comes from a little wine store there known as *Il Paradiso.*"

Giuseppe laughed and said, "That is my father's store."

"Really," she said. "I can't believe it. I'll have to tell him I met you. I don't think he has ever been to your store. He usually convinces business partners who have dealings in Palermo to stop there for him."

"We get a lot of people who stop in as they journey along the road either to or from Palermo. My father always says our wine shop sits in a very lucky spot.

She asked, "Do you like living there?"

"It's a special place. One day you must come see it. I'll give you a tour like you gave me a tour of this terrace and the wonderful views."

"I would like that. You have a deal. I have always wanted to see your village. Is this your first time in Monreale?"

"No. I go to high school at *St. Ignatio.*"

With a sparkle in her eyes, she said, "You do. Well, maybe we will run into each other again."

"*Spero.* I hope so," Giuseppe said. "Perhaps, if I come up here to the terrace after school on Monday, you might be here."

Maria replied, "*La vita è piena di sorprese.*" (*Life is full of surprises.*)

Giuseppe looked out toward the *Conca d'Oro* and then into her eyes, saying, "I could look at this view for the rest of my life."

For the second time that day, she blushed. The two of them left the terrace and made their way out of the Cathedral and into the *Piazza Guglielmo* where Padre Mancini and Rodolfo were waiting.

"Where have you been?" Rodolfo inquired.

"We were up on the terrace. I was showing Giuseppe the view."

Rodolfo asked, "Wonderful, eh?"

"*Si*," replied Giuseppe, all the while staring at Maria.

Rodolfo said, "Padre Pietro tells me you're quite an opera enthusiast and that you go to school at *St. Ignatio*. Whenever you're free, I would love to spend time talking to you about opera."

"I would like that very much."

"I work with my father over there in that candle store. Come by. We live above the store."

"I will. It was very nice meeting the both of you."

AS PADRE MANCINI and Giuseppe made their way back to Bellafortuna, all of Giuseppe's thoughts were of Maria. He was completely smitten. She was beautiful, nice, funny, and smart. He was barely paying attention to the conversation Padre Mancini was having with him.

The priest finally asked, "Did you hear me? Or have you been struck dumb by lightning, like St. Paul?"

"*Mi scusi*. I'm just tired. What did you ask me?"

"What do you think about Rodolfo's voice?"

"Truly wonderful. I can't believe he has been unable to have an operatic career."

"I can't explain it."

"Padre, what's most amazing is that he looks somewhat like Caruso."

"Really. Well, but for your little napkin drawing he gave you many years ago, I don't think I have ever seen a picture of Caruso. I bet you and your father are the only people in the village who even know what he looks like. I mean, it's not like we have a major newspaper like Palermo."

"You're probably right, Padre. But trust me, if you ever saw Caruso, you would agree that Rodolfo Giulini does resemble him. Since meeting the great tenor many years ago, I have followed his career very closely. Whenever I travel to the mainland with my father and see an article about him, I always read it."

Giuseppe and Padre Mancini continued speaking during the return trip. The little cart finally reached the narrow dirt road that led to Bellafortuna. With the sun setting in the distance over the Sicilian hills, Giuseppe sat in the cart, dreaming of Maria Giulini.

13

THE DEBATE OF THE SOCIETÀ DELLA LIBERTÀ PER BELLAFORTUNA

*A*s he promised, Giuseppe went to the terrace of the *Duomo* on Monday, hopeful of seeing Maria. When he arrived, she was already waiting for him in the same spot where they had spoken to each other the day before. They talked about their lives and dreams.

Maria recently turned seventeen. She was a junior at *Sacro Cuore*, an all-girls school located on the opposite side of Monreale from Giuseppe's school. She was the only daughter of Giancarlo and Renata Giulini. The family lived above Giancarlo's small candle shop, just a few yards from the front door of the *Duomo*. Maria was in charge of the household chores so that her mother could work downstairs in the shop.

Giuseppe saw Maria every day after school that entire next week. It quickly became obvious to both that there was a strong connection developing between them. Maria was captivated by Giuseppe's knowledge. He spoke to her about his travels to the mainland of Italy about his love of opera - an art form that she loved as well, because of her brother.

Likewise, the daughter of the candle maker completely fascinated Giuseppe. She had a kindness that was immediately recognizable. For the first time in his life, a woman had touched Giuseppe's soul.

LATE FRIDAY NIGHT, the *Società della Libertà per Bellafortuna* had its first meeting at Signor Renato Silveri's barn located down in the valley, close to the entrance of *Antica Campanèlla*. The barn was lit with kerosene lamps. Bales of hay were used for seats. The cackling of chickens punctuated the meeting.

All forty-five members of the society were in attendance. Giuseppe found a seat next to Biaggio and listened as Luigi welcomed everyone.

About a third of the members believed action should be taken now to try to remove the Vasaios from power. Another one-third believed they should wait until the right time presented itself. Giuseppe and Biaggio, as well as Dondo, Antonio and Luigi, were in this group. The last one-third didn't know which way to go, with a few in that group leaning toward the position that no action should be taken at all.

At one point, Alberto Capecchi, the owner of an olive grove, stood up to address his fellow society members. "I agree with all of you. Never before has our village been brought together as it has since the performance of *Nabucco*. Verdi's stirring words lit a fire under all of us. But that fire must be tempered by reason. If we act and fail in removing the Vasaios, we run the risk of making things even worse."

Turiddu stood up immediately, grabbed his son's shoulder and emphatically said, "And if we do not act, if we don't try to do something, then for the rest of our lives, as well as our children's lives, this village will be ruled by oppression. No, I say we must act now."

People began to yell out their support for either position. Alberto Capecchi finally regained control of the floor. He said, "All of us living or working down in the valley are in the same boat. We live at the whim of Vittelio Vasaio. He can foreclose on our loans at any time because we are always behind in our payments. If we act and fail, he will foreclose on those who tried to do something."

Arguments broke out throughout the barn. It finally quieted down when Antonio stood up to speak. "I do agree with Alberto on one point. But I would state it a different way. *'Noi non possiamo fallire'. (We cannot fail.)* Therefore, when we act, we must act only when the time is right. And that time has not yet presented itself. For those who say act now, I say we have no plan. For those who say don't act, I hope you mean don't act now and not that we should never act. The time will come. And when it presents itself, we will have our plan in place."

Fiorenza asked, *"Caro*, Antonio, I agree we must act when the time presents itself. I have yet to hear a plan."

Antonio replied, "We have to find a way to rebuild the Boccale Winery and olive presses. Once we have done that, we can finally generate income that will bring this village out of debt."

Giacomo Terranova asked, "Even if we could do that, how

would we be able to sell the wine and olive oil that we produce?"

Antonio said, "Through my connections with producers and distributors, we will be able to export our wine, and either through some of those same distributors or through people with whom they are connected, we will likewise be able to sell our olive oil. Once again, *Olio e Vino di Bellafortuna* will make this village thrive."

Dondo Spatalanata stood up and said, "I like what Antonio is saying. The problem is finding a way to make it work. The only real way it will ever work is if the interest rate charged by the Vasaios is reduced."

Antonio smiled and said, "Dondo has dropped the cheese on the macaroni. That is our ultimate solution. Somehow, we have to get Vittelio Vasaio to agree to lower the interest charges and refinance the terms of all of the debts. If we can get him to do that, Giuseppe and I have the funds to rebuild the Boccale winery and olive presses. With the reduced interest charge, we can easily produce the oil and wine to meet those payments. A portion of the remaining profits can then be used to reduce the principal on the debts. Over time, our business will continually grow, we can develop vintage wines, and we will be in a position where we can pay back all of the debts and achieve liberation from the Vasaios."

Turiddu shouted, "How in God's name can you expect that bastard Vittelio to reduce his interest charges and refinance the terms?"

"I don't know, Turiddu," replied Antonio. "But I believe that is our only hope."

Giacinto Bordelli said, "Antonio, that will never happen. I

mean, what are you going to do, walk over to the *Palazzo Vasaio* and say, 'Vittelio, drop the interest charge, please?'"

Antonio replied, "Perhaps. I will do whatever it takes."

The debate raged for another hour with really no decision being reached. Antonio said toward the end, "For the time being, we must keep our fellow villagers in the same mindset they have adopted - the feeling that liberation is close. Some of the members of this group are in the orchestra. Please continue to play Verdi's song at the concerts with the same passion you have shown."

As everyone began to leave the barn to return home, Antonio was physically exhausted from the debate. He was also disappointed in the way things had gone. Luigi noticed this and told his friend, "Antonio, don't be dispirited. It will take time. The key is that the discussions have begun, and our neighbors are involved."

ON SUNDAY OF THAT WEEK, after Giuseppe had finished his musical training with Padre Mancini, Giuseppe and Biaggio went fishing down by the *Stagno Azzurro*. As usual, they sat amid the remnants of the old chapel near the pond and talked while they fished. Giuseppe brought his violin along and played some arias. After Giuseppe completed one aria, he said to Biaggio, "I haven't seen too much of you."

"Just tired lately. What have you been up to?"

"When I went to Monreale with Padre Mancini last week, there was a wonderful singer in the choir who sang some solo parts. His voice was magnificent. When the performance was over, Padre Mancini introduced me to the singer, Rodolfo

Giulini, as well as his sister, Maria. I have never laid my eyes on a more beautiful sight."

"What does she look like, Giuseppe?"

"Her hair is as golden as the setting sun over the Tyrrhenian Sea. Her skin is soft like lamb's wool. Her eyes, oh her eyes, they are as blue as this pond. I would give anything to stare into those two eyes of blue every day."

Biaggio laughed and said, "Oh, it sounds to me like you have it bad, *amico*."

"Indeed. I can't wait for you to meet her. She would like to come to the village one day. When she does, I'll introduce you to her."

"I would like that. Does she have a sister?"

Giuseppe laughed and said, "Nope, just a brother."

"Darn. Well, I guess I could always give in and start dating one of Signor Terranova's daughters."

"You can ask one of them out at the next concert in the Piazza. They're always on the prowl."

"You do know I'm joking, Giuseppe."

"I know, Biaggio. My father says the store has been busy. How's it going?"

"Giuseppe, I love working at *Il Paradiso*. Your father is such a nice man. I have learned so much about wine. I'm really having a good time. I owe both you and your father so much."

"No, Biaggio. You don't owe us anything. I'm glad you could help my father while I'm in school."

Biaggio said, "I love working the concerts with you. Those concerts have come to mean the world to the villagers of Bellafortuna. I don't know what they would do without them now. It gives them such an opportunity to escape from all of their troubles. I'm still moved when they end the concert with 'Va, pensiero', with all of the villagers and the members of the orchestra standing, facing the *Palazzo Vasaio* and singing the chorus with such passion. You did a good thing, Giuseppe, by stealing the music to that chorus."

"I would never steal, Biaggio," Giuseppe said with a sheepish grin.

"Giuseppe, what your father has done for this village will never be forgotten. My father says that on his own, your father has brought a chance of freedom that has never before existed."

As they continued to fish and talk, Giuseppe thought about Biaggio's words. He was correct. Antonio had really taken the lead in trying to bring freedom to the village.

After a short while, Biaggio said, "Let's go home, Giuseppe. With all of your violin playing, the fish aren't biting today, and I'm very tired."

The two friends left the pond and made their way home. Giuseppe couldn't wait for the day when he could introduce Biaggio to Maria.

A VISITOR TO BELLAFORTUNA AND ANTICA CAMPANÈLLA

For the past few weeks, the *Scagnozzi* had been making reports to Vittelio Vasaio about a whole new feeling that was brewing in the village, a feeling of defiance. Vittelio believed that it wouldn't take much action on his part to quell the villagers' emotions. He thought that when push came to shove, the villagers would have no backbone.

Giuseppe, in the meantime, was spending more time in Monreale than he had at any time before. That was because of his relationship with Maria. She showed Giuseppe all of the sights around Monreale. Giuseppe also had the opportunity to meet her parents when he was invited to their home for dinner.

Giancarlo was a very nice, older gentleman, and Renata was a beautiful woman who loved her family. They lived a comfortable life in Monreale because of Giancarlo's hard work. Giuseppe was immediately aware that both husband

and wife wanted nothing but the best for their children. For Maria, they wanted her to marry someone who could provide for her and, like their own marriage, someone whom she loved and who loved her in return.

As for Rodolfo, they were concerned he would never leave home. He had dated a lot while growing up but had yet to find that one person who made his heart sing. Rodolfo's dream was to become an opera tenor. His family believed that his voice was good enough for him to realize that dream. So, while he waited for his break, he continued singing with the well-known choir for the *Duomo*.

Although years apart in age, Rodolfo and Maria had a very close relationship. Giuseppe and Rodolfo enjoyed talking about different operas, composers and singers. They had hit it off right from the beginning. On a few occasions, Giuseppe would ask Rodolfo to sing for him.

———

MARIA'S PARENTS agreed to let her visit Giuseppe's village for the day. Giuseppe hooked Caruso up to a small cart and journeyed on the first Saturday morning in December to meet her. Her father, Giancarlo, arrived with her at 8:00 a.m. at the junction of *Corsa Calatafimi* and the *Via Valle*, the road that led to Bellafortuna.

As Giuseppe approached in his cart, a look came over Maria's face, which her father had not seen before. At that moment, he knew she was falling in love with the young man from Bellafortuna. Maria said *addio* to her father and climbed into Giuseppe's cart. Her father said he would be back at that spot at 5:00 p.m. and expected them to be on time. Giuseppe said he would have her back on time as he sent Caruso up the dirt road heading toward Bellafortuna.

As they neared the village of Bellafortuna, Maria noted the vast vineyards on each side of the road that stretched for miles all the way to the village of Bellafortuna. Rows and rows of grapevines lined the road and ran as far as one could see.

As they passed the vineyards, Giuseppe told Maria who owned each one. He also made a passing mention of the Vasaio clan and how they controlled the lives of his fellow villagers.

At a bend in the road, right before a clump of trees, the road turned slightly east. Right at that point, one could see where an old road made its way to the west. Giuseppe told Maria that the old road once led to the village of Campanèlla before its destruction by an earthquake.

As they made the turn going away from *Antica Campanèlla*, and after passing the clump of trees, Maria got her first glimpse of Bellafortuna, rising in the distance. Giuseppe pointed and said, "There it is - my village of Bellafortuna."

"I had no idea it sat up so high. I can't wait to see it."

The road began to climb, and the vineyards on the slope of the hill were joined by the olive groves located all along the slope of the hill. Workers were hard at work, but they stopped to yell their hellos to Giuseppe as he passed.

When they reached the very top of the hill, Giuseppe pulled Caruso around, allowing Maria to view the entire valley below.

"*Gran Dio.* I now know why the village is called

'Bellafortuna'. This is the most beautiful view I have ever seen in my life," she said.

From their vantage point, the vineyards were lined up in perfect rows. The homes of the vineyard owners were interspersed throughout the valley. There were also a number of farms below, raising the livestock and growing the food that were used by the villagers.

Off to her far right, down in the valley, Maria noticed the bluest pond she had ever seen. Next to the pond were some old ruins, as well as what looked like an old amphitheater. Giuseppe told her, "That is *Antica Campanèlla*. Before we leave today, I will take you down to the old village. It's a wonderful place to visit."

Giuseppe pulled Caruso around and drove the cart to the village of Bellafortuna, through the *Piazza Santa Croce* to the Pandolfini stables behind *Il Paradiso*, where he introduced Maria to his uncle, Onofrio Pandolfini before they entered the wine store from the back door.

"PAPA, I would like you to meet *Signorina* Maria Giulini," Giuseppe said as they entered the wine store.

His father was working behind the counter. Antonio looked at the young woman and said, "You are just as beautiful as Giuseppe described. It's a pleasure to meet you."

"*Grazie, Signor* Sanguinetti. It's nice to finally meet you as well."

"How was your trip to our lovely village?"

"Magical, *Signor*. The valley is so beautiful. And the views from the village are truly spectacular. Giuseppe promises to show me more."

"Giuseppe, Mamma Lucia will be coming down shortly. I know she is anxious to meet Maria as well."

While they waited, Giuseppe showed Maria around the wine store. She was amazed at all of the bottles of wine and the way they were arranged to perfection. She also noticed the Victrola and, above it, the napkin with Caruso's drawing. Giuseppe told her about his meeting Caruso in Milan. She said, "My brother would die if he saw this."

Giuseppe replied, "I know it's hard to see because it's a caricature, but it's uncanny to me how much your brother resembles the great singer."

She laughed, saying, "They both have the same kind of face. I guess you can say they do resemble each other, but only in looks, Giuseppe, not in voice."

"Maria, your brother has an exceptional voice."

As they continued to speak, Mamma Lucia came from upstairs and into the wine store. She immediately hugged the young girl from Monreale. She told her, "We have heard so much about you. Can you cook?"

Antonio laughed while Giuseppe looked on, mortified.

"I can, *Signora*."

"*Va bene*. Giuseppe is my *figubeda*," Mamma Lucia responded. When she had a moment alone with her grandson, she told him how much she approved of his choice. "You will have fair children," she said to Giuseppe, referring to Maria's blonde hair. He blushed.

Giuseppe and Maria left the wine store and took a stroll around the village, with Giuseppe giving the tour and introducing her to the people they ran across. There was one store in the Piazza they had to go into, at Maria's request. It was Fiorenza's clothing store, Meridiana. Maria thought she was in heaven once she was inside the store. Fiorenza showed her some of the different outfits she had designed herself. When they left the store a short time later, Maria had two bags full of clothes that Giuseppe put in the wine store to be picked up later.

They spent the rest of the early morning seeing all the sights of the village. When Giuseppe took her into the *Chiesa della Madonna*, Padre Mancini was very excited to see Maria. He did not know that the two of them were dating but was thrilled for the both of them. After all, both came from good families.

On the street between the *Chiesa* and *Meridiana*, leading out of the Piazza, Giuseppe showed her Tomaso Gianfala and Nicolo Bonura's barbershop, Vito Anzalone's butcher shop, Marco Tumminello's grocery and the village grammar school, *Benedetta Vergine*.

He took her to see a flower shop and a very small library. He also took her to the northern side of the village from which she was able to look toward Palermo and the Sea in the far distance.

She said, "Giuseppe, I thought the greatest view in the world was from the terrace of the *Duomo* in Monreale. It is nothing compared to the views Bellafortuna affords. I could spend all day taking it all in."

Soon they were back in the Piazza, sitting on a bench near the statue of Enzo Boccale, awaiting the arrival of Biaggio so they could have lunch with him before embarking on their tour of *Antica Campanèlla*.

Maria looked toward the *Palazzo Vasaio* and asked Giuseppe, "Who lives in that big place?"

"*Bastardi*. That is who lives there. That is the home of the Vasaios."

Giuseppe then said to Maria, "Enough about them. Let's talk about us." He nervously cleared his throat and said, "We have been seeing each other for over a month now, and I want you to know that the time we spend together is very special to me."

Maria smiled and touched Giuseppe's hand, which was resting on the bench. Giuseppe continued, "I have also gotten to know your family, and I like them immensely."

Maria smiled again, saying, "They like you, too, Giuseppe. My brother loves speaking to you about opera."

Giuseppe stood up from the bench and began to pace back and forth. He said, "I have never had a girlfriend before."

"I've never had a boyfriend before, Giuseppe."

He said, "I consider myself very lucky to be with you. From the first time I laid my eyes on you, I wanted to be with you. Since that day, my dream has come true. I guess what I'm trying to say is . . ."

Maria cut off his words and replied, "*T'amo*, Giuseppe."

Giuseppe took a deep breath, more out of relief, and said, "That is what I was hoping to hear. I love you, too."

"Giuseppe, you're so adorable when you get nervous."

Giuseppe walked back over to where Maria was sitting and kissed her. He said. "I'm so glad you came today." Their conversation was cut short by the arrival of Biaggio.

Biaggio shook hands with Maria, saying, "For the past few weeks I have heard Giuseppe talk about nothing else except the girl he had met in Monreale. I now know why he only spoke about you."

"*Grazie*, Biaggio. When I'm with Giuseppe, he talks about you a lot."

The trio made their way over to Bellini's to have an early and quick lunch. Turiddu was in rare form, ranting and raging about the Vasaios the moment they entered the small *trattoria*.

After they placed their order, Biaggio told Maria about Turiddu's daily habit of shouting at Vittelio in the *Palazzo Vasaio* and peeing on his home after the Angelus. She loved the story.

Each one had a plate of lasagna and a glass of wine. The conversation between them never stopped. After lunch, they got into the cart and traveled down to the valley and onto the road that led to *Antica Campanèlla*. After passing vineyards, the road came to some farms and the granary that stored most of the food products consumed by the villagers. A granary had always stood on this very spot dating all the way back to ancient times. It reminded the villagers of Bellafortuna how long their ancestors had worked these same fields and how tied to the soil their lives had always been.

A little further along, past the farms and the granary, was another vineyard and a small home located near the road. Giuseppe said to Maria, "This is Biaggio's vineyard and home."

Maria replied, "Biaggio, it's wonderful. It's a lovely vineyard."

Biaggio said, "*Grazie*. My father takes great pride in it. At one point in our history, before the Vasaios came to power, my family was quite successful. See those buildings over there. They are the remnants of the Boccale Winery, which once existed here in Bellafortuna. Our village was once a great producer of wine, as well as olive oil. It all came to an end with the rise of the Vasaios."

A few hundred yards from the Spatalanata home were the ruins of the Boccale Winery and the storage sheds. Giuseppe told Maria, "It was in this very spot where *Vino di Bellafortuna* was once produced and sold throughout Sicily and Italy by our ancestors. Now it is just a shamble."

The road went on a little further, past what had been the Occipintis' vineyard until it came to two Greek columns located on either side of the road. One of the columns had fallen over. However, the words on both columns could still be read: *Benvenuto Campanèlla.*

Biaggio said, "Here we are, Maria. Welcome to *Antica Campanèlla.*"

Giuseppe stopped Caruso and tied him to a tree after they had exited the cart. As they did so, Maria looked down the road that ran through the old village. There were a few buildings - all overgrown with weeds and bushes - that were still standing. However, most of the buildings were nothing more than rubble.

As they walked through the old village, Biaggio remarked to Maria that the reason so many of the buildings were in disarray, besides being destroyed in the earthquake which had forced the move, to begin with, was because some of the building supplies for the new homes came from here when Bellafortuna was being built high up on the plateau.

"In that way, a part of this old village still lives on," added Giuseppe.

The trio continued to walk down the main road through

the village. Giuseppe and Biaggio took Maria inside a few of the homes that were still standing. It was obvious that at one time, people of wealth lived in them. Giuseppe showed to Maria one area that was completely barren. This was the ancestral home of the Sanguinettis.

They continued walking through the village along the main road, which led directly to the *Stagno Azzurro* and the *Cappella di C*ampanèlla. As they climbed over the ruins of the chapel, Maria said, "This is the pond I saw from the crest of the hill by the village. I've never seen a pond this blue."

Giuseppe said, "This is the pond where Biaggio and I fish every weekend."

"I couldn't imagine a more peaceful spot," Maria said. "I have been here only a short time, but it's as if this entire old village still has a life. It's hard to explain."

Biaggio smiled and said, "No need to explain. Giuseppe and I know exactly what you are talking about. There is still a spirit about this place."

Past the chapel, Giuseppe led Maria to the amphitheater. As they climbed among the granite benches, Giuseppe told her, "This is the spot where the villagers of old had the opportunity to see plays. One day, I want to turn this into a venue for opera. I have always envisioned the day when these ancient ruins could be refurbished and where operas could be held on a regular basis. The setting on the shore of *Stagno Azzurro* for nighttime performances would be splendid."

Maria said, "That would be wonderful. The way the pond looms behind the stage would make this a beautiful location."

Giuseppe said, "Maria, you have to hear the acoustics."

As Giuseppe made his way to the stone stage, Biaggio sat

next to Maria on the bench. He told her, "You are a very lucky girl. I know I'm biased, but that boy is just about the most caring person you will ever know."

"I know, Biaggio."

"What he and his father are trying to do for this village will never be forgotten."

"What is he trying to do?"

"Rid us of the Vasaios, once and for all. To let the vineyards once again grow our grapes with pride. I love him like a brother and ask that you never hurt him."

"I love him as well, Biaggio. I promise I won't hurt him."

Before Biaggio could reply, Giuseppe was on the stage singing "La donna mobile" from Verdi's *Rigoletto*.

The trees around the amphitheater acted as a natural enclosure for any sound coming from the stage. It truly would make a remarkable place for opera. Midway through the aria, Maria turned to Biaggio and said, "I love him, Biaggio. But not that voice."

Biaggio laughed and agreed that Giuseppe's voice was one of a kind.

A short time later, the trio left *Antica Campanèlla* and made their way back to the village of Bellafortuna. This time, as they passed the vineyards and the olive groves on the slope of the hill leading to the village, Maria noticed that not a worker was to be seen. Biaggio explained that it was siesta, and most of the workers were up in the village.

"Doing what?" she asked.

"Just wait and see," replied Giuseppe. "We are on our way back to the village right now."

Maria had no idea that a concert was about to take place

in the Piazza. Giuseppe and Biaggio wanted her to see it before she left for the day.

MARIA ENJOYED THE CONCERT IMMENSELY. While sitting in the *Piazza Santa Croce*, she quickly became aware that the concerts held by the villagers were not just for entertainment. These concerts gave the villagers hope. It gave them life. These concerts gave the village a soul that would live on for future generations.

After enjoying each other's company as they relaxed in the Piazza taking in the concert, the trio then made their way out of the village and down the road heading toward the junction with the road that led to Monreale. While Bellafortuna was still visible, Giuseppe told Maria, "Look at the village now."

She turned in the cart and looked over her shoulder. High on the hill, glistening in the beginning of a setting sun, was the village of Bellafortuna. In such a light, the entire village gleamed in the distance as though it was made of gold.

"*Paradiso*," she said.

Giuseppe shook his head in disagreement and replied, "It only looks like Paradise. It will be like Paradise again if we can force the Vasaios to release their grip on our people." Biaggio agreed.

Maria thanked both Giuseppe and Biaggio for her wonderful day in the village as well as for the Bordelli painting of the *Piazza Santa Croce* that Giuseppe had bought for her. Biaggio said how nice it was to meet her and that he now understood why his good friend had been spending so much time in Monreale.

The trio continued to talk the rest of the trip to the junction where Giancarlo Giulini was waiting.

After leaving Maria with her father, Giuseppe and Biaggio made their way back home. With the sun setting, Biaggio, who thought he was getting influenza, was cold, so Giuseppe gave him a blanket. Shivering, Biaggio asked point-blank, *"Vuoi sposarla?"* *(Will you marry her?)*

"Sì," was Giuseppe's simple reply.

"Bene," said Biaggio.

The small cart continued down the *Via Valle,* amid the vineyards of Bellafortuna, carrying two dear friends back to their beloved village of Bellafortuna.

15

CON LA MIA MORTE, TROVATE LA LIBERTÀ

*B*y mid-December, Giuseppe had not seen that much of Biaggio because his friend was bedridden, suffering from influenza-like symptoms. On December 16th, Giuseppe returned home from Monreale one late afternoon and found his father having a conversation with Dondo Spatalanata in the wine store. There were tears on Dondo's face.

Giuseppe asked, "Papa, what is wrong? Dondo, what have the Vasaios done to you?"

Dondo turned to Giuseppe, and with great difficulty, told Giuseppe, "*Il tuo amico è moribondo, Giuseppe.*" (*Your friend is dying, Giuseppe.*)

Giuseppe shook his head in disbelief and replied, "What are you talking about? Where is Biaggio? He's just been tired the last few weeks."

Dondo turned away as the tears continued. Antonio looked compassionately at his son and said, "*Vero.* It is true,

Giuseppe. He is very ill. A specialist from Palermo came to see him today. There is nothing that can be done. His frail body is ravaged by disease. He is dying."

Giuseppe covered his face with his hands and cried uncontrollably for a long time. When he finally composed himself, he asked Dondo, "*Signor* Spatalanata, can I see him?"

"He would like that. I'll take you to him right now."

As they made their way to the Spatalanata home, Giuseppe was in a state of shock. He said to Dondo, "I saw him just four days ago. He looked ill, but ...," he was unable to finish the sentence.

Dondo patted his son's good friend on the back and replied, "It is cancer, Giuseppe. We never knew it, but it has finally been confirmed that he's had it for years. He has fought bravely his entire life to overcome it. He has finally lost the battle."

"Is there nothing that can be done?"

"*Nulla.*"

Giuseppe said, "If money is an object, I could speak to my father. We can send him to the best doctor in Italy."

Dondo shook his head and replied, "Giuseppe, there is no hope. If there were, I would sell my entire vineyard, trust me. But the cancer is too far along."

Giuseppe bit his lip as he tried to hold back the tears while the cart continued down the road.

Dondo led Giuseppe inside the home and walked with him to Biaggio's bedroom door. Dondo slowly opened it and went in, followed closely by Giuseppe.

In the sparse bedroom was Biaggio's bed, situated in the middle of the room. Biaggio was asleep under heavy covers up to his neck. His face was as pale as a ghost. His breathing was somewhat labored. Victoria, his mother, was sleeping in a chair next to the bed, her hand clasping her son's on the bed.

Dondo walked over to the bed and whispered into his son's ear. "Biaggio, Giuseppe is here to see you."

Biaggio's eyes fluttered open, and he turned his head to the right. As his eyes focused, they landed upon the image of Giuseppe. A smile came to his face. "*Amico,*" he said.

Giuseppe hurriedly went to his side and knelt next to the bed. Victoria woke up and thanked Giuseppe for coming. After a few moments, Biaggio asked his father and mother to leave the two friends alone.

Giuseppe began to cry the moment Biaggio's parents left the room.

Biaggio looked at his good friend while patting his arm and said, "*Non piangere,* Giuseppe. This is all of God's will. He has a purpose in my dying."

"Biaggio, have they tried everything? My father will pay for whatever you need."

A smile came to Biaggio's face. "I know he would, Giuseppe. But it is finished. My time is up. There was talk of sending me to a specialist in Bologna. My poor father knew he would never be able to pay for that and keep up the vineyard. But he was prepared to do whatever was necessary. But the specialist from Palermo, after looking me over from head to toe, decided that nothing could be done. In a way, Giuseppe, I was thrilled to hear that Bologna was not an option because my father would have been in financial troubles and the Vasaios would be eager to foreclose on his beloved vineyard.

"You see, Giuseppe. My father is a simple man who

loves God and his family. He takes great pride in his vineyard. My one wish in life was to see him have the opportunity to have his grapes produced and sold here in Bellafortuna like his ancestors had done. That is all I ever wanted for him. Because of you and your father, there is now a glimmer of hope that it could be achieved. No, Giuseppe. Tell your father he does not need to pay for any specialist for me. Save his money and spend it on rebuilding the Boccale Winery and olive presses. Free the village from the Vasaios. That is my one and only request to you. Bring freedom to my father. Promise me you will continue to try."

"Biaggio, I promise. I will do what I can."

"Giuseppe, I know I can trust a promise from you. I'm so tired. Just sit with me for a while. Don't leave me. Let me sleep while you're with me."

"Sure, Biaggio. I won't leave you."

"*Ti voglio bene, amico.*"

Biaggio drifted asleep. When he woke up early the next day, Giuseppe was still sitting next to his bed.

GIUSEPPE STAYED home from school the entire next week. He spent all of his time at Biaggio's side. As the week progressed, Biaggio grew weaker and weaker. Both Dondo and Victoria were visibly upset as well as Biaggio's sisters. With no hope of recovery, all they could do was to keep a vigil watching their loved one die.

On December 22nd, Giuseppe was getting dressed at his home, after spending all night at the Spatalanata home.

Suddenly, the door to his room flew open, and Biaggio's older sister, Anna, rushed in.

"Giuseppe, my mother said to come at once and bring the Monsignor."

Giuseppe ran over to the Church to get the Monsignor. However, Padre Mancini informed Giuseppe that the Monsignor had left for Rome two nights ago to spend a month there celebrating his seventy-fifth birthday and his fifty years as a priest. So, the young priest came with Giuseppe instead. Meanwhile, Antonio had gone to the Pandolfini stables to get his cart for them to use. The three men and Anna went as fast as Caruso would go to the Spatalanata home.

When they got there, Biaggio was in bed. Beads of sweat were on his brow. His face was even much paler than before. But a slight smile came to rest on his lips when he heard Giuseppe's voice.

Padre Mancini went over to the bed and immediately performed the last rites, to prepare Biaggio's soul for his journey to Paradise. After the oil of salvation had been put on Biaggio's forehead, the priest bent down and whispered a prayer into his ear. The priest then went to offer his sympathy to the family. Antonio stayed off to the side of the room.

With all the strength Biaggio could muster, he called Giuseppe over to him. Giuseppe rushed to him and said, "*Sono qui.*" (*I am here.*)

With trouble, Biaggio spoke, "*È finita*, Giuseppe."

Tears began to flow down Giuseppe's face. Biaggio continued, "Listen carefully to me. By the *Stagno Azzurro*, across the pond from the amphitheater, there is a small knoll, covered with trees. Bury me there so that I can always look upon my pond. And the day you make the amphitheater into a venue for opera, know that I will be listening to that first performance from across the pond."

Giuseppe's hand went up to his mouth as he cried uncontrollably. Biaggio shook his finger, saying, "Don't cry, Giuseppe. Remember your promise to me regarding my father."

"I will do my best."

Biaggio's breathing started to become erratic. Giuseppe was about to stand up to get his parents when Biaggio reached out and pulled him close. He whispered into Giuseppe's ear the last words he spoke on this earth, pronouncing every word emphatically. *"Con la mia morte, trovate la libertà."* (*Through my death, find freedom.*) He then fell back lifeless.

"No," Giuseppe yelled as Dondo rushed to the bed. Victoria fell into Antonio's arms. Padre Mancini made the sign of the cross. Giuseppe grabbed Biaggio's hand and shouted again, "No, Biaggio. *Resta con me! Resta con me!"* (*Stay with me!*) Finally, Giuseppe, overcome with emotion, fell limp on the floor next to the bed.

Later that day, the bell of the *Chiesa della Madonna* tolled across the valley, letting all the villagers know that a fellow villager had died.

BIAGGIO'S FUNERAL was held on Christmas Eve morning. It was a gloomy day with the clouds heavily laden with rain. The entire village turned out to attend the services at the *Chiesa della Madonna*. Those who could not fit in the Church remained out in the Piazza. Such a showing of love on the part of the villagers gave the Spatalanata family a feeling of comfort and the knowledge that their son had led a good life.

Giuseppe had spent the day before in Monreale with Maria, grieving. She accompanied him back to Bellafortuna for the funeral. She had slept with Mamma Lucia.

With the Monsignor out of town, Padre Mancini celebrated the Mass and delivered the eulogy. He spoke about the loving family with which Biaggio had been blessed. He also spoke about the importance of friendship on this earth, and the wonderful friend Biaggio had in Giuseppe Sanguinetti. There was a rumble of laughter at one point when the "Sanguinetti slap" was mentioned.

He ended the eulogy with Giuseppe's words. The priest said, "During the last week of Biaggio's life, his friend hardly ever left his side. After one particularly rough night, I ran into Giuseppe as he made his way home to change his clothes and get a quick bite to eat. I asked about Biaggio and was informed it was just a matter of days. I could tell Giuseppe was upset, so I spoke to him at length. He summed up Biaggio's life in one word better than I ever could have. He said, 'Padre, Biaggio is irreplaceable.'"

During communion, Giuseppe walked onto the altar with his violin and played one of Biaggio's favorite pieces of music. He had grown to love the *Intermezzo* from *Cavalleria Rusticana* by Pietro Mascagni since working at *Il Paradiso* during the concerts in the Piazza. Giuseppe played it very beautifully, crying the whole time he played. When he took his seat back in the pew, Maria told him how wonderfully he had played.

At the end of the service, Giuseppe and some of Biaggio's

relatives took their place next to the casket in the middle of the Church aisle. Together they hoisted the casket onto their shoulders and began to proceed outside. The organist, Salvatore Licindoro, was playing an old liturgical funeral dirge.

As the men reached the midway point of the aisle, the congregation, on their own, began to sing softly, 'Va, pensiero'. Walking behind the casket, Biaggio's family was in tears. As the casket was carried out of the Church, the bell tolled for the loss of a fellow villager. The Piazza was filled with villagers, all there to say their final farewell. The casket was loaded into the back of a cart, decorated with black bunting. Caruso was the horse that had been chosen to pull the cart.

Everyone filed out of Church and lined up behind the casket. The cart was pulled a little forward to allow room for everyone filing in behind. Giuseppe was standing next to the casket on the right side of the cart.

As he waited for the procession to the burial place to begin, something made him look up toward the *Palazzo Vasaio*, which he was facing. While 'Va, pensiero' continued to be sung, Giuseppe noticed a face peering out from one of the windows. There was a look of sadness on that face as the person looked down on the moving events taking place in the Piazza.

Giuseppe wasn't sure, because he had seen him only a few times in his life, but he thought the person peering out of the window was Vittelio's son, Santo, who attended boarding school in Taormina and who rarely was ever in Bellafortuna. Giuseppe thought that he must have been in town for Christmas.

Slowly, the procession began to move through the village, down the road leading to the valley, through *Antica Campanèlla*, to the knoll located on the opposite shore of *Stagno Azzurro*, directly across from the amphitheater; the final resting place of Giuseppe's good friend, Biaggio Spatalanata.

When the burial had been completed, and all of the mourners returned to their duties in the village, two lonely figures stayed behind by the burial plot. Sitting on the knoll, looking out across the pond, Giuseppe Sanguinetti, with Maria Giulini holding him tightly, was spending his last moments with his dear friend. In his head, the last words of Biaggio Spatalanata echoed, *"Con la mia morte, troverete la libertà."*

If it were at all possible, Giuseppe would bring freedom to the village.

16

THE BELL TOLLS AGAIN

*T*he days following Biaggio's death were very difficult for Giuseppe. Shock turned to grief; grief turned to anger. He began to ask the question that most survivors ask after the death of a loved one; how could God allow this to happen?

Giuseppe became a recluse during the Christmas and New Year holidays. At midnight on New Year's Eve, he walked aimlessly around the streets of Bellafortuna, not in any mood to attend a party welcoming the New Year. As he walked the streets that night, while his fellow neighbors were throwing their dishes out of the windows of their homes onto the street below - an old custom of Sicilians to scare off the evil spirits for the New Year - Giuseppe thought about Biaggio. He would dearly miss spending time with Biaggio.

During his time off from school for the holiday, when he was not helping his father at the wine store, Giuseppe would sit for hours among the ruins of the *Cappella di Campanèlla,* looking out over the *Stagno Azzurro*, toward the knoll and the simple cross that marked Biaggio's grave. Other times, he would sit on the knoll with his violin and play music, usually with tears in his eyes as he thought of his good friend.

One day, while he was still on holiday from school, Giuseppe stopped in the *Chiesa della Madonna* to say a quick prayer. While he was in a pew, Padre Mancini came on the altar to fix a few candles whose wicks had disappeared and were no longer able to be lit. The priest noticed Giuseppe sitting in the pew, crying. The priest walked over to Giuseppe and sat down in the pew directly in front of him.

"Giuseppe, it's good to see you. *Come va?*"

"It's been rough, Padre."

"I'm sure it has been. Have you seen Dondo or Victoria lately?"

"No. I can't bring myself to see them."

The priest said, "I went to Biaggio's home the other day to check on the family. Dondo is holding up as well as can be expected. Victoria, on the other hand, has not been doing well. Men like us have no idea the feeling of loss a woman must have when the life she brought into this world is extinguished before her own. A life she created and carried in her own body. Her pain is deep, Giuseppe. Just as I am sure, yours is."

Giuseppe asked, "Why did God allow this to happen? *Perchè* Padre?" (Why Padre?)

"Giuseppe, I will be completely honest with you. If you would ask the Monsignor that question, he would tell you, like he has done at numerous funerals, that God allowed it to happen so that we, the ones who are still living, can learn from death to appreciate our life a little more and to have an awareness of our ultimate destiny.

"The Monsignor is a very experienced priest, Giuseppe. He truly believes God speaks to him. On the other hand, I'm just a young priest in a small village. Simple humility compels me to believe that God makes His presence known to me in the same way He makes His presence known to every person. Our faith teaches us that God has given to me a special calling. If that is the case, I should try to live my life with even more humility. I became a priest because I truly believed it was my best way to help people. And I have learned that through my ministry of Jesus's sacraments to the people and that by showing them goodwill and sympathy in Jesus's name, I am providing a great help and solace to them. There is no need for me to look beyond that for meaning in my priestly life.

"I don't try to pretend that I have the answers to all of humanity's questions. My explanation to you of why God allowed Biaggio to die would be that I have none. To even try would be nothing more than a guess. I know God acts in different ways in different situations. It's pointless to even try to figure out why he allowed something like this to happen. Instead, I do know that we have to continue to live. And that is what you must do. The pain of your loss will subside, and so will your anger. However, your love of Biaggio will grow, and he will never be forgotten in your heart. And by living, you will find a purpose in the loss of Biaggio. It will take time, but you will. And perhaps, that purpose was why God acted."

Giuseppe thought for a second before he replied by saying, "Biaggio's last words to me were, '*Con la mia morte, troverete la libertà'*. He asked me to swear to him that I would bring freedom to the village; that I would rid our village of the Vasaios. Since his death, I now know this is what I must do. I have dedicated my life to bringing this about."

The priest looked at Giuseppe with awe and asked, "Are you really going to try to take them on? They are very powerful."

"I am Padre. When the time is right, I will act. All of my fellow villagers are prepared as well. We have formed a group, the *Società della Libertà per Bellafortuna*. We will come together to remove the shackles of oppression and throw the Vasaios out. Will you help me?"

"Giuseppe, you know how close the Monsignor is to Vittelio Vasaio. If I did help you, God only knows what the Monsignor would do to me. The Vatican would probably send me to some outpost in America, probably all the way in California. No, Giuseppe. What you want to do is noble, but there is no way that I can be a part of it."

Giuseppe said emphatically, "Padre, the Vasaios bring misery to our people."

"Giuseppe, you're asking me to do something that I cannot do. I will pray for your success, and your secret desire is safe with me, but I cannot and will not help you or your fellow neighbors in this plan. *Grazie*, no."

"*Perdoni me*, Padre. I do not understand. But you will always be my good friend, and I will hold you to your promise of prayers for these people and me."

———

WHEN GIUSEPPE WENT to bed that night, he couldn't sleep. He

understood why Padre Mancini felt that he was in a position where he could not help him. Yet, Giuseppe still was disappointed in the priest. If a priest wouldn't stand up to fight oppression, then why become a priest in the first place?

After midnight, Giuseppe was finally able to fall asleep. He was awakened around seven the next morning, Wednesday, by the slow tolling of the bell from the tower of the *Chiesa della Madonna*.

Bong...

This was the same bell that had tolled less than two weeks ago for Biaggio. Why was it tolling now? Which villager had passed away during the course of the night?

Bong...

Giuseppe quickly got dressed and made his way to the Piazza to hear the news. He did not yet know that the bell was tolling for a death in the family.

Bong...

A DEATH IN THE FAMILY

*B*ong…

Giuseppe made his way from his upstairs room down to the wine store. He did not see his father or Mamma Lucia. He continued out of the front door of the wine store and into the Piazza.

Bong…

People were milling all around the Piazza. Ahead of him, by the statue of Enzo Boccale, he saw Turiddu speaking with Giacomo Terranova.

Bong…

He headed in that direction. As he approached, he asked Turiddu, "Who died?"

Bong…

Turiddu, with a smile on his face, replied, "Carlo Vasaio has finally met his maker."

Bong…

The bell tolled for the last time. Giacomo Terranova said, "He died early this morning."

Turiddu said, "I'm not attending that person's funeral. I spit on him and his family." With that, he cocked his head back and spat forcefully on the ground.

Giuseppe noticed his father at the far end of the Piazza speaking with Mamma Lucia and Graziella Pandolfini, the wife of the stable master where Caruso was kept. Giuseppe excused himself from his conversation with Turiddu and Giacomo and made his way over to where his father was standing.

Antonio inquired, when Giuseppe walked over, "Have you heard the news?"

"I have."

"Tonight a special meeting of the *Società* has been called. We are to discuss the event that just occurred and what our response should be."

"I can tell you that Turiddu thinks we should not attend the funeral."

Antonio said, "I've been hearing a lot of the same talk. We must pay our respects to Carlo Vasaio, even if he brought misery to the village."

"Papa, I knew you would feel that way. I agree with you. We must pay our respects."

THE *SOCIETÀ della Libertà per Bellafortuna* met that night at the Silveri barn. All of the members were in attendance. Luigi Tavelo was the first to speak that night. It was a raucous crowd he had to speak to.

Luigi said, "The funeral is set for tomorrow. As most of you know, the Monsignor is still in Rome and will be there for a few more weeks. Therefore, Padre Mancini will be saying the Mass. I've heard rumblings that none of us should go. I disagree. We should pay our respects to the deceased."

Turiddu stood up at this point and began to speak very passionately. He said, "Since the first time we came together and formed this little group, every meeting has been filled with discussions and examples of the misery caused by the Vasaios. Now, when one of the leaders of those hateful people dies, there is talk of forgiveness. Talk of respect for him. I say they do not deserve respect. Let the Vasaios roll their loved one out of Church and out of this village to his grave with an empty Church and empty streets. Let them know we have no respect for them. Let them know their loved one has to answer to God alone."

Fiorenza stood up, cutting off Turiddu, saying, "Turiddu, but what about the Monsignor? If he were here, he would expect us to be at the funeral."

Turiddu smiled and replied, "*Bella Signora*, he's not here. So it is our decision. It is always easier to ask for forgiveness than permission. If we are wrong, we can say how sorry we were. But I vote we do not go."

Giacomo Terranova stood up and said, "I agree with Turiddu. We owe nothing to these people. I vote as well that we don't go."

The crowd murmured back and forth, with some concerned about what Vittelio might do if they didn't go to his father's funeral. Luigi tried to regain control of the floor but to no avail. Just as it reached a fever pitch, Dondo Spatalanata stood up from the hay bale he was sitting on. He had been quiet the entire night. The moment he stood up, the barn was silenced. He began to speak, and everyone listened.

"Less than two weeks ago, my son died. It was a devastating loss. When you lose someone, the feeling of helplessness is truly overwhelming. I know because I am experiencing it. The Church tells us in a time of need to turn to prayer, for God will help us.

"Prayer is a good thing. But that alone is not what gets you through the pain of the loss. It's also the support of people. Walking down the aisle of the Church as well as stepping out into the Piazza and seeing all of you there for Biaggio meant everything to Victoria and me. It gave us the strength to continue on.

"So, no Turiddu. I vote we go to the funeral. Not for the Vasaios, but because it's the right thing to do."

Turiddu fired back, "They were not there for your son's funeral. We should not be there for Carlo's."

Dondo replied, "Even more reason why we should go, Turiddu."

The debate raged on. People were arguing back and forth until Giacinto Bordelli, the good-looking tailor and painter, spoke. He said, "All of you are missing the point. Dondo, with all due respect to you and your family who are suffering at this time, we went to the funeral for your son because we loved him and you. Not one Vasaio came. We, the members of this *Società*, have been asking when is the right time for action. The time is now. With the death of Carlo, we can make our feelings known like we have not been able to do so before. Let Vittelio Vasaio know once and for all that his control is waning. Let his father roll out of this village as if it were just an ordinary day."

Cheers echoed throughout the room. Luigi finally got control of the floor and asked Dondo, "What do you think about Bordelli's words?"

Dondo's head was bowed. He slowly lifted it and said, "I have complete trust in Antonio's leadership. I will agree to follow whatever he believes is the best course of action."

Agreement echoed throughout the room as all eyes turned toward Antonio. Antonio sat on a bale of hay in contemplation, as everyone begged him to speak. Antonio had not spoken throughout the entire meeting. His reasons for silence, which only Giuseppe could understand, were because of Antonio's father's business dealings with Carlo Vasaio in the past. He felt it was not his place to get involved in this argument. He thought the villagers should go to the funeral, but also thought that if he strenuously argued the point, it would be viewed as payment for an old debt the Sanguinettis owed to Carlo Vasaio.

Now that the spotlight was on Antonio, he stood up and softly said, "I have listened to the arguments on both sides, both of which are very persuasive. So much so, that I find that this is neither mine nor any individual's decision to make. It should be a decision as a group. Therefore, I say a vote should be taken for a final decision of this matter."

There was universal agreement that this was the best choice. By a show of hands, the *Società della Libertà per Bellafortuna* voted 36-7 not to attend the funeral of Carlo Vasaio, with Antonio not voting as the head of the *Società* except in case of a tie.

Word spread quickly throughout the village that tomorrow the villagers of Bellafortuna would be making a statement by not attending the funeral.

As Giuseppe and Antonio made their way home that night, Giuseppe asked his father, "Do you think they were right, voting that way?"

"No, Giuseppe. But it's understandable."

LATER THAT SAME NIGHT, there was a loud knock on the front door of the Sanguinetti wine store. Giuseppe ran downstairs and found Padre Mancini at the door.

"Ah, Giuseppe, just the person I was hoping to see."

"*Buona sera*, Padre. Would you like to come in?"

"*Si*. Just for a moment. I need to speak to you briefly about something."

Giuseppe let the priest inside the wine store. As the priest walked inside, he said, "I know you heard the news today about Carlo Vasaio dying."

"*Si*. I heard the news."

"Well, with the Monsignor still out of town, the funeral preparation has been left to me. Vittelio and Santo Vasaio just left a meeting with me about preparations for the funeral tomorrow."

"Padre, how does this concern me?"

"Giuseppe, you played the violin so beautifully at Biaggio's funeral that I thought it would be nice if you did the same at Carlo's."

Giuseppe's face took on a hard look. Shaking his head, he replied, "Padre, I cannot."

"Cannot or will not?"

"Both."

"I do not understand your reaction, *amico*."

Giuseppe thought momentarily and finally replied, "You are my friend, and therefore, I owe you an explanation. But what I am about to tell you must be kept secret. You must treat it like a confession. You must never tell the Monsignor. I want to tell you this, and I trust you."

"Giuseppe, you know you can trust me. What you tell me will stay with me."

"The *Società della Libertà per Bellafortuna* voted tonight as a group not to attend the funeral of Carlo Vasaio."

Forcefully, the priest said, "Giuseppe, the vote that was taken tonight is wrong."

"I asked my father what he thought about the vote. He disagreed with the result but told me it was understandable. I agree with him. The Vasaios have brought this village nothing more than pain and suffering. It is too much to ask to have these people stand together and celebrate the life of the person who persecuted them. It's too much to ask."

"But Giuseppe, that is exactly what God asks of us. It's easy to take the path that is not dangerous. However, God wants us to take the path upon which we would not dare to tread. I know it's too late for me to convince the entire village to change their minds and attend the funeral. But it's not too late for you. Please play the violin tomorrow."

"Padre, I appreciate everything you have said. But I cannot, unless if by my playing, Vittelio Vasaio stops hurting my people."

"Giuseppe, you never know what happens when an act of kindness is done. And that is what I am asking for, an act of kindness. Kindness has no boundaries. You never know what shore it will wash up on."

Giuseppe stood before the priest dumbfounded. Perhaps,

through kindness, a door could be opened that might allow freedom into the village. With those simple words of the priest, Giuseppe's mind had been changed.

"I will play, Padre. *Giocherò*."

"*Molto bene, amico*." The priest hugged his friend and left for the night. Giuseppe returned upstairs to relate his decision to his father. He knew his father would agree with it. As for the rest of the villagers, Giuseppe would just have to wait to see their reaction.

SANTO'S LAMENT

*T*he morning of Carlo Vasaio's funeral was exceptionally beautiful. The sky was a deep blue, without a cloud anywhere in sight. As Giuseppe walked to the Church, he noticed that the Piazza was crowded with his fellow villagers going about their daily chores.

Giuseppe arrived at the Church an hour before the funeral was set to begin. Padre Mancini was on the altar getting everything ready. When Giuseppe approached the altar, the priest thanked Giuseppe for agreeing to play at the funeral. He also said to Giuseppe, "Young di Franco's son, Gennario, was supposed to be my acolyte. It came as no surprise when his father came by an hour ago to inform me that his son was 'sick' and unable to serve. These people really hate the Vasaios, Giuseppe. After the funeral Mass, will you aid me at the gravesite?"

Realizing that he had already committed himself to

something that would be displeasing to his fellow villagers, Giuseppe stated with resignation, "*Si.*"

"*Grazie*, Giuseppe."

Giuseppe went up to the choir loft to warm up while Padre Mancini continued to get things ready for the Mass.

The first people to arrive at the Church to say their final farewell to Carlo were Vittelio and Ada, who walked into the Church holding hands. Santo and a few other relations soon joined them.

Lastly, the *Scagnozzi* arrived. No one else came into the Church.

At precisely 10:00 a.m., Padre Mancini walked onto the altar. Directly in front of the altar, in the middle of the aisle of the Church, lay the remains of Carlo Vasaio. On either side of the casket sat the Vasaios and their employees. Padre Mancini looked out across the rest of the Church, which was completely empty. Even though Giuseppe had made him aware of the villagers' intentions, he was still surprised that not one villager was in attendance.

During the eulogy, Padre Mancini apologized on behalf of the Monsignor who would have wanted to be there for the Vasaio family at their moment of grief. The rest of his sermon concerned how death is not really the end, but the beginning of a new life, a life with Christ.

As Padre Mancini spoke, Giuseppe could not help but reflect on how different the eulogy was for Biaggio's funeral. Padre Mancini had made Biaggio's much more personal. But without an overpowering show of love in the Church, what else could Padre Mancini do, Giuseppe thought. The priest couldn't speak of how loved Carlo had been and all that he had done for the village, although Giuseppe was sure that is what the Monsignor would have said if he had been giving the eulogy instead.

A little later, as Santo and a few of his relatives carried the casket containing the remains of Carlo Vasaio out of the Church, Giuseppe played a small part of the Overture to Verdi's *Sicilian Vespers*.

As the procession came out of the Church, the pallbearers stopped dead in their tracks. The Piazza was completely deserted. As the rest of the Vasaios came out of the Church, they, too, were astonished to find the Piazza empty.

AFTER THE BURIAL, Giuseppe and Padre Mancini returned to the Church. The priest was grateful for Giuseppe's help with the funeral. As Padre Mancini went into the sacristy to change, Giuseppe went up to the choir loft to get his violin.

Just as he came down the stairs of the choir loft at the back of the Church, he noticed Santo Vasaio also walking toward the sacristy.

Santo was tall like Giuseppe. He was well built, with heavy, dark eyes and thick, black wavy hair. Giuseppe quickly followed, but he stayed outside the sacristy within listening range.

Santo thanked the priest for saying the Mass "Padre Mancini, on behalf of my entire family, I wanted to thank you for your kind words at the funeral of my grandfather."

"*Prego*, Santo. I know the Monsignor will be upset that he missed it when he gets back in town."

"No, Padre. I'm glad we had you. You did a wonderful job."

"Santo, *molta grazie.*"

"Also, Padre, my father advised me that you might be able to help me with my plans."

"If I am able. What do you need?"

"As you know, I go to school in Taormina. However, since I've been home for Christmas, with grandfather ill during my entire stay, I started speaking to my father about transferring to a high school in Monreale, a Jesuit school, *St. Ignatio.* That way, I could help my father, now with grandfather deceased."

Giuseppe listened intently from his hiding spot, imagining what it would be like to have Santo in his class. Santo continued, "My father grew tired of fighting me about it and said I could do it if the school would agree to the transfer. I know you have connections with the school. Could you help me?"

Padre Mancini said, "If you want, I will go with you to Monreale tomorrow to meet with Padre Molinari, the headmaster. I will see if it will be acceptable to him."

"*Grazie*, Padre. I will owe you for this."

"*Prego*, young Vasaio. How is your family holding up after the loss of Carlo?"

"To be honest, Padre, they were doing well until the funeral. After you left the gravesite, my family spoke about the way that none of the villagers of Bellafortuna had come to the funeral. They shunned my family."

Padre Mancini took a breath and said, "Santo, these people are good people. They believed they were doing the right thing. They did not love your grandfather."

Giuseppe's mouth dropped open from his hiding spot. Padre Mancini had said something to a Vasaio that let them know all was not well in the village. However, the reaction of

Santo to the words of Padre Mancini shocked Giuseppe even more.

Santo said, "Padre, my family has always felt that it has done good things for the villagers. Today has shown me that at least in the villagers' minds, that belief is wrong. Just a few days ago, I watched the funeral for a young man who had died. The outpouring of grief and love for that boy was overwhelming. Today was the exact opposite. I told my father that I don't want to bury him to the sound of silence that I witnessed today."

Giuseppe was leaning forward, trying to hear, when by accident, his violin case struck the sacristy door.

Both Santo and Padre Mancini stopped talking and looked toward the door. Giuseppe, knowing his cover was blown, quickly walked into the sacristy, apologizing for the intrusion because he wanted to tell the priest goodbye.

Padre Mancini said, "Santo, this is Giuseppe Sanguinetti, the violinist at the service today."

Santo extended his hand and said, "You played beautifully. Thank you for playing. Sanguinetti? Are you any relation to Salvatore?"

"He was my grandfather."

"I've heard a lot about him from my grandfather, Carlo. He really liked him."

With a touch of sarcasm, Giuseppe replied, "Thanks."

Santo turned to the priest and excused himself, reminding him of their date tomorrow for Monreale. The moment Santo left the sacristy, Giuseppe smiled at the priest and said, "Did you hear what he said to you, Padre? He knows his family is not liked around Bellafortuna. That is what we have been waiting for. For the first time, there is an opening in the armor of the Vasaios. Santo is that weak link. Through Santo, we may be able to get to Vittelio."

Padre Mancini asked, "Were you listening to our conversation, Giuseppe?"

"I cannot lie to a priest. I most certainly was listening."

Padre Mancini smiled and bid Giuseppe a good day.

As Giuseppe made his way home, Biaggio's last words came to mind. Indeed, Biaggio's death had made an impact on Santo Vasaio. Perhaps, through Biaggio's death, the village would find freedom.

GIUSEPPE'S NEW CLASSMATE

*G*iuseppe saw Padre Mancini the very next night. Giuseppe asked him about his trip to Monreale with Santo. Padre Mancini said in reply, "As I said before, I cannot get involved in your endeavor with your fellow villagers. However, I will report to you that without question, the villagers' response, or non-response actually, to the death of Carlo truly had an effect on Santo. He spoke to me about it both to and from Monreale."

"Padre, do you think it really had an effect on him? Do you believe he is sincere? After all, he is a Vasaio. We must always keep that in mind."

"I do think he is, Giuseppe. I can see it in his eyes. He has opened up to me, like never before. He told me that he spent an entire night talking to his father and mother about his feelings and raised the question of why his family was so hated by the villagers. Giuseppe, Santo has begun questioning things in his mind."

"Well, let's just hope he finds the right answers."

Padre Mancini laughed and replied, "We will see, Giuseppe. Perhaps you can help him find the correct answers, as you say. You will soon get to know him a lot better. The headmaster has agreed to allow Santo to transfer."

"You're kidding? I can't believe it. I will be going to school with a Vasaio." Lo and behold, just like that, Giuseppe had a new classmate.

Giuseppe spent the last weekend of his holiday break hanging around *Antica Campanèlla*. He thought a lot about Biaggio. He looked forward to going back to school and seeing Maria, although he could not quite come to terms with the notion that Santo Vasaio would be in his class.

He was also looking forward to going back to school for another reason. Ever since the funeral, he felt like a few of the villagers stared at him more. Maybe he was being overly sensitive because he expected people not to be happy with him for playing the violin at the funeral of Carlo Vasaio.

Giuseppe found it strange that first day back in school when the teacher announced to the class the addition of a new student, Santo Vasaio. Giuseppe avoided Santo the entire day

When school let out later that day, Santo found Giuseppe and asked, "Sanguinetti, care to have some company on your return trip home?"

"No, Santo. I'm not going home just yet. I'm going to see someone."

"What about in the morning? Would you like to travel together to school?"

"No, I will not be able to do that. I have too many chores to do before I leave. But I'll see you at school."

With that, Santo and Giuseppe parted company. There was no way Giuseppe was ever going to come to school with Santo Vasaio.

AFTER DEPARTING FROM SANTO, Giuseppe met Maria in the Piazza near her home. He held her in his arms for a long time. It felt good to hold her. She reached into her pocket and pulled out an envelope addressed to him from her brother. Inside was a newspaper article from the Monreale newspaper. The headline read, Caruso to be recognized by the Order of Persephone in Palermo the last Sunday of July. The article related that Caruso was to receive the Golden Palm of Persephone as the outstanding Italian in the world for last year, 1907. Persephone was the mythological Greek goddess who had Sicily as her domain.

When he finished reading the article, Giuseppe said to Maria, "Caruso is coming to Palermo this very summer. How wonderful. Too bad he has no plans to sing. He is just receiving the honor. I will have to go to Palermo to try to meet Caruso and remind him about my special meeting with him in Milan years ago. I'll have to post this article in the wine store so that everyone will know that the great tenor will be at nearby Palermo."

She asked, "Will he remember you?"

"I truly believe that he will because he showed such surprise by what I told him that night. It was just a moment in time, but he would remember."

As they walked, Giuseppe told her all about the events surrounding the death of Carlo Vasaio and how Santo was now a fellow student. She smiled knowingly and said, "The Lord sometimes does work in strange and mysterious ways."

He went on to tell her about his conversations with Padre Mancini and how Santo was questioning things. She asked him, "Do you trust Santo? Do you think he could change?"

"No. He is a Vasaio. I cannot and will not ever trust a Vasaio."

They reached her home, and Giuseppe went in to spend more time with her and to say hello to her family. He truly loved this young woman and was happy to be spending time with her once again.

EVERY DAY, for two weeks, Santo asked Giuseppe to either go to or from school with him. Every day, Giuseppe declined. One day, as Giuseppe was making his way to school, Santo surprised him when he jumped from behind a tree.

Santo said, "Giuseppe, please talk with me."

"What do you want from me, Santo?"

"All I want to do is speak with you."

"Well, keep up if you can."

While the two walked side by side, Santo asked, "You don't like me, do you?"

"I don't like the way your family treats the villagers," replied Giuseppe.

"So you hate me for the actions of my family."

"What this village once had, is now long gone. And it's because of your family." Gesturing with both his hands, Giuseppe pointed to the fields on either side of the road. He then said, "The ancestors of the villagers worked these same fields, and they thrived. They had a good life - a life devoted to God and family. Today, these same fields are worked to line the pockets of your father. Do I hate you? No. I pity you."

Santo said, "My father, like his ancestors before him, has tried to help the people in the village. If it weren't for my family, the villagers couldn't make it on their own. They have relied on the generosity of my family for years."

Giuseppe grimaced, saying, "Is that what you call it? Generosity? You can tell your father we don't want any of his generosity."

"Giuseppe, my family has done wonderful things for the village."

Giuseppe turned toward Santo. "That is where you are wrong, Santo. Your family has brought nothing but misery to the village. That's all. At an early age, you were shipped off, like the rest of your ancestors, to school in Taormina. A clever trick on the part of the Vasaios to assure that their children never become close to any of the villagers over whom they will one day rule. You spend just a few days out of the year in Bellafortuna, and all of it at your father's home. You don't know what it is like to live under his control, especially for someone living in the valley. Next time you have a chance, walk to the edge of the village on top of the hill and look down upon the slope and the valley below. You will immediately notice how rich and fertile this land is and how abundant its harvests are.

"After taking in that view, go down into the valley and see how these people live. With such fertile soil and bountiful harvests, ask yourself why they live in such squalor. Talk with them. Get to know them. Most, if not all, of these people have no idea who you are. Go speak to Dondo Spatalanata, a vineyard owner, and see what happens to him every harvest. Ask Dondo to show you the nearby remnants of the old closed down winery. This was the winery that once brought honor and respect to the village as well as financial rewards. Your family took all of that away. *Tutto.* They left us nothing but debt.

"After you leave the valley, go look at your father's books and see how much interest he charges the villagers on their loans. See how much blood he is taking from us; see his generosity for yourself.

Santo replied, "Every morning, the owner of the *trattoria* in the village is yelling at my father's house, asking if my father died during the night. He pees on our house. These people have no respect. I thought you were different. Now in talking with you, I realize that you're just like the rest of them. You don't know what lengths my family has gone through to help this village or how much money my father has loaned to help the villagers get by."

"Get by? Those loans and their high-interest charges are the means used by your father to control the villagers."

"You're mistaken, Giuseppe."

"Just do what I'm asking you to do. Pay attention. See for yourself." Giuseppe then said forcefully, "Leave me alone until you do that. But you won't do it. You don't want to know the truth."

Santo angrily replied, "Fine. Don't worry. I won't bother you again."

"Good." With that, Giuseppe kicked his pony and, picking up the pace, left Santo behind.

Giuseppe's words stung Santo. He wondered why his family was hated so much?

On either side of him were the vineyards of Bellafortuna. Since it was January, the fields were not as overgrown, so one could see from one end to the other as the fields stretched for miles.

Right near the road was the home of one of the vineyard owners. Santo, at first, thought the home was abandoned but realized when he got closer that a family still lived in the dilapidated home. Behind the home was the owner's grapevines, lined row upon row. Santo asked himself how someone with that much land could live in such conditions.

Instead of continuing to Monreale for school that day, Santo left the road and brought his pony into the front yard of the home. He dismounted, pulled a hat from one of his saddlebags, pulling it down on his head, and walked to the front door. He knocked on the door. The owner of the vineyard, Ettore Fizzarotti, answered it. He was a very old man who had worked these fields for many years.

Santo said, *"Scusi, signor.* My family and I are visiting your lovely village, and we are thinking of moving here. May I come in for a second to ask you what life is like here?"

The old man opened the door and let Santo in.

2 0

SANTO'S DILEMMA

*A*bout two weeks later, in early February, Giuseppe
was working late at the wine store doing inventory
for his father, who had gone to Palermo for the night to meet
with some of his wine distributor friends. Mamma Lucia had
already retired to bed. The hour was growing late, and
Giuseppe was becoming tired.

As Giuseppe worked, the Victrola located in the store had
the singing voice of Caruso emitting from the large horn. The
great tenor's voice swelled throughout the wine store.

Since the purchase of the first record for the Victrola,
Antonio's record collection had grown. He now possessed a
large number of records of Caruso, singing arias and songs.
The voice was truly God-given.

Suddenly, above the sound of Caruso singing 'Celeste
Aida', there was a loud knock on the front door of the wine
store. When Giuseppe opened the door, he was surprised to

find Santo Vasaio standing before him in a large coat, protecting him from the cool, damp, February night.

"Giuseppe, I need to speak to you."

"I'm sorry I can't. I have too much work to do. I'll see you at school tomorrow."

Giuseppe began to shut the door, but Santo had put his elbow against the door, pushing it inward. Santo said, "Please talk with me."

Giuseppe reluctantly opened the door and let Santo in. Once Santo was inside, Giuseppe walked toward the Victrola to turn it off. Santo followed closely behind him.

While Giuseppe was putting the record away, Santo said, "You and your father sure do love opera. Some of the people who work for my father comment all the time how they love walking past the store when Caruso is singing. They have even said that you and your father met him. Is that true?"

Giuseppe pointed to the drawing in the frame above the Victrola and said, "It is true. We met him in Milan when his career was just beginning. He gave me this napkin that night. Since then, it has sat on this wall as a memento of that evening. But, Santo, I'm sure you did not come here to listen to the voice of Caruso. Whatever the reason, please let me get back to work. Just go ahead and leave." Giuseppe turned his back on Santo and walked over to one of the wine racks.

"I went to the valley, Giuseppe, and did what you told me to do."

The comment caught Giuseppe by surprise. He turned back toward Santo and replied with sarcasm, "Good for you."

Santo said, "I have spent the past few weeks speaking to your fellow villagers, mostly those living in the valley. They work hard in the fields every day, with little financial rewards to show for it."

"And that is because of your family," interjected Giuseppe.

Ignoring the comment, Santo said, "Giuseppe, your family is very well respected. The people living in the valley know how much you and your father help them. However, there are people who believe your family could be forced to leave Bellafortuna, like what happened to the Boccales."

Giuseppe bit his lip and then spoke harshly to Santo, saying, "Is that why you came here tonight? Is that why you came to see me? Did your father send you to threaten me; to let me know the Vasaios will try to do to the Sanguinettis what they did to the Boccales? I knew you could never be trusted. Listen to me, even if we were forced out, it truly doesn't matter, Santo. Even if we left, others would take our place. The winds of change have blown through our village."

"Giuseppe, I did not come here tonight to threaten you. I came to tell you about my talks with your fellow villagers."

"You spoke to them?" Giuseppe asked.

"I did. These people did not know I was a Vasaio, so they spoke freely with me."

Giuseppe asked, "What did they tell you?"

"They all spoke about the glory days when Bellafortuna produced its own wine and its own olive oil, and they longed for those days once again. But most of what they told me was their dislike for my family. Example after example was given to me of the hardships these people were forced to endure because of the greed of my father and his family.

"I spoke to many different villagers. Some even hired me for the day to help with some chores out in the fields."

At that comment, Giuseppe couldn't help but laugh out loud at the thought of a Vasaio working in the fields. "You did not?" he asked.

"I most certainly did. I refused their pay and took a free meal instead. The conversations at dinner were real revelations.

"I also began to dig around a little bit in my father's house and looked at my father's books. I was shocked by the amount of money he was bringing in from the villagers, with the high-interest charges paid by the villagers and the immense profits from the sale of their harvests. This forced me to look at my father and my entire family in a different light. For the first time in my life, I began to understand why my family is so disliked."

Giuseppe's mind started to race. What was Santo Vasaio saying? Had he really been touched by his visit to the valley? But he quickly reminded himself to never trust a Vasaio. He said, "*Semplice parole*. Those are mere words, Santo."

Santo continued, "With so much land and fertile soil, I was amazed at the poor conditions under which these people had to live. I began to wonder where their money from the harvests went."

"Santo, take my word for it, their money went into your father's pockets."

"I came to believe that, Giuseppe. I went to seek guidance from Padre Mancini. I told him about our conversation and how you told me to speak to the people living in the valley. Through my conversation with Padre Mancini, it all finally made sense. The priest had let it slip that you overheard our conversation regarding my seeing the funeral of that boy who had died just a few days before my grandfather.

"You told me to go speak with Dondo Spatalanata, which I did this morning. You tricked me, Giuseppe. You knew he was the father of that boy whose funeral had affected me. I should be mad for being used like that. But through my conversations with Dondo, I have become at peace with myself. His words moved me more than any other."

"What do you mean, Santo?"

Santo said, "I'm still not sure if Dondo knew I was a Vasaio or not. Unlike the other villagers down in the valley, he didn't speak to me about how much wealth his family had before the arrival of my family. Instead, he spoke to me about the value of family and about the loss of a great thing that mattered to him, his son, Biaggio. All he had hoped for in life was to take pride in his work and provide for his family. But he felt the Vasaios had taken that all away.

"But what they could not take away was the love of family and the pride he held in his heart for his family as well as for his fellow villagers. He worked hard for his family and tried to raise his family to the best of his ability.

"He took me to the grave of his son. As I sat on the knoll with him, Dondo put it this way, 'All we can do and all we must do is lead a good life. And the only way that can be done is through service to others. My son was not a leader of great armies or a politician leading a country; he was nothing more than a God-fearing individual who cared for others. He tried to live a good life. And in living that simple life, he made this world a better place. At the end of the day, that is all one could hope to be able to say about a loved one'.

"Giuseppe, my family is disliked by the villagers, and now I believe that feeling is justly earned. I know my father has treated the villagers badly. Carlo did too. All they cared about was money. Carlo is now dead. My father lives on. I don't want my father to die like his father, as an old, hateful person, disliked by all. Deep down, I know my father is a good person. But his upbringing caused him to be the way he is. He had no chance to be any different. I will not be like him. I will be different. I want him to be different. I want him to change his ways."

Giuseppe asked, "What makes you think you can be different? You had the same upbringing."

Pointedly, Santo asked Giuseppe, "Why are you so different from your grandfather? I know your grandfather worked with my family."

"By choice, Santo. Like my father, I choose to do good instead of bad."

"Don't I get the same opportunity to make that choice for myself?"

"Yes, but you must change your father's ways first. My grandfather had already changed his ways when my father had to make that choice. Your father, on the other hand, still remains in control, unchanged."

"What are you driving at, Giuseppe?"

"Get your father to drop his interest charges, and then he would be a changed man. You see, Santo, my grandfather, Salvatore, betrayed his fellow villagers when he went into business with your family. However, he later realized he was wrong and walked away from it. With that action, he was welcomed back into the community. When he died, he had a funeral with an outpouring of love. He had changed. Carlo, as was very obvious, did not. Don't let your father make the same mistake. Help him change."

"How could I ever do that?"

"You know him better than I. Find a way."

"Giuseppe, I know my father will not listen to me. But the way you speak with such passion, he may listen to you. If I get you a meeting with him, would you come with me and talk to him?"

"Me talk to your father? I wouldn't know what to say."

"I know the funeral of his father upset him immensely. He now knows fully how deeply disliked we are in the village. I think the time is ripe. He may listen to you if you present a reasoned proposal regarding lowering the interest charges."

"Sure, he may listen. But he will want something in return."

"Not if my feeling is correct. I truly believe that. The time to act is now."

Giuseppe thought momentarily and finally said, "If you can get me an audience with him, I will go speak to him."

"I will get him to agree to the meeting. Just you wait and see."

"For better or worse, Santo, I put my trust in you."

When Santo left later that night, Giuseppe's emotions were mixed. Was Santo really touched by everything he had experienced down in the valley or was this all a game? Some plan, drawn up by Vittelio, to use his son to get to Antonio; to hurt him somehow? "Never trust a Vasaio" was the saying that Giovanni kept running through his head. Yet, there was something tugging at Giuseppe that made him believe, deep down in his gut, that perhaps Santo was being genuine. But how would Giuseppe know? How could he truly know? For the present, Giuseppe was relying on hope more than assurance.

If Santo could somehow get his father to agree to a

meeting, Giuseppe knew he would first have to seek approval from the *Società* for the proposal that would be put forth. He was aware of his serious obligation to receive their input and approval because the results of that meeting would affect them all.

But what were the chances that Santo could really convince Vittelio to have such a meeting? Slim to none was what Giuseppe believed. He would soon find out if his belief was correct.

A DIVIDED VOTE

*G*iuseppe did not have long to wonder. The very next morning, on his way to school, Santo met up with Giuseppe and told him his father had agreed to the meeting. Giuseppe was stunned.

Santo said, "Giuseppe, I believed that after a lengthy discussion and a good bit of battling, I might be able to convince my father to have this meeting. My conversation with him had only just begun when he cut off the discussion and advised me to arrange the meeting."

"Thank you for arranging the meeting, Santo," Giuseppe responded.

"I'm really not sure what I did, Giuseppe. Be careful when you have that meeting. How quickly my father agreed to it, concerns me. Be prepared with your proposal and stick to it."

"Before I attend that meeting, I must get approval from my fellow villagers to see if they want me to go and, if so, what exactly our proposal will be. Will you be at the meeting with your father?"

"*Si.* Giuseppe, the only stipulation my father gave, is that you are the only villager invited to attend the meeting and to represent and negotiate for the villagers, no one else. The meeting will not take place if anyone else comes with you."

"I understand. But let me ask you this. Do you think your father will even consider any proposal I put before him?"

"I still believe he will. He knows change is occurring in the village. I think he wants to change too. I hope I'm not wrong."

"Me too, Santo. Me too."

For the rest of the day, all Giuseppe kept asking himself, was what could he have possibly gotten himself into? Santo did exactly what he said he would do. He got his father to agree to the meeting. Was Santo actually trying to change Vittelio? Giuseppe knew that he would find out soon enough. First, he would have to go to the *Società della Libertà per Bellafortuna* and tell them the news.

THE FOLLOWING WEDNESDAY NIGHT, in the barn of Renato Silveri, the *Società della Libertà per Bellafortuna* was involved in a lively debate regarding the financial stranglehold the Vasaios held on the village. Alberto Capecchi stood up and inquired, "We keep speaking about our hope of one day forcing Vittelio to lower his interest charges. I don't think Vittelio will ever agree to lessen those charges. What if we refinanced the loans ourselves? We may be able to get a bank in Palermo to loan us the funds at a much lower rate. Then we could pay Vittelio off and be done with him."

There were a few cheers in agreement when Alberto concluded his remarks. The clapping stopped, however, when Luigi took the floor. "Alberto has a wonderful idea. But it can go nowhere. We do not know what banks in Palermo, if any, are not influenced by the Mafia. As we all have said in the past, we don't want to do anything by our action that will bring the scourge of the Mafia to our beloved village."

Turiddu stood up and said with disgust, "I'm tired of talk. The time for action is now. All we do is sit around and discuss options. I say the time to take a chance has come. Let us do something to change our way of life."

There was a small amount of applause. Antonio said, "Turiddu, we have to be certain the time is right. We have to be certain of the action we are taking."

Turiddu replied, "I'm tired of words. We want freedom."

Luigi replied, "That is what we all want, Turiddu."

Turiddu said, "Then let's get it."

Fiorenza asked, "But how, Turiddu? That is our problem. You are correct; all we do is talk about the possibilities. But at least we are doing that. Perhaps, through our discussions, we will find a way."

Turiddu asked in return, "How?"

At that moment, Giuseppe, who had said not a word all night, stood up on the bale of hay upon which he had been sitting. With a strong voice, he said, "I may have a way."

There was complete silence throughout the barn. All turned toward Giuseppe. Antonio looked at his son with surprise. Giuseppe continued, "As many of you know, I played the violin at the funeral of Carlo Vasaio."

At Giuseppe's statement, there were rumbles of disapproval by some of the people in attendance. Giuseppe said, "Our decision to not attend the funeral of Carlo Vasaio stung that family deeply. So much so, Santo Vasaio sought me out to find out why his family was so disliked in the village. I told Santo to go down to the valley and see how the people lived there under the crushing hand of his father. He did so. He probably spoke to many of you, without your realizing that he was a Vasaio."

The look of surprise on a few of the faces in the room was almost laughable as it dawned on them that Vittelio's own son had eaten at their homes and worked in their fields.

Giuseppe turned to where Dondo was sitting and said, "Many of you said things to Santo, which I believe made him see his family in an entirely different light. He knows the heartache his family has brought to the village. More importantly, he wants change. The moment for us to come together and find freedom for the village is now. Santo has gotten his father to agree to a meeting, a meeting to discuss our financial conditions."

Turiddu replied, "Ha. And you trust a Vasaio?"

Giacinto Bordelli spoke out also, "There is no such thing as a good Vasaio. They cannot be trusted."

Giuseppe replied, "I know it's tough to believe, but I trust Santo. I could see it in his eyes. He knows his father better than any of us. He knows the effect Carlo's funeral had on him."

Some members shook their heads in disagreement.

Luigi said, "Are some of you not paying attention to what young Sanguinetti has said? This is what we have been waiting for. This is our chance to put forth a proposal to

Vittelio. Perhaps, with the backing of his own son, he may not only listen but also agree to give relief to us, and then we will have the best of both worlds. We would move toward freedom and, at the same time, retain the wealth, power and influence of the Vasaios to keep the Mafia out."

Giacomo Terranova replied, "I agree with Luigi. We can send a whole delegation to meet with Vittelio. Lay it all on the line and try to swing a deal."

Cheers echoed again throughout the room as the people for the first time began to get excited about the news Giuseppe had just related. Giuseppe's next sentence quickly quelled the excitement. "Only I can go. No one else. If not just me, then there will be no meeting."

People began to shake their heads. Turiddu said, "You're just a young boy. Vittelio is a conniving son-of-a-bitch. He will eat you up alive. No, we need someone with more experience. Someone like your father or me."

Antonio stood up and said, "I would go in a heartbeat, but the stipulation is that only Giuseppe will be received. Unfortunately, we know the Vasaios; the terms of the meeting are set, and Vittelio will be adamant about any attempted change. I can understand your grave concern, which I share, in having Giuseppe deal alone with Vittelio. He either goes alone, or we have no meeting."

The arguing continued back and forth, with most saying Giuseppe was too inexperienced to handle Vittelio Vasaio. As the arguing reached a fever pitch, Dondo Spatalanata stood in the middle of the room and spoke. "I wish all of you could hear yourselves. 'Giuseppe is this, Giuseppe is that'. Well, my friends, Giuseppe took it upon himself to try to give us a chance at freedom. I think this group is afraid to take any action. The time is now. I met with Santo. I didn't let on that I knew he was a Vasaio. I took him to the grave of my son, and I could see compassion in his eyes. Perhaps we will fail. So be it. Giuseppe somehow was able to get this meeting. I say let him go."

Turiddu replied, "He is too young, and he is telling us to trust a Vasaio whom he has now befriended."

Luigi said, "Enough talk. I say we take a vote. Antonio and Giuseppe will abstain."

With the two abstentions and one member out with sickness, there were 41 members of the *Società* present for the vote. With a show of hands, the final vote was 20 for and 20 against.

This meant the acting head of the meeting, who was normally Antonio, had the final vote. Tonight it fell to Luigi. He smiled over at Antonio before rising and saying, "I give my blessing and my vote for Giuseppe to attend the meeting."

A number of members rushed up to Giuseppe and patted him on his back. Antonio sat next to Luigi with mixed feelings of pride and concern for his son. He also had fear for the society members and his fellow villagers. He spoke softly to Luigi, saying, "There is no going back now. We all are in this together. We are like the Americans in their struggle for freedom. Upon signing the Declaration of Independence, Benjamin Franklin wisely said, 'We must all hang together, or most assuredly we shall hang separately'."

The rest of the meeting that night was spent setting forth the proposal that Giuseppe would present to Vittelio Vasaio. As the meeting was finally coming to a close and the proposal had been hammered out and given to Giuseppe, Turiddu ended the discussion with these words. "Giuseppe, whatever you do, do not make any concessions to that bastard. Put our proposal before him and see if he bites."

"I will, Turiddu. No concessions."

Fiorenza D'Arcangelo, with her woman's instinct, sensed the extreme burden of pressure and responsibility being assumed by Giuseppe. She believed it important to let him know that they were with him. She rose and was recognized. She moved that the *Società* now give a vote of support and confidence to Giuseppe and his task. Luigi said the motion was in order. The vote was taken. It was forty yeas and no nays.

So ended a very long but fruitful night down in the valley of Bellafortuna, a small village that for once believed freedom was possible and put its faith and fate into the hands of Giuseppe Sanguinetti.

22

THE MEETING

he meeting between Vittelio and Giuseppe was set for that Saturday morning, February 17th. The entire village was alight with excitement as word spread to all of the villagers.

After school on Friday, Giuseppe stayed in Monreale to have supper with the Giulini family. Before supper, Giuseppe and Maria walked toward the *Via Benedetto d'Acquisto,* a shopping area in Monreale, very close to where Maria lived. While walking arm in arm, Maria asked Giuseppe, "Are you nervous about tomorrow?"

"Sono terrorizzato dal domain. (I am terrified of tomorrow.) I know it all rests on my shoulders. But since Biaggio's death, I know this is my destiny. Now, my chance to fulfill that destiny has presented itself, and I must remain strong."

"Giuseppe, I am so proud of you."

"I truly love you, Maria. I'm so happy I found you and that you found me."

"I love you too, Giuseppe. I wish you luck tomorrow."

Giuseppe told Maria, "When you came to Bellafortuna, Biaggio asked me if one day I would marry you. I told him I would."

Maria blushed and asked, "What did he say in response?"

"*Bene*. He approved wholeheartedly."

"Good, because I would, too."

"*Ti amo*, Maria," Giuseppe said as they fell into a long kiss.

They continued talking the rest of the early evening before returning to the Giulini home for supper. Maria told her family about the meeting that was about to take place on Saturday in Bellafortuna and of the importance of the meeting for the small village. They all wished Giuseppe luck.

After supper, Giuseppe returned home to Bellafortuna to get a good night's rest before the big meeting at 10:00 a.m. Saturday morning.

GIUSEPPE DID NOT SLEEP WELL at all that night. At 5:45 a.m., he finally decided that sleep was not an option. He quickly got dressed and made his way over to the Church for Mass. A little divine intervention could never hurt.

The Monsignor said the Mass. Giuseppe prayed the entire time that his meeting would be a success and that he would serve the villagers of Bellafortuna well.

When Mass was over, he noticed Padre Mancini near the front of the Church. He told Padre Mancini about his meeting set for that day.

The priest said, "I know all about your meeting. People have been speaking about it for two days now."

"Pray that it goes well, Padre."

"I can do that. I do wish you luck, Giuseppe."

"*Grazie.*"

When Giuseppe had walked a few feet away, the priest yelled out to him, "I'm proud of you, *amico*. Very proud."

"That means a lot, Padre. I hope everyone will feel that way after my meeting."

"I'm sure they will."

Giuseppe returned home and waited until it was time to make his way over to the *Palazzo Vasaio*.

At 9:45 a.m., Giuseppe came down to the wine store to tell his father goodbye. Antonio told him, "Giuseppe, no matter what happens, I am very proud of you. Be careful of Vittelio. Be strong when you put forth our proposal. And whatever you do, don't give in to him."

"I won't, Papa. Do you think this will work?"

"Yes, I do. I have faith in you, my son."

With that, Giuseppe left the store and made his way to the *Palazzo Vasaio*.

GIUSEPPE NERVOUSLY APPROACHED the front door of the *Palazzo*. He grabbed the doorknocker that was in the middle of the door and knocked on the door. The door was quickly answered by a *Scagnozzo*.

"I am Giuseppe Sanguinetti. I have a meeting with Vittelio Vasaio this morning."

"I am aware, sir. He is awaiting your arrival."

Giuseppe walked into a foyer that was truly magnificent. A huge staircase, which led to the second floor, came cascading down into the foyer. A massive chandelier hung right above the spot where Giuseppe was standing. A grandfather clock stood off to one corner. To Giuseppe's left was a closed door. On his right was the entryway to what Giuseppe guessed was the main dining area. Straight ahead from where Giuseppe was standing, pass the staircase, was the entranceway to the rest of the house. Giuseppe noted that the house was immaculate.

Just at that moment, Santo came down the stairs. "*Benvenuto*, Giuseppe. *Come Va?*"

"I'll be doing better in a little while, I hope."

"Italo, I'll take Signor Sanguinetti to see my father."

"As you wish," the man responded.

With that, the Scagnozzo turned and walked out of the foyer. Santo asked Giuseppe, "Are you ready?"

"I think so."

"Giuseppe, everything will be fine. Come, my father is waiting for us in the study."

They turned to the left, and Santo knocked on the closed door. "*Aperto*," a deep voice from within responded. Santo opened the door and led Giuseppe in.

The study was a large room decorated with very dark, heavy, opulent furniture. Bookshelves located on the four walls were filled with books. Huge portraits of the Vasaio ancestors hung on each of the walls as well. A portrait of Alessandro hung on the left wall, below which was a large fireplace; Aldo on the wall across from the doorway; Carlo on the next wall; and on the wall next to the door was a portrait of Vittelio.

Tucked into the corner of the room by the fireplace was a large desk, behind which was a window facing the Piazza.

Seated behind the desk sat Vittelio. He stood up when Giuseppe entered the room.

Vittelio was now in his sixties. He had always been a big, rotund man with a very large bushy mustache. With age, he had not lost any of his weight, which gave him the appearance of still being very full of life. He always had a swagger and a look of arrogance about him.

"*Buon giorno, Signor Sanguinetti,*" Vittelio said.

"*Buon giorno, Signor Vasaio.*"

"*Grazie. Sedete,*" Vittelio said as he pointed to two chairs across from the desk.

"*Prego,*" said Giuseppe as he and Santo sat down.

Vittelio said, "You have your grandfather's eyes. I was a much younger man when Salvatore worked for my family. But I do remember him. He was a fine man."

"That he was *Signor.*"

"How is your father? The wine business is going well?"

"He is fine, and his business is doing well."

"My son has told me why you wanted this meeting; to discuss the vineyards and the olive groves. You are here to speak on behalf of your fellow villagers. I will listen to what you have to say. Proceed."

Giuseppe rearranged himself in the chair. He took a deep breath and then began to speak. He spoke very clearly, making sure every word he used was the correct one.

"As you know, the people of this village work hard every day down in the valley. For years their families have worked these same fields. A long time ago, when Bellafortuna produced its own wine and olive oil, its residents thrived and were able to have pride in themselves as well as in their village.

"However, since the closing of the winery and the olive presses, that pride has been lost. These people now only work to pay off their debts. They are all thankful to you, *Signor* Vasaio, for the loans that you provided to them at very bleak times in their lives. However, they are under the belief that the interest charges are much too high for them to ever get out of debt."

At these words, Vittelio leaned back in his chair and closed his eyes as he continued to listen.

Giuseppe continued, "Please understand, *Signor*, they are not trying to get out of paying the debt that they owe. What they are asking for is a reduction of the interest charges. They are asking for relief.

"As you know, from year to year, the interest rate you charge fluctuates from 15% to 18%. What we are asking is that the annual interest rate be dropped to 6%. By your doing this, Bellafortuna could then rebuild its winery and olive presses. We could start production. For five years, you must agree not to call in any loan of a villager who is paying the annual interest or to foreclose on any villager in instances where their vineyard or grove harvests have been affected by a disaster. At the reduced interest rate and the sale of their own harvests, I believe every villager will be able to make their annual interest payments and eventually liquidate the debts, especially once we all are again producing *Vino di Bellafortuna e Olio di Bellafortuna.*"

Vittelio, with his eyes still closed and leaning back in his chair asked, "And who will rebuild the winery and olive presses?"

"My father will advance the funds interest-free. With the

money coming in from the sales, the winery and olive presses will eventually pay for themselves."

Vittelio waved his hand for Giuseppe to continue. Giuseppe said, "During those five years, our wine production will continue to grow, and we will soon have vintage wines that will make a small fortune for the village. We believe that, within that five-year period, all of our debts to you will be paid off. Once all of the debts have been satisfied, we will pay you for five more years a percentage, say 6%, of the money coming into the winery and olive presses, in appreciation for your assistance in the past. If you allow this to happen, if you agree to our proposal, once again this village will thrive. Once again, pride will reign in the hearts of the villagers. And with your help, the winery and olive presses will be hugely successful, which in turn, will bring you money."

Vittelio opened his eyes. He looked directly at Giuseppe and asked, "*Finito?*"

Giuseppe nodded his head.

Vittelio leaned forward in his seat and said, "For four generations, my family has provided for the people of Bellafortuna. And yet, at the death of my father, not one person, not one, had the respect for my family or for me to show up at his funeral."

Santo quickly said, "Giuseppe did. And that is why I wanted you to speak with Giuseppe, Papa. To get the people to respect us by changing our ways."

Vittelio quickly shot a glance toward Santo, shutting his son up. Vittelio turned once again to Giuseppe and said, "These people have always needed my family, but as of late, they have refused to give my family the credit and respect that we deserve. Now, throughout the village, I am told there is a feeling of defiance growing. There is even a group that was formed to stir the people in the village to action."

Giuseppe's face showed surprise.

Vittelio said, "Oh, yes, I know about the *Società della Libertà per Bellafortuna*. Nothing in this village can be kept secret from me, nothing. This feeling of defiance all started with those concerts out in the Piazza that end with that infernal song being sung by the villagers at the top of their lungs."

Vittelio looked toward his son and said sadly, "And now that feeling of defiance has even entered my home." He turned back to Giuseppe and said, "These people disgust me. They cannot do anything for themselves. They need me just as they have always needed my family. In the future, they will need Santo."

Giuseppe sat in his seat in shock at the words of Vittelio. The anger in Vittelio's voice scared him. But this was his moment to fulfill his promise to Biaggio. He said in reply to Vittelio, "You say these people can do nothing. I say that's because you have never given them a chance. That is what we are saying. Give us a chance."

Vittelio stood up from behind his desk and walked over to the fireplace. Leaning against the mantle, he lit a cigar he had pulled from a gold box that was sitting above the fireplace. As he did so, he looked up at the picture of Alessandro. He then turned back to Giuseppe and said, "You are just like the rest of the villagers. Do you not realize what my family has meant to this village? Do you, of all people, not realize what my family has meant to your family? Without us, the Sanguinetti wine store would be selling vinegar. We have given your family a life here in the village. Yet, your grandfather turned his back on us. He walked back into the open arms of his fellow villagers and disrespected us. Now, your father walks around this village, stirring trouble with his concerts. Who does he think he is? Why does he think he is so important? Pretending that the Sanguinetti family knows Enrico Caruso. Playing Caruso records all day long. Selling his wine in a store that we deserve the credit for its success. Your father is nothing."

Santo looked mortified at his father's words. Giuseppe had heard enough. He stood up from his chair and replied, "It is you who are nothing, you, *Signor*. You are probably correct. Without your family, the wine store would not be as successful as it is. However, if it were not for my grandfather coming to his senses and walking away from your family, then his soul would not have been saved. He rectified his life. He tried to make it up to his fellow villagers. They accepted him back. You say my father is a nothing. At least when he dies, people will show their love for him at his funeral."

Vittelio's eyes flashed with anger as he said, "You little bastard! How dare you speak to me that way!"

Santo stood up from his seat and put his hands out in front of him and shook them, while he said, "*Aspetta*, Papa. I was the one who asked Giuseppe here. I arranged this meeting. I thought you wanted to hear their proposal. I thought you would be receptive to the idea. This is my doing. Do not take it out on Giuseppe." One could feel the tension in the room subside as the gentle voice of Santo echoed off the walls.

Vittelio walked back to his chair. "*Mi scusi. Sedete,* Giuseppe."

"*Aspetto,*" Giuseppe said antagonistically. Santo stood next to him.

"Fine. Let us speak to each other as friends. You come to me with a proposal. I have listened. Because of the lack of respect for my family by the villagers, I have given you the reasons why the proposal is preposterous. Yet, I know my son disagrees with me and thinks I should give in. He thinks the time has come to change. Because of him, I will agree with this proposal with a condition."

Giuseppe, surprised, asked, "What is that?"

"I will let you know my reasons upfront for this condition. You had the gall to come here and approach me with this ridiculous proposal. The reason you could do this is because of your feeling that somehow I cannot touch your family and that I have no control over you. There was once a family who lived here who felt the same way with my ancestors."

Vittelio turned toward the window and looked at the statue of Enzo Boccale. He turned back to Giuseppe, saying, "They were wrong."

"What are you saying, *Signor* Vasaio?"

"It's time your family gets put in its place. I will agree to the proposal but it will be wholly conditioned on one thing and only one thing. If you can pull it off, you will be a hero in the village. Fail, and you and your father will be the reason why the proposal failed."

"What is the condition?"

Vittelio said, "As I'm sure you are aware since you and your father supposedly know him so well, Enrico Caruso is coming to Palermo the last weekend in July to receive an honor. Every July 28th, the Festival Boccale is held out in the Piazza in Bellafortuna in remembrance of Enzo Boccale.

Every year, there is a concert. If you can get Enrico Caruso to come sing one aria on the concert stage, I will agree to the proposal."

Santo said, "Papa, that's not realistic. You're just trying to embarrass them."

As Santo continued to speak on Giuseppe's behalf, young Sanguinetti stood with his head bowed. His mind was racing. He thought back to the night he met Caruso in Milan so many years ago and the words Caruso had told him: "If you ever need me, please feel free to call me." Maybe, just maybe, Giuseppe could pull it off. He could write to Caruso and get him to come; after all, the great tenor would be in nearby Palermo. He would just have to start writing letters to him early. During the summer, Caruso always returned to Italy. He could write to him in the early part of the summer in Italy and ask him to come to Bellafortuna while in Palermo. He could even write to him now in New York and let Caruso know about it early on. He would remind Caruso of that meeting many years ago. What did Giuseppe have to lose? His fellow villagers would be no worse off if he failed. Vittelio didn't understand these people. They wouldn't blame Giuseppe. They would thank him for trying.

With Santo still speaking, Giuseppe, realizing he had much to gain and little to lose, picked his head up and said, "*Signor* Vittelio, Caruso will come. You have a deal."

Santo said, "Giuseppe, you…"

Giuseppe cut him off, "Santo. It's fine. He will come, and the village will find glory once again."

Vittelio said in reply, "*Bene*. We have a deal. If he comes, I will agree to everything you proposed. Everything."

Giuseppe started to turn to leave the room when Vittelio said, "One more thing, Giuseppe. What's in this for me?"

"Your debts will be paid off, and within a few years, you will get a percentage of what is produced."

"No. I mean if Caruso doesn't come. I have given you a chance for change. I am giving up something to you. In return, if you fail, I want something."

"What is it that you want?"

"I want the *Società della Libertà per Bellafortuna* disbanded. I want the *Opera Orchestra di Bellafortuna* disbanded as well as the assurance that no concert will ever be given in Bellafortuna again. That will put an end to that song that has raised these people's so-called hope of freedom."

Giuseppe shook his head in disagreement and said, "Those concerts have come to mean the world to these people. It gives them a break from a hard week's work. It gives them joy. It gives them hope."

Vittelio said, "What I am agreeing to, if you can pull it off, which I doubt, will give them freedom."

Santo said, "Giuseppe, don't do it. You have no idea if Caruso will come. Since I've been living back in the village, I have come to know what these concerts mean to these people. Don't allow my father to take them away."

Giuseppe paused and thought about Biaggio and the mission Biaggio had entrusted to him. He wanted to believe that he could get Caruso to come. With both fear and faith, he made the decision to take the gamble. "No, Santo. *Verrà. (He will come.) Signor* Vittelio, I accept the wager. But since you made an unexpected last-minute condition that I was not prepared for, then this part of the wager will be subject to my last-minute condition: that you will not disclose this last part of the wager to anyone until after the Festival. If you break your word on this, I will not be bound by the last part of the wager."

Vittelio paused before responding. After reflecting on Giuseppe's condition, he said, "I accept your condition. *"La scommessa è fatta."* *(The wager is on.)*

Giuseppe immediately turned around, left the room, and departed the premises.

"YOU KNEW IT. This was your plan all along. You used me to bring this about, to catch Giuseppe in this trap," said Santo to his father after Giuseppe had left.

"You must learn, Santo, that no one questions the integrity of this family. The villagers must learn this. I have listened to you the past couple of weeks. Your whining about Carlo's death. Your feeling that we don't need any more money, and that we have enough. That we can lower the interest charges. Don't you see? Giuseppe Sanguinetti hooked on to you to put these poisonous ideas in your head? You are weak. I will make you stronger. You are a Vasaio. Act like one. The Sanguinettis will fail. Because of that, all of their respect in the village will dwindle away. And hopefully, like the Boccales, they will leave this village, taking their poison with them. They will fail because, just like the rest of the villagers, they are useless. They cannot do anything for themselves. I have given them a chance. But they will not capitalize on it. You will come to see why these people have always needed us."

"No, Papa, you did not give them a chance. You gave them an impossibility."

"That is not true. My people tell me how the Sanguinettis put forth this image that they know Caruso. This gives them respect. This, in turn, allows those concerts to continue in the Piazza. Those concerts must be stopped. I knew this was the perfect way to do it."

"So you used your own son."

"*Si* . . . . . These villagers will learn. It is payback as well for Salvatore Sanguinetti. He walked away from our family like we were evil. He became a hero around the village. They will all learn who controls this village. "

"Papa, with all due respect, I hope they can pull it off. I hope Caruso comes. After all, he will already be in Palermo."

"That is all the more reason why it will be fun to see them fail with Caruso being so close. Your friend, Giuseppe, has been taken up with his own importance. For someone who knows Caruso like he says he does, he forgot that Caruso, for whatever reasons, has not publicly sung in his homeland since 1903. These people have no chance. They cannot do anything without me. After they fail, you have to prove to me that you can rule them. I did not work hard all these years so that you could throw it all away. No, Santo. You will learn that I am correct. You will come to despise these people as I do. You will follow in our footsteps."

Santo walked out of the room. He hoped, come July 28th, the voice of Enrico Caruso would reverberate throughout the Piazza and the *Palazzo Vasaio*.

23

GIUSEPPE MAKES HIS REPORT AND WRITES HIS LETTER

*A*s Giuseppe walked across the Piazza toward the wine store, he thought about the meeting that had just taken place. Could he get Caruso to come? Deep down, he truly believed he could. He would write to the great tenor and tell him about his predicament. He would explain to Caruso how the Vasaios ruled the villagers. He would remind Caruso about meeting him when his career was just starting, and what Caruso had told him. He would tell Caruso that his village was very close to Palermo, so while he was there, it would be a short trip to Bellafortuna.

But if Caruso didn't come to Bellafortuna, if Giuseppe couldn't get him to come, what had he done to the villagers by agreeing to Vittelio's proposal? Why did he fall into the trap set by Vittelio? It started to make sense now. That was why Vittelio jumped at the chance to have the meeting. He never intended to give in to the demands of the villagers. Instead, he was going to use the opportunity to put an end to one thing in the village that gave the villagers hope and determination, namely the concerts, and at the same time discredit Giuseppe and his father. And Giuseppe had played right into his hands.

Giuseppe reached the wine store and entered. Antonio, Turiddu and Luigi were inside awaiting his return. Antonio spoke first, "Well, Giuseppe, how did it go?"

"Papa, Vittelio was still very upset about no one going to the funeral of Carlo. He believes his family has no respect."

Turiddu said, "Good. I'm glad he figured that out."

Giuseppe continued, "After much debate, he finally agreed to the proposal."

Luigi and Turiddu both replied simultaneously, "What! You are joking?"

"I am not. However, he agreed with one condition."

Turiddu said, "Giuseppe, I warned you not to make any concessions."

Giuseppe said, "This is not a concession. If we can get Enrico Caruso to come sing at the Festival Boccale, he will agree to our proposal."

The feeling of disappointment in the room was palpable. Luigi said, "How can we do that? He won't come here?"

Giuseppe said, "He will come. As you know, Caruso will be in Palermo that weekend. I will begin writing to him, advising him of our needs. I will ask him to come. I will beg him. I believe he will come. I've never told anyone this. The night my father and I met Caruso, the great tenor told me if I ever needed him, I could contact him. Well, I need him now. That is why I agreed to Vittelio's proposal. Caruso will come."

Luigi turned to Antonio and asked, "Do you really think he will come?"

Antonio said in reply, "I don't know. The one fact we have to live with is that Caruso does not sing in Italy. For five years now, he has not done it."

Giuseppe said, "Papa, I completely forgot about that."

Turiddu interjected, "Then we have no chance of winning this wager."

Antonio said, "Who knows. I never knew Caruso told him that if he ever needed him, he could call upon him. I know that Caruso did speak to him. Giuseppe can write to him and see if he will come. However, we are no worse off if he doesn't come. We tried. We have made our feelings known to Vittelio for the first time. Perhaps, down the road, that may help us. And remember that we have made giant strides with Santo for him to realize what his family really has done to our people; that cannot but help us in the future. As for now, who knows, Giuseppe may be able to pull this off. It's obvious to me, Vittelio feels threatened by us. He is using this to try to embarrass Giuseppe and me. He is hoping that we cannot get Caruso to come, and the villagers will turn against us for our failure to do so."

"Papa, that is exactly what Vittelio told me. There is no doubt about it."

Turiddu said, "If that is what Vittelio is trying to accomplish, it will not work. I agree, Antonio. We are no worse off by Giuseppe agreeing to this deal. He made no concessions. He offered our proposal, and Vittelio virtually rejected it. But instead of just saying no, he made this offer, thinking he could hurt the Sanguinettis. But really what he did was to give us an opening, a chance. I don't know if Giuseppe can pull it off or not, but at least we will try."

Luigi said, "I'm going to tell everyone else in the village what happened at the meeting. I'm sure they will be dejected. But Antonio, you are correct. At least we made our feelings known. It was a dream to think Vittelio would agree to our proposal. However, his arrogance has opened a door for us, a very small door. Giuseppe, I think you should get started drafting your letter."

"I will. When it is done, I will show it to all of you. Once approved, I'll send it to all the places where I know Caruso will be within the next few weeks and months. I'm bound to find him at one location."

Turiddu said, "*Grazie, amico.* I thought you were too young to face Vittelio. I thought you would give in to him. I thought he would take advantage of you. You did well. You told him we were unhappy. That took courage."

Luigi said, "Giuseppe, I'm sure Caruso gets inundated with requests to sing here or sing there and is under constant pressure to sing in his homeland. Tell him in the letter that if he sings here, the villagers of Bellafortuna swear to never let it be known outside of our village. In that way, Caruso will know that by agreeing to do it, he will not be bombarded with future requests."

Giuseppe said in reply, "I will put that in. Do you really think the villagers won't say anything if Caruso does come?"

Luigi laughed and said, "Let's get him to come first. *Addio*, Sanguinettis."

Turiddu and Luigi then left the store, leaving Antonio and Giuseppe alone. Antonio said, "I'm proud of what you have done, Giuseppe."

"I'm glad, Papa. Because of what has transpired, I don't think I will be able to go with you on your trip to Italy in July. I should probably stay here and prepare for the Festival and hopefully the arrival of Caruso."

Antonio chuckled and said, "I bring wine back to the villagers from my trip. What you can bring them is freedom. I think it wise you don't come with me in July as well. But take my word for it, I'll be back as usual in time for the Festival."

Giuseppe made his way upstairs. Perhaps he was wrong in not telling them, and especially his father, the whole deal. He just couldn't do it. If Caruso came, the villagers would never know that the concerts and the *Società* were the bargaining tool.

But would Caruso come? As Giuseppe reflected on the meeting with Vittelio, he became aware that Vittelio had controlled the meeting to such an extent that Giuseppe had forgotten that Caruso had not sung in Italy since 1903. The more he reflected on the meeting, the more convinced he became that he had been a fool and had fallen right into Vittelio's trap. However, because of his meeting with the great tenor in Milan many years ago, Giuseppe believed that Caruso would come. Caruso had to come.

THE NEWS of the wager spread very quickly throughout the village. By Saturday night, Giuseppe couldn't go anywhere in the village without someone asking if he had written to Caruso and if he really thought Caruso would come. The villagers all knew Caruso would be in Palermo that same weekend of the Festival Boccale, so it wasn't such a stretch to think Giuseppe could get the great tenor to come.

Giuseppe was glad to be leaving the village on Sunday to spend the day with Maria. He woke up early that morning and hooked Caruso to the cart. He made his way to Monreale and met Maria. Her family believed that, after Mass, the young girl was going to spend the day at a friend's house in the city. That was not the case. Giuseppe and Maria wanted to spend a few hours alone together.

They traveled a short distance outside of Monreale to the western summit of *Monte Cuccio* that separated the village of Bellafortuna from Monreale. After climbing the path through piney woods up the slope of *Monte Cuccio,* they came to Castellaccio, a 12th century Norman castle.

The same ruler who had constructed the *Duomo* in Monreale, William II, had built the castle. The castle was eventually abandoned and turned over to the Benedictine Monks, who turned it into a fortified monastery. It was finally abandoned for good after it was severely damaged by the earthquake of 1752, the same quake that destroyed Campanèlla.

One could still enter the castle and explore the ancient building. Giuseppe and Maria made their way up a long flight of stairs and stood on the parapets, which offered spectacular views in every direction, including toward Bellafortuna in the very far distance.

While there on the parapet, Giuseppe told Maria about the events of the day before. He did not tell her about the concession he had made at the meeting with Vittelio. When he finished, she asked, "Do you think Caruso will come? Do you even know how to contact him?"

"All these years, I have followed his career very closely. I spent all of last night looking over newspaper articles from Italy that I had kept regarding his career. Luckily, his schedule is somewhat predictable now.

"From the autumn through early summer, his time is spent in New York. He is a fixture at the Met every year during those months. When he is not at the Metropolitan, he travels to Philadelphia and other nearby American cities. However, New York is his base. That is where his apartment is. I will write to him care of the Metropolitan Opera, and perhaps with luck, he will receive it.

"By the early part of the summer, he is usually in London for performances at Covent Garden. I will send him a letter there as well.

"However, my best chance of reaching him is in Italy. After London, he always retires to Italy to recover from his grueling schedule. He lives at his villa, Le Panche at Castello, right outside of Florence. He is there the whole summer. That is where I know I can get a letter to him. That is where he will agree to travel from Palermo and come to Bellafortuna for July 28th. He will come to help us."

Maria said, "I hope so, Giuseppe. Do you know what your letter is going to say?"

"No. I thought you could help me write it. I brought my pen, inkwell and paper. Let me start to write, and I'll let you see it when I'm done and you can let me know what you think about it."

"That's fine. I'm going to look around the castle. You will be up here?"

"*Si.*"

She kissed him goodbye and went down the stairwell to

the inner rooms of the castle. Giuseppe turned and looked toward Bellafortuna. He reached inside a bag he had put next to him and pulled out some paper. He knew this was the most important letter he would ever write in his entire life. He sat down and began to write.

Meanwhile, Maria walked through the old rooms of the castle. There was no furniture anywhere, probably looted over the years, she thought. The one thing that caught her attention was that every room had windows in them that offered wonderful views over the landscape of Sicily.

She made her way to the yard in the middle of the castle. There were old stables off to one side, a small chapel on one side, and a huge kitchen. Maria enjoyed exploring the old castle. For a building that had been abandoned for so long, it was still in very good shape, probably because of the fact that it was so well built.

After spending about an hour roaming around the old castle, Maria returned to the parapet where she found Giuseppe, with crumpled papers all around him, finishing the letter. His fingers were covered with ink.

"*Finito?*" she asked.

"*Si.* I want you to read it and tell me what you think."

He handed the letter to Maria. It consisted of three pages, written in script. Maria sat down next to Giuseppe and began to read:

---

18 February, 1908

Commendatore Caruso:
    My name is Giuseppe Sanguinetti from Bellafortuna,

Sicily. I have loved opera from a very early age because of my introduction to it by my father. My absolute passion for the art form, however, can be traced to one event. That was the first night I ever witnessed an opera on the stage. I was nine years old then. It was the premiere of Giordano's Fedora in Milano.

When you walked on the stage that night and sang the aria, "Amor ti vieta", I was enraptured. Never in my life have I heard a voice like yours. Never has a voice moved me like yours. That night was very magical to me and has lived with me ever since.

Later that same night, my father and I went to dinner at a Milano restaurant. While there, you came into the same restaurant. I sat in awe when I realized that the owner of the greatest voice I had ever heard was sitting close to me.

Upon leaving the restaurant, I approached your table and told you how wonderful your voice was. I also told you that "Vesti la giubba" should be your signature song. You were touched by my words and drew for me a caricature of yourself as a clown. You also very kindly told me that if I ever needed you, I could call on you at any time.

That time is now.

My village of Bellafortuna is located just a few miles from Palermo. It is a wonderful place with wonderful people. The villagers grow grapes and olives. They also have a love of music that I know you would find very touching.

The people of my village are also very poor. Their status in life is not the result of their own actions. It is because of the ruling family in the village. They have kept my people in debt with high-interest charges. All of their harvests go to this family, with little rewards coming to them.

I know you were born in Naples and had a hard life growing up. Yet you made it. You worked hard and are now at the top of your profession. You had a chance; you took it and became successful.

The villagers now have a chance at freedom. After a personal tragedy in my life with the loss of a dear friend, I had a meeting with the man who rules our village. He made a wager with me. If I win the wager, he will lower the interest charges and will allow my people once again the freedom to sell their own wine and olive oil. The wager is that I have to get you to come to the village to sing one song at a yearly festival we have in the village, set for July 28th.

That is the purpose of this letter. I took this wager, perhaps stupidly, but I remembered what you told me. "Whenever you need me, call me." I need you on July 28th. My village is only a short trip from Palermo. You will be in Palermo that same weekend receiving the Golden Palm of Persephone.

If you are able, please come to my village. Help bring my village freedom. I will meet you in Palermo and bring you to my lovely village. I humbly make this request to you. You can send your response to me directly at a friend's house in Monreale, Piazza Guglielmo #12 since it will be quicker for your response to get there than to my small village. Once you respond to me, I will follow up with you on the details.

I can only imagine the many requests you receive like this one asking you to lend your assistance to multitudes of worthy causes and the impossible burden which would be involved in attempting to satisfy them. The villagers of Bellafortuna have authorized me to give to you their assurance that your appearance will not be disclosed or publicized, in order to avoid this from being used as a precedent for others to make demands upon you for assistance.

Saint Augustine always said to sing is to pray twice. I sing all day, praying that you will be able to meet my request.

Your great admirer,

Giuseppe Sanguinetti

UPON COMPLETING THE LETTER, Maria looked at Giuseppe and said, "*Bèllo.* It's a very moving letter. It's very well done."

"I just hope Caruso feels the same way."

"Just have faith, Giuseppe."

"That is all I have, Maria."

They had a light picnic lunch before returning to Monreale in the early afternoon. While driving back to Bellafortuna, Giuseppe only thought about his letter. Was it good enough to make Caruso act? He really would never get that answer until he received word from Caruso that he was coming. All Giuseppe could do was to pray for that response. He didn't know why, but deep down, he had the feeling that Caruso would indeed come.

THAT NIGHT, Giuseppe showed his letter to Antonio and Luigi. They both agreed it was a very good letter and neither had anything to add to it. Giuseppe retired to his room, where he handwrote three neat copies of his letter. He addressed each letter as follows: *Commendatore* Enrico Caruso, Metropolitan Opera, New York; *Commendatore* Enrico Caruso, Covent Garden, London; and *Commendatore* Enrico Caruso, Villa Le Panche, Castello.

He would mail the three letters tomorrow from Monreale when he went to school. Then in the middle of each month thereafter, he would mail them out again. He would keep this schedule until he received word from Caruso that he was coming.

Before going to bed, he went to his father's bedroom.

"Not in bed yet, Giuseppe?"

"No, Papa."

"You wrote a good letter. After you left, Luigi told me how impressed he was with it."

"Papa, do you think Caruso will come?"

"You have written a wonderful letter. There is nothing more you can do. Now it's in God's hands."

"I know, but is there more I can do?"

"*Figlio mio*, do you think he will come?"

"I do, Papa. He will come because he will remember that night I met him. I truly believe that."

"Then there is nothing more for you to do. You have made me very proud, Giuseppe. After what your grandfather did to these people in our village, I never thought we could make it up to them. When the opportunity came for you to attend this meeting with Vittelio, I was struck with fear. I will now admit to you that I was dreading your meeting with him because I did not want another Sanguinetti to do anything that would hurt these villagers again. My fear was baseless. I should have trusted you. What you have done has given us all a chance at freedom. And best of all, this chance comes with our losing nothing if we fail. How you pulled that off I will never understand. But you did. Since you have brought us this far, if you believe Caruso will come, I would put my money on the fact that he will."

Giuseppe was quiet for a moment, not even looking at his father. He finally spoke and said, "Papa, um…there was one thing about the meeting that I have not told you."

"I'm sure you had trouble remembering everything that occurred."

"I guess."

Antonio said, "I think even Turiddu will admit that he was proud of what you accomplished. Now, what is it that you wanted to tell me?"

Giuseppe rubbed his brow with his left hand. As he did so, he changed his mind with what he was going to say. He quickly replied, "Just that Vittelio said I had grandpa's eyes."

"That may be true. But your heart is different. You have the heart of a lion. You did well, Giuseppe."

"That means a lot coming from you. *Buona notte*, Papa."

"*Buona notte*, Giuseppe."

Giuseppe walked over and kissed his father good night and retired to bed.

AFTER GETTING Caruso readied Monday morning, Giuseppe met Santo in the valley, and the two young men rode to Monreale together. Santo apologized for the way his father had treated Giuseppe and the way he had used the young Sanguinetti to try to discredit him and his father.

Giuseppe said at one point, "No one in the village knows what happens if I can't get Caruso to come."

"You never told them?"

"I couldn't, Santo. You know what the orchestra means to these people. You have witnessed for yourself how much they love those concerts. I just couldn't bring myself to tell them that I wagered the only thing they have left. I just couldn't."

"But if he doesn't come…"

"He will come, Santo. He must come. Look, here are my letters I'm mailing today to him. I pray they reach him."

"I hope they reach him as well."

They continued down the road together on their way to school. From that day forward, the two young men traveled to school together. Despite their different backgrounds, both were becoming increasingly aware that they were of a kindred spirit.

24

NO WORD FROM CARUSO

The weeks passed, and Giuseppe heard nothing from Caruso. In mid-March, Giuseppe sent out the second set of letters. He hoped with these that Caruso would respond. He began to be questioned almost daily by his fellow villagers if he had heard anything from Caruso. He would always tell them that he had no word yet but reassured them that it was still early.

Well, March turned into April, April turned into May, and still, he had not received any word from Caruso. Giuseppe had now mailed out three sets of letters. July 28th was getting nearer and nearer, and still there had been no response.

One Saturday in May, Giuseppe was working behind his father's table during the concert, selling wine and cheese. As the concert was underway, Giuseppe noticed Luisa Canali, an elderly villager, who owned a very small olive grove. Her husband had passed away a few months ago, and in his memory, she kept the little olive grove going. However, rumors were that at this year's harvest, she would not be able to pay her debts, and Vittelio would foreclose.

She made her way over to the table to order a glass of wine. As she approached, she said to Giuseppe, "*Buon giorno,* Sanguinetti."

"*Buon giorno, Signora* Canali. Wonderful concert today, huh?"

"*Molto bello.* Sanguinetti, is he coming?"

"Caruso?"

"*Si.* It's my only chance I have left to save my olive grove. Is he coming?"

"I haven't heard yet, Signora. But I believe he will."

"*Allora.* Well, the Vasaios may take our land, but at least they can never take our souls. We will always have our music."

Giuseppe felt like someone had punched him in the gut. *Signora* Canali took her wine and made her way back to her seat to enjoy the concert. When she had left the table, Giuseppe looked around the Piazza.

The faces of the villagers told the story. Smiles. A type of joy could be seen in those faces which only music can bring. Music that enriches and touches the soul. Music that brought happiness, for a fleeting moment, to these people.

As he looked out over the faces, Giuseppe thought about the wager. What had he done? How could he have allowed Vittelio to take advantage of him like that?

When the concert ended, the villagers, as usual, stood up in place, turned toward the *Palazzo Vasaio,* and began to sing their song of freedom. A tear rolled down Giuseppe's cheek. A little more than two months was all he had left. If Caruso didn't come, these concerts would come to an end all because of Giuseppe.

While the crowd continued to sing, Giuseppe turned from the table and sadly made his way into the wine store. Tomorrow he would do another mailing. Perhaps Caruso would respond soon.

On May 21, 1908, Giuseppe graduated from *St. Ignatio*. Antonio, Mamma Lucia and Maria all attended the ceremony in Monreale. Sitting a few seats away from them were Vittelio and Ada Vasaio, witnessing their son graduate as well.

After the ceremony, Antonio congratulated his son. Mamma Lucia and Maria kissed him. While they were all talking, Giuseppe noticed Santo shaking hands with Vittelio and hugging Ada.

When Maria had a moment alone with Giuseppe, she told him how proud she was of him.

He said, "Well, now I'll go to work full time with my father. All these years, he has tried to teach me the trade of wine selling. He is putting me in charge of the inventory. Eventually, within a year or two, I will be going alone to the mainland of Italy to buy the stock."

"You must be excited?"

"Maria, I will be in about a year when you graduate from high school. Once you do, I want to marry you."

"I want to marry you too, Giuseppe."

Holding both of her hands in his, he replied, "Maria, my life is in Bellafortuna. I want you to be part of that life. But, I would not ask you to move to Bellafortuna as long as the Vasaios remain in control."

Maria kissed him before replying, "I will live with you, wherever that may be, either with or without the Vasaios. Wherever I live with you, I will be happy."

Giuseppe was taken aback and left totally speechless by Maria's statement until he broke out into a broad grin and simply replied, "*Ti amo, piccina mia.*"

"I'm going to miss seeing you after school on a regular basis, Giuseppe."

"I'm going to miss that too. But we will have the weekends."

They kissed deeply before they returned to where Giuseppe's family was standing. Giuseppe said goodbye to a few classmates. He and Maria also walked over to where Santo was standing and congratulated him.

Santo said, "I'm going to miss our talks as we traveled to and from school, Giuseppe."

"I will too."

"I'm going to miss you, Giuseppe."

"Santo, we live in the same village, in the very same Piazza."

Santo said, "Worlds apart, Giuseppe. I know we can never become close friends living in Bellafortuna. At least not now. But that could all change."

"You never know, Santo. Hopefully, it will change."

The two friends hugged. Maria again congratulated Santo on his graduation. Then Maria led Giuseppe and his family over to her parents' home so that they could meet. It was a wonderful afternoon filled with conversations and food.

Antonio hit it off with Giancarlo as Mamma Lucia helped

Renata in the kitchen. Mamma Lucia was amazed at how little olive oil Renata used. She finally grabbed the dispenser at one point and showed Renata how good Sicilian food was made.

Antonio also had a long conversation with Rodolfo. They spoke about opera. By the end of the evening, Rodolfo even sang a few arias. Antonio was floored at the absolute beauty of his voice.

As the Sanguinetti family made their way back home later that evening, Antonio and Mamma Lucia both told Giuseppe how wonderful Maria's family was and how much they had enjoyed the entire day.

Antonio said, "And Rodolfo has a lovely voice. You should invite him to sing at one of our concerts. The villagers would love his voice."

"You are right, Papa. I never thought about that before. Don't you think it's uncanny how much he resembles Caruso?"

"My God, now that you said it, he certainly does."

Mamma Lucia said, "All I know is he does have a beautiful voice."

Antonio agreed.

The cart continued down the road traveling to Bellafortuna. Their conversation finally turned to the Vasaios and the fact that Giuseppe still had no word from Caruso.

Antonio said, "Wait, Giuseppe. You said he gets back to Italy at some point during the summer. That is where he will get your letters."

"I hope so, Papa. I hope so." The little cart made its way up the slope of the hill to the beautiful village of Bellafortuna.

As it did so, Giuseppe thought to himself about his

conversation with Maria. He would not ask her to live in Bellafortuna as long as the Vasaios were in control. Caruso had to come.

AT THAT EXACT MOMENT, in New York City, an entire continent and ocean away, the great tenor, Enrico Caruso, who at age thirty-four was at the absolute pinnacle of his career, was boarding the *S/S Kaiserin Augusta Victoria*, bound for London. He had a concert scheduled there for May 30th and a single performance of *Rigoletto* set for June 11th in Paris. After that, he would retire to his villa outside of Florence to spend time with his wife and children and recuperate from his long season. His only scheduled event that summer was a trip to Palermo the last weekend in July to be presented with that city's highest honor, the Golden Palm of Persephone.

A CONFESSION

*B*y the end of May, Giuseppe had heard enough questions regarding Caruso. He was bombarded with them at work all day long by customers.

July 28th was now two months away, and there had not been a word from Caruso. Giuseppe began to have trouble sleeping. He thought about July 28th constantly. Perhaps he was wrong in not telling the villagers or at least the members of the *Società* the complete truth about the meeting with Vittelio. But how could he have done that?

He was not the only person having a rough go of it. Since graduation, Santo settled into his new life. He had no specific job in his father's business, other than paying close attention to all aspects of the business and learning what it took to run it so that he could take it over one day. Santo's lack of interest was telling and resulted in his father berating his son almost daily.

Santo also began to feel the pressure of July 28th. That

was his one chance of redemption; his chance to break free of the life his father had written for him already. But if Caruso did not come, then all would be lost. The people would lose their music, and Santo would lose his chance at a new life.

With all of these thoughts, and no one in his family to go to, Santo finally went to seek comfort and support from Padre Mancini, a man he both liked and respected. He met with the priest and told him all of his feelings. Like everyone, the priest already knew about the meeting Giuseppe had with Vittelio. But Santo, asking that what he said be kept in confidence, told Padre Mancini what the wager truly was between his father and Giuseppe. Padre Mancini's mouth dropped open when Santo informed him.

He asked Santo, "Does anyone know about the real bet?"

"No. Giuseppe told no one. Not even his father."

JUST A FEW DAYS after that meeting, Padre Mancini went to see Giuseppe one night as he was closing the wine store. At the priest's request, they went to Bellini's to have a glass of wine while they discussed an urgent matter about which Padre Mancini needed to speak to Giuseppe.

After they found a spot in a quiet corner of the *trattoria* and after the wine was poured, Padre Mancini went right to the point of the meeting, "Someone who cares about you and the people of this village has informed me about your meeting with Vittelio, all of it."

"What do you mean by 'all of it'?"

"No concerts, no orchestra, no Verdi chorus."

"Santo, damn him. Padre, I could not bring myself to tell these people. If Caruso comes, they will never have to know."

"And if he doesn't come, then what?"

"I don't know, Padre. At the time, it seemed like the right thing to do. Not to tell them. Now, even if I thought I should, I can't. It's too late."

"Giuseppe, you have to tell these people. If you feel that you cannot tell all of the villagers, you at least must tell the members of the *Società*. After all, these were the people who put their trust in you."

Giuseppe said, "And these were the very same people who told me not to give anything up to Vittelio."

"Giuseppe, you played right into his hands."

Angrily, Giuseppe responded, "At least I tried to do something, Padre. At least I didn't sit by quietly while people suffered around me."

Padre Mancini's eyes bore in, and he said, "What are you saying, Giuseppe?"

"Oh, Padre. Forgive me. I'm so tired. I don't know what to do. I'm at my wit's end. *Mi scusi*. I shudder to think what will happen if Caruso does not come. I try not to think about it, and yet that is all I think about. I cannot let these people down. No, Padre, I respect your wishes, but I just can't tell them the truth."

"Giuseppe, don't be mad at Santo for telling me. The guilt he is carrying is a lot. After all, Vittelio is his father."

"I'm not mad at him. I won't even tell him that you told me."

With a look of deep compassion, Padre Mancini said, "Giuseppe, I know it will be hard, but you have to tell the members of the *Società* the entire truth about your meeting with Vittelio. I want you to tell them what happens, what you gave up if Caruso does not come."

"Padre, anything but that."

"No, Giuseppe. That is what I want you to do. That is what you must do."

There was a long moment of utter silence until Giuseppe finally said, "I can deny you nothing. I will do want you want, Padre. I promise. Just say some prayers for me."

They finished their glass of wine before retiring for the night.

GIUSEPPE FACES THE SOCIETÀ

*T*he next meeting of the *Società* was scheduled for the Monday of the following week. As the days passed leading up to the meeting, Giuseppe eagerly awaited word from Caruso; none came. It was now mid-June. Giuseppe thought Caruso was probably just getting to his villa outside of Florence to rest for the summer. Maybe there he would get the letters and respond.

On Sunday, Giuseppe went to Monreale to spend the day with Maria. He was in a very anxious state. That night he intended to sit down with his father and tell him about his wager with Vittelio. He knew his father would be upset when he heard the news. For now, Giuseppe needed time away from everyone in Bellafortuna, time to collect his thoughts. He needed to confide his fears to someone. Maria was his most logical choice.

On that Sunday, they walked around the streets of

Monreale as Giuseppe told Maria about the condition of the wager as well as his conversation with Padre Mancini.

Giuseppe said, "I must follow his request and tell everyone in the *Società* what happened between Vittelio and me. I fear the members of the *Società* will not understand why I never told them. I'm not even sure if I know the reason why I never told them. Was it fear? Or is it that I knew what I had done was wrong?"

Maria grabbed Giuseppe's hand tightly, and while smiling lovingly at him, she said, "Giuseppe, you did not tell them the whole story because of your friendship with Biaggio. Since his death, you committed your life to bring freedom to your village. You were given a chance, and you took it; a chance to fulfill your destiny. There is no shame in that. The concerts certainly mean a lot to your people, but freedom will mean more."

Giuseppe said, "But when freedom fails, all that is left is hope. These concerts provided hope for the people. That is what I have possibly destroyed. That is what I used to bargain with Vittelio. The villagers will not understand why I did not tell them what Vittelio and I agreed to. That is what will upset them. They trusted me, and in return, I bargained the only thing they had left and followed that up by lying to them."

"Giuseppe, I agree with Padre Mancini that they should be told. But I understand why you didn't tell them. You are such a good, loving person. You care and are willing to use your talents to help others. I believe they will understand why you did not tell them the whole truth. Besides, for those who don't understand, it won't matter if Caruso comes."

"Not 'if' Maria, but 'when' Caruso comes. Caruso must

come to the village. That is the only thing that will let these people forgive me for what I have done. I owe it to them, and I owe it to my father. I have never told you about my family. But by my doing so, you will understand why I fear the results of my action."

Giuseppe went on to tell Maria the history of his grandfather's relationship with the Vasaios. As he spoke, she began to understand why Giuseppe had such a drive to bring change to the way of life for his fellow villagers. As he finished relating the story, he said, "My father worked hard to build respect in the village after what his father had done. And within a matter of minutes, I threw all of that away."

"Giuseppe, you took the bet because you truly believed Caruso would come. You must still believe it. You have to."

"I do, Maria. I have no other choice than to believe it."

She said, "That is what you tell the *Società* and your father. Tell them the truth about the meeting and emphasize that it doesn't change anything because you always believed Caruso would come. Leave it at that."

"And if he doesn't come?"

"We will cross that bridge when we get to it."

"We?"

"*Sì*, Giuseppe. I'm in this with you. I will help you in any way that I can. My life is your life. We are together forever."

"I knew you would understand my actions. That is why I had to speak to you today. I greatly needed your support. It means the world to me that you understand why I never told them the truth."

"I do understand. You loved Biaggio like a brother. There is nothing else to explain to me."

"*Grazie, Maria. T'amo.*"

She kissed him before they continued walking along the streets of Monreale. Giuseppe left her in the early afternoon, to make his way home so that he could speak to his father and prepare his speech for the meeting Monday night with the *Società*.

———

ANTONIO SANGUINETTI WAS EXTREMELY quiet the night of the meeting of the Società. He sat at the very back of the barn, totally alone. His face had a blank stare. Before the meeting started, a few people, including Luigi, asked the elder Sanguinetti if he was feeling all right. He only nodded his head without a word being spoken.

The meeting was called to order by Luigi. After some housekeeping items were taken care of, Luigi turned the floor over to Giuseppe Sanguinetti, who had asked to be allowed to speak at the meeting.

As Giuseppe made his way to the front of the crowd, he caught a glimpse of his father. Last night, he had told his father the truth about the meeting with Vittelio. His father was very upset by the news related to him by his son. But by now, anger had turned to hurt. His father was looking straight down at the ground. Antonio would assume that position the entire time Giuseppe spoke.

Giuseppe reached the front, and before uttering one word, was asked by a chorus of four or five individuals, "Have you heard from Caruso yet?"

Giuseppe took a deep breath before responding. "Not yet. However, as I have said at earlier meetings, Caruso would have just gotten to his villa outside of Florence a day or so ago. I recently mailed letters to him there. I know he will get those since he always spends his summers there, relaxing, practicing and learning new roles. He will respond shortly, I'm sure."

A few cheers broke out across the room. Giuseppe raised his hands and asked for quiet. Once it was silent, Giuseppe said, "You gave me the authority to attend a meeting with Vittelio Vasaio and put forth our proposal. As you are aware, I did that."

Salvatore Licindoro yelled from the back of the barn, "And you did a fine job."

Giuseppe continued, "However, Vittelio said that in order to have the proposal accepted, we would have to get Caruso to sing at the Festival Boccale. This is exactly what I reported to you when I spoke to everyone after the meeting took place. Sadly, that was not the entire truth."

Alberto Cappecchi asked, "What do you mean?"

Giuseppe took an even deeper breath and said, "After I took Vittelio's bet, he made a condition on the bet itself. If Caruso does not sing, then the Società must be disbanded; the orchestra must be disbanded, and no more concerts will be allowed. Those were the terms put forth by Vittelio." Giuseppe looked down and said, "I agreed to his terms."

Murmuring could be heard throughout the room. Luigi stood up and said, "You did what?"

Turiddu, whose face was red with rage, said, "I knew it. I said he was too young to go. I said Vittelio would eat him up alive. How could you give in to him?"

"I gave in to Vittelio because I truly believed Caruso would come. I knew that if I didn't agree, our proposal had no chance. So I took the gamble."

Turiddu said, "Even when I said to you to accept no concessions. You had no right."

Giuseppe said in reply, "I did not think it was a concession because I thought I could win the first part of the bet. I still believe that. Caruso will come."

Turiddu responded, "But you're just guessing you can get Caruso. We all thought your getting him was a long shot. Before tonight, that didn't matter. We were no worse off if he didn't come. But tonight we learn differently. Tonight we learn that if he doesn't come, which is most likely, the village will lose the only thing we have left, its spirit."

Giacomo Terranova asked, "I want to know what Antonio thinks about this?"

But Giuseppe stepped forward and said, "My father has nothing to do with this. Like you, he did not know the truth about the meeting. I told him last night."

Luigi spoke up and asked, "Giuseppe, Vittelio wants our *Società* disbanded. How does he know about it?"

"The *Scagnozzi* keep him informed. Somehow he knows."

Turiddu said, "He probably knows from his son, Santo. Giuseppe befriended him. You can trust no Vasaio. Take my word for it. I knew it was a bad thing when I saw the two of you spending time together."

Giuseppe said, "Signor Turiddu, Santo Vasaio had nothing to do with any of this."

Fiorenza D'Archangelo stepped forward and threw out a question to the entire assembly. "Is there some way we could go back to Vittelio and tell him that we do not agree with the condition accepted by Giuseppe?"

Luigi immediately replied, "No, unequivocally no. It is not even worth trying."

Turiddu followed, "Giuseppe acted on our behalf. We are bound by what he agreed to."

Dondo Spatalanata stood up and looked kindly at Giuseppe. He said, "I ask all of you to put yourself in Giuseppe's shoes. What would you have done when presented with a chance for freedom? Most of you, if not all of you, would have taken it also. We put our trust in Giuseppe because we believed in him. Well, I still believe in him. All of our hopes for a free village must rest on the ability of Giuseppe to somehow get Caruso to come to our village. At least, because of Giuseppe, we have a shot, a chance at freedom. Be it a sure thing or a long shot, a chance is better than nothing."

Turiddu replied, "I would agree, Dondo, if we had nothing to lose. But now we do. You know what these concerts mean to everyone. You know how important this Società has become. Don't forget that it was the very members of this group who voted not to attend Carlo's funeral, and that fueled the entire idea of putting forth a proposal to Vittelio."

Dondo said, "You are correct, Turiddu. And Giuseppe carried forth our proposal to Vittelio. He acted in what he thought was our best interest at that moment. Was he wrong? I don't know, and I don't care. At least he had the courage to act."

Turiddu replied, "Even a fool can have courage."

Giuseppe shot a glance over at Turiddu. Luigi quickly told Turiddu to take a seat and tried to wrap the meeting up since there was really no point in discussing it anymore. "What was done was done," Luigi said.

When the meeting ended, the members filed out of the

barn, very dispirited. Giuseppe walked over to Dondo and said, "Once again, you come to my aid in front of these people. I want you to know how much I appreciate that."

Dondo leaned over and whispered into Giuseppe's ear, "For yourself and your father, just get Caruso."

Giuseppe closed his eyes and nodded his head affirmatively.

Before leaving the barn, Giuseppe went up to Luigi and apologized to him for not telling him the truth, especially because of the closeness between him and his father. Luigi said, "Giuseppe, I'm sorry for my reaction at the meeting. I know you meant well. But this orchestra has been in Bellafortuna since the 1700s. We cannot lose it."

"I know. I will do my best."

Giuseppe and Antonio left the barn and walked alone on the road up from the valley to the village. Hardly a word was spoken for some time until Giuseppe said, "I'm glad that's over. Papa, are you still mad?"

Antonio looked at his son and said in reply, "I'm just glad you finally told them and me the truth. They had a right to know."

"Indeed, they did, Papa."

"You must promise me that you will never withhold anything from me again."

"I promise. You don't have to worry about that. I will tell you everything from now on."

Antonio smiled at his son for the first time since being told the truth and said, "Now let us just pray that Caruso comes."

"Amen to that, Papa. Amen to that."

THE CHAUFFEUR

*O*ne day thereafter, Giuseppe was in *Il Paradiso* and standing by the Victrola. He was listening to a Caruso record. Spellbound by the magnificent voice of Caruso, he had his eyes closed, virtually moved to tears by the passion and majesty of the voice.

Suddenly the door to the wine store flew open. Giuseppe opened his eyes and saw Maria running toward him. In her left hand, she held a telegram. Crying, she ran into his arms and kissed him, saying, "He is coming. Caruso sent word that he is coming."

Before he could respond, always at this point in the dream, Giuseppe would wake up and then count in his head how many days were left before the Festival Boccale. After the meeting with the *Società* a few weeks ago, this recurring dream played itself over and over again in Giuseppe's head.

It was now July 10th. Time was running out. If he didn't

hear in about a week's time, then he would have to accept the fact that Caruso was probably not going to come. He still held out hope, though. Antonio, meanwhile, was preparing to leave on his annual July trip the following day. Giuseppe was staying home from the trip, hoping to hear the news that Caruso was coming. Instead, the news he received brought hope to its knees.

———

ON THAT HOT, July 10th, mid-morning, two bankers from Palermo, on their way home from Monreale, stopped in Bellafortuna to pick up some cases of wine from the Sanguinetti wine store. One of the men was very tall and distinguished looking. The other was much smaller and fatter.

Antonio was helping the two men pick the wine. He spoke to them of different vintages and which were the better wines for them to purchase. As they walked down the aisles, Giuseppe returned to the store from making a small delivery in the village. His father introduced the two men to Giuseppe, who, in turn, welcomed the two visitors to the village.

Antonio informed Giuseppe of the two men's choices of wines. Giuseppe went to get the crates to put the bottles in for the men's return trip to Palermo. When Giuseppe came back with the crates, he set them down in the aisle and began to fill them with the bottles. As he was doing so, the gentlemen walked over to the Victrola and noticed the napkin drawing. Giuseppe heard one of the two men ask Antonio while pointing to the napkin on the wall, "Do you know Caruso?"

"My son and I met him a very long time ago, years before his career took off to the heights that he now occupies."

The taller of the two men from Palermo chuckled at Antonio's words and said, "Well, the great tenor has fallen from those heights."

Giuseppe stopped putting the wine into the crate and walked over to where the men were speaking. Antonio asked, "What do you mean?"

The smaller man replied, "My friend here hates people more popular and successful than he. Please excuse him. You have not heard the news about the great tenor?"

Before Antonio could respond, Giuseppe, who was now right next to the man, said, "No. What news?"

The smaller man replied, "Times have been rough on the great tenor as of late. After a hugely successful year in America, the great tenor returned to Europe in May. While making the crossing on board ship, Caruso learned that his father had died in Naples. After singing engagements in London and Paris, he went to Naples to be with his brother and step-mother at their time of bereavement."

Giuseppe looked at his father and said, "Naples with his brother and step-mother. That is why he hasn't responded as of yet. He's been there with them and not in Florence."

Antonio smiled and nodded his head in agreement toward Giuseppe. A look of relief was on their faces. They still had a chance.

The taller man said to the Sanguinettis, "*Aspetta*. The story is not finished yet."

The other man said, "After spending time with them in Naples, the great tenor returned to his summer villa outside of Florence, to relax with his wife and two children. Immediately upon setting foot inside his villa, he discovered that his wife had run off with his chauffeur and left him to care for the two children alone."

The faces of both Giuseppe and Antonio showed shock. The taller man said with glee, "He is the greatest tenor in the world, and his love and the mother of his two children runs off with his driver. Can you imagine the humiliation? I mean, what type of Italian man is he that cannot control his woman?"

The smaller man said, "The press has been hounding him since the story broke. Caruso has gone into seclusion. Yet, the press will not leave him alone."

Giuseppe asked anxiously, "Do you know if he is still coming to Palermo? Is he still coming?"

The smaller man responded, "The article I read said it was still on. Probably would do him good to get away from the controversy. Can you imagine the embarrassment that poor man is going through?"

Antonio didn't answer the question directly. He merely said, "The chauffeur. Caruso's spirit must be totally destroyed."

The taller man smiled and said, "I know, isn't it wonderful?"

Giuseppe walked back to the crates and finished putting the bottles in. He loaded the men's wagon, which was parked in the Pandolfini stables, and they left the village. Giuseppe said to Antonio, "If what they say is true, Caruso will never come to sing here. That is true even if he comes to Palermo at all. *Tutto è finito.* It is over. Our problems in the village will mean nothing to him because of his own personal tragedy. I have failed you, Papa."

"Giuseppe, the men said he was still coming to Palermo. There still is hope."

"Papa, can I have the rest of the day off? I need to get some fresh air. I need to think. I need to get away for a little while."

"Certainly you may, Giuseppe. I'll see you tonight."

"Papa, when the villagers hear this news, they will believe Caruso will not be coming."

"But, at least they will understand why you couldn't get Caruso."

"Perhaps, Papa."

Giuseppe grabbed his violin case and walked out of the wine store into the Piazza. His father closed the door behind him. He felt bad for his son. He knew the turmoil going on inside of him. The news today had to have been a fatal blow to Giuseppe.

GIUSEPPE MADE his way down to the valley, then through *Antica Campanèlla* to the knoll opposite the amphitheater. There he sat down on the ground next to the cross above Biaggio's grave.

He stared out across Biaggio's beloved pond, thinking of all the days spent here with his friend. He took out his violin, and as he had done on numerous occasions with Biaggio, he played a few arias while sitting by the *Stagno Azzuro*. Finally, overcome by those memories as well as the news he had just received about Caruso, tears began to flow down his face. These were not just ordinary tears; they were tears of absolute despair. He stopped playing the violin and cried hard. After a short while, when he had composed himself, he began to speak to his old friend, as he often did when he would come to this spot.

"*Amico*, I have tried to fulfill your dying request to me. I have failed. Vittelio used me to try to embarrass my father, and I allowed it to happen. In return, I also have allowed the only thing the villagers have left in the world to be taken away from them. I don't know what to do. I wish you were here. I miss you so much. I have learned that Caruso is currently involved in a personal tragedy. He will not come to the village to sing. All I keep thinking about is the day of the Festival Boccale and the look that Vittelio will have in his eyes when he finds that Caruso is not coming. After that, Vittelio's power will become immense. He will know no one can stand up to him.

"I truly believed Caruso would come. I guess I was stupid. I know everyone in the village will be distraught, but the one person I'm most concerned about is my father. You know more than most what my failure will do to him. Again, he will have to answer to the villagers of Bellafortuna for the actions of a relative.

"Biaggio, please help me. Ask God to help me. Do not abandon me. I did this for your father. I did it for my father. I did this for everyone. But most of all I did it for you. You asked me to bring freedom to the village. I tried. I took a chance. But now there is no hope. I need you now. I need your help. Please, please help me. Tell me what I can do to rectify what I have done. Show me what I can do to still achieve freedom. Tell me how I can get Caruso to come here." Giuseppe covered his face with his hands, and lay on the ground, overcome with grief.

Suddenly, from across the pond, a single bird began to sing, sending forth its high-pitched voice over the entire area surrounding the pond. Giuseppe lifted his head from the ground and looked across the pond. He noticed the bird as it flew from its treetop perch over the stage of the amphitheater toward the remnants of the chapel, still calling to other birds with its beautiful song as it flew. The bird's call was answered by another identical looking bird as it too flew over the stage in the same direction. The two birds were now flying next to each other. Each sang differently, but to Giuseppe, they resembled each other so much that he couldn't tell them apart.

As Giuseppe listened, he momentarily forgot his troubles and simply enjoyed nature's serenade. From his vantage point, he could see the stage in the amphitheater perfectly. His eyes locked on the stage. For whatever reason, while listening to the song of the birds and looking at the stage, a plan was born in Giuseppe's very soul, a plan that, if it worked, would indeed bring freedom to the village. As if someone had just opened a curtain to let light in a dark room, Giuseppe suddenly could see the plan fully in his mind. There was still a way to have Caruso sing from the stage at the Festival Boccale. There was still a way to win the wager. At the Festival Boccale, Enrico Caruso would grace the stage and sing one aria, "Vesti la giubba".

Giuseppe smiled to himself. He looked at the cross on the

grave and said to Biaggio, "It might just work. With a lot of luck, I may be able to pull it off. It is my only chance now."

Giuseppe stood up from the knoll. His earlier desperation now had changed to resolve. As he made his way back to the village, some element of confidence again began to swell within his heart. It might just work. It had to work.

ANTONIO REACTS TO A DESPERATE PLAN

*G*iuseppe made his way back to the village and the wine store. When he entered, his father asked, "You're not still upset about the news you heard today from those two men from Palermo?"

"No, Papa."

"That's good. You still must believe Caruso will come. He still may answer you and come to the village."

"That's what I wanted to talk to you about. After the news we heard today, I know Caruso will not be coming. Papa, you know Caruso is not coming. You know it. I know it. But I'm not upset because I thought of a plan."

"What type of plan?"

Giuseppe said in reply, "My plan ensures that come the day of the Festival Boccale, Enrico Caruso will indeed grace the stage in the Piazza."

"I don't understand, Giuseppe. You just told me that you think Caruso will not be coming."

"That's correct. Caruso will not come."

"I'm very confused."

"Don't be. Let me explain. No one in this village has seen or heard Caruso live, including most especially the Vasaios. The only way anyone has heard his voice is on your Victrola. I have seen operas with you all over Italy and Palermo. We have seen many wonderful tenors in those productions. And yet, the best tenor voice next to Caruso's I have ever heard is the tenor voice of Rodolfo Giulini. Luckily, for my purposes, Rodolfo not only has a wonderful voice, he resembles Caruso, as you yourself have seen. I will get Rodolfo to sing from the stage on the day of the Festival Boccale as the great tenor, Enrico Caruso. I will have *Signora* D'Archangelo make a clown costume for him to wear for greater effect."

Antonio asked, "You are joking?"

Giuseppe, without the hint of a smile, said, "I've never been more serious in my entire life."

Antonio's demeanor changed, and he became more serious. He said to Giuseppe, "It would never work. I mean, Rodolfo does not sound like Caruso."

"But these people won't know that from one song. Rodolfo has a beautiful voice. At the concert, 'Caruso' will walk out of the wine store and sing 'Vesti la giubba'. After the aria, he will accept the accolades of everyone and then quickly leave the village under the ruse of having other engagements back in Palermo. With that, Vasaio will lose the wager."

Antonio said, "You cannot do this. You know the precarious position we are in living in this village because of your grandfather. We cannot do anything that will hurt these people again. Your plan will not work. Put it out of your mind. You cannot do it. I say no."

"Papa, I have already hurt these people by bargaining away the only thing that they have left, hope. The other day you told me never to keep anything away from you again. I promised I wouldn't, so I wanted to tell you my plan before you left for Italy. I have told you as you ordered. But I'm not asking for your approval. I'm merely telling you what my plan is."

Steadily getting angrier, Antonio said, "I don't care if you ask me or not. You will not do this. I won't allow it. This is the most ludicrous, stupid plan I have ever heard. Are you crazy? *Sei matto?*"

Giuseppe said, "I swore to Biaggio on his death bed that I would do anything in my power to bring freedom to the villagers. So when Vittelio put forth the Caruso condition to our proposal, I took the chance. I had no option. But now I see the harm that I will cause the villagers if I fail. Papa, every single day I am asked by the villagers, 'Have you heard anything? Is he coming?', until it gets to the point that I avoid seeing people in the village. Imagine what would happen if we lost the bet. These people will hate us and not respect us. I will not let that happen to you. My plan will work. Sometimes desperate times need desperate actions."

"I agree, Giuseppe that your plan is desperate. But you must realize if Vittelio finds out it is not the real Caruso, he will come down hard on the villagers."

"Papa, if we lose the bet, he will feel all-powerful and will still come down on the villagers. He will never give us a chance at freedom again. Thus, we cannot afford to lose. We must do everything in our power to bring it about. Caruso must sing from the stage. That will happen with my plan."

"How in God's name did you come up with this 'plan'? I beg you to rethink it. It will not work. You will embarrass me even more than if Caruso does not show up and we lose the bet."

Giuseppe said, "But if I can pull this off, your embarrassment for the actions of your father will go away. Freedom would have been achieved."

"And at what cost, Giuseppe? I never knew I raised a deceiver and a fool. This will never work."

Giuseppe walked over to the frame on the wall containing the caricature of Caruso. He pulled it off the wall and returned to his father. He said, "I have nowhere else to turn, Papa. What would you have me do? Stand on the stage during the Festival and say we lost. This is the last time they will hear the orchestra play, an orchestra that has been in existence since the 1700s. This is my only chance to save the concerts and the *Società*. This is our last chance to make amends for the actions of Salvatore. This is our last chance to bring freedom to the villagers. My plan will work." Giuseppe lifted the frame and held it near his father's face. He said, pointing to the picture, "Rodolfo resembles Caruso. It's worth the chance."

Antonio brought his hand up and moved it to the left in a motion meant to dismiss the thought out of hand. However, in so doing, his hand made contact with the frame, sending it tumbling to the floor. The glass for the frame shattered into many pieces.

"Papa!" Giuseppe yelled as he looked at the broken glass on the ground. Antonio tried to explain that it was an accident, but Giuseppe would not listen. He walked out of the wine store to his bedroom upstairs.

Damaging the frame took the fight out of Antonio. He went to get a broom and swept up the remnants of the glass. As he did so, he couldn't help but think about his son. He was just a kind person who found himself in a terrible situation. Would his plan work? Almost certainly not. But Antonio was fully aware of the pressure his son was under.

After sweeping up the glass, Antonio bent down and picked up the cloth napkin with Caruso's caricature drawing on it. Very carefully, he folded it and put it in his pocket for safekeeping.

Antonio then went to his son's room. He entered and again apologized for breaking the frame. Giuseppe just nodded his head. Antonio said, "Giuseppe, I do know the pressure you are under. I know you mean well. But your plan will not work. I'm leaving to go to Italy. I will be back in time for the Festival. I beg you not to do this. But if you decide you must, I cannot be a party to it. I hope you decide not to go through with it. If you do it, at least know that I understand why you did it, but I will never agree with it."

Giuseppe went to his father, hugged him, and said, "That's good enough for me."

Antonio patted his pocket and said, "I have your Caruso drawing here. I will get it reframed for you."

Giuseppe softly smiled and said, "No hurry. If I go through with my plan, the last thing I want is a picture of the real Caruso up on a wall."

Antonio smiled in reply. He said, "I love you, Giuseppe. Just do the right thing. I think you know what that is."

"I love you too. I will do what I believe is the best thing for me to do."

"We will leave it at that, *figlio*."

"No matter what, Papa, I won't let you down."

"Nor I, Giuseppe. Nor I."

29

RODOLFO'S DECISION

One week later, on Wednesday, July 18th, only 10 days before the Festival, Giuseppe went to Monreale to see Maria. The entire week before that visit, Giuseppe found the pressure around the village very intimidating. Some of the villagers came into the wine store every day to see if Giuseppe had heard word from Caruso. It got so bad that Giuseppe became more convinced that the plan with Rodolfo was the right thing to do. He had to have a Caruso sing in the village.

He met Maria outside of her school. He kissed her when he saw her. Maria could tell Giuseppe had not been sleeping well. He asked, "No word from Caruso?"

"None, Giuseppe. I'm sorry."

"This is all my own doing, Maria."

"It took courage to even go before Vittelio Vasaio, Giuseppe. Always remember that."

"What I am about to ask you, please understand I ask this

only because I have nowhere else to go." He proceeded to tell her about the news he had received regarding Caruso and the personal tragedy in his life. When he finished relating the story to Maria, he said, "I cannot let my villagers down. I cannot let my father down. I cannot let Biaggio down. That is why I now turn to you with this question."

"You can ask me anything, Giuseppe."

"It concerns your brother."

"My brother? What about my brother?"

"I want him to sing one aria at the Festival Boccale as Enrico Caruso."

Maria said quizzically in reply, "You mean 'as him'. Like everyone will think he's the real Caruso."

"*Si.*"

Maria asked, "And you think it would work?"

"I don't know. But I have no other option. He resembles Caruso. He has such a good voice. One aria and he leaves. My hope is Vittelio will be in such a state of shock, he will not pay close attention to the voice."

"Have you spoken to Rodolfo about this?"

"No, not yet. I want you to be there when I do."

"Giuseppe, I will do whatever you want me to do. But as for my brother, I don't know if he will agree to do it or not."

"It's my only chance. I cannot fail these people."

"My brother as Enrico Caruso. It would be unbelievable if it works."

"No, Maria. Believable. That is the key. If we do it, Vittelio must believe it is Caruso. That is all that matters."

"Will you tell the other villagers your plan?"

"No. No one will know, except for my father. I can't afford to have the word slip out."

"That's probably wise. Have you given up hope that the real Caruso will come sing?"

"Yes. Rodolfo is where my hope lies."

Maria said, "He's in the candle shop right now. Do you want to go see him?"

"Yes. Come with me."

They walked over to the candle shop together.

"YOU WANT ME TO DO WHAT?" Rodolfo asked when Giuseppe told him of his plan.

Giuseppe said, "Sing as Caruso."

"Have you been sipping too much of your father's wine?"

Giuseppe said, "You resemble him. You have a great voice. You only have to sing one aria. Everyone will think you are the real Caruso."

"And what about Padre Mancini? He knows who I am."

Maria said, "I didn't think about him."

Rodolfo said, "I don't think either of you have thought at all about this entire plan."

But Giuseppe said, "Rodolfo, Padre Mancini will see you only when you take the stage to sing. At that point, he will know not to say anything. He knows what is at stake. Like the rest of the villagers, he will not question it. He will know that to do so would mean the end of any chance for freedom."

"And what about your Vasaio fellow? You really believe he will think I'm Caruso?"

"We must convince him of it. You must become Caruso. We can even put you in a clown costume, though leaving your face unpainted since you resemble Caruso. But the costume will even add to the mystique. With that costume, you sing the aria from *Pagliacci* as the broken-hearted clown. When the aria is complete, you will only have to shake hands with Vittelio and say a few words to him. I will make certain that some villagers will come quickly forward who want to speak to you. And you will leave the village to return to Palermo for other commitments. After you leave, the word will spread that Caruso has a condition of his appearance, one already agreed to by the village, that his visit could not be disclosed or publicized. That way, Rodolfo, you sing your one song, and then it is finished. It will not be talked about. You would have helped bring freedom to my people."

"I cannot do it, Giuseppe. I would love to help you, but I cannot."

"Rodolfo, you are my only chance. Please help me."

"Giuseppe, your plan is a stretch. I understand your problem, but I just can't do it."

Giuseppe looked at Maria, who shrugged her shoulders. Giuseppe said to Rodolfo, "I understand, Rodolfo. You're probably right. The plan is a stretch. Thanks for listening anyway."

Rodolfo said, "I'm sorry, Giuseppe. I wish I could help you."

"I know. I'm sure you would if you could. Take care."

Giuseppe and Maria walked out of the candle shop into the Piazza. Maria said, "I'm sorry, Giuseppe."

"Don't be. I know my plan was desperate. But I am desperate."

"Look, Giuseppe. We still have ten days before the

Festival. I will work on Rodolfo. Perhaps I can convince him otherwise."

"I hope you can. Let me know if he changes his mind."

"Giuseppe, have you considered what you will do if the day of the Festival does come, and you have neither Caruso nor my brother?"

"A part of me will die that day, Maria. I don't even know if I can be in the village to see Vittelio relish in his victory."

"I will work on my brother."

Giuseppe said, "Please do. Make him change his mind. In the meantime, just in case, I need to get Fiorenza D'Archangelo working on a clown costume."

30

THE LAST MEETING OF THE SOCIETÀ

The very next day, July 19th, Giuseppe went to Meridiana to meet with Fiorenza D'Archangelo. He asked her if she had time to make a clown costume for the Festival Boccale to be worn by Caruso.

"Is he coming?" she asked.

"I have not heard from him yet. But you never know. I thought it would be appropriate if he wore a costume on the stage when he sings 'Vesti la giubba'."

"That should be no problem. I'll have it finished by the end of next week. What size to make it?"

"Since it's a clown costume, you can make it baggy. Make it a big size. It doesn't have to fit perfectly."

"Do you want it to look any particular way?"

"No. I tried to find the drawing he had given me to show you what the collar looked like, but my father broke the frame the other day, and I don't know where he put the drawing."

"That's all right. I'll just make a ruffled clown collar."

"That would be perfect."

"Giuseppe, I hope the costume is used the day of the Festival."

"Me too, *Signora*."

She said, "*Addio*, let me get started. I'll see you at the meeting of the *Società* this coming Monday?"

"*Si*. I'll be there."

THAT MONDAY, July 23rd, was the last scheduled meeting of the *Società della Libertà per Bellafortuna* before the Festival Boccale. Giuseppe sat nervously near the back. It wasn't long before Giuseppe was called to the front to let the crowd know if he had heard from Caruso.

As he had made his way to the front, a solitary figure entered the barn and sat back in the shadows, unseen by the members who were anxiously waiting to hear what Giuseppe had to say.

"I have not heard from Caruso," he said. "However, *Signor* Caruso, as some of you may know by now, has suffered a personal tragedy in his life. His wife ran away with his chauffeur, leaving him alone to care for his two children. I think it's safe to say our problem here in the village means nothing to him at this terrible time in his life."

Turiddu said, "Then he is not coming. Vittelio will not accept our proposal, and we lose our only chance at freedom."

Giuseppe said, "No, Turiddu. There is a chance that he still may come. Caruso is still going to Palermo. I will go there this Friday night before the Festival and find him. I will ask him to come. He will not turn me down if I can face him in person. Come the Festival, he will be here."

Giacomo Terranova asked, "And if not? What happens?"

Giacinto Bordelli stood up and said, "I want to know that, too. We put our faith in this young man once before. We got lied to in the process. His father is not here tonight, so I feel we can speak freely. Giuseppe, you let us down. You will let us down again."

Giuseppe sat quietly as more and more members stood up and commented on the situation. As the condemnation of Giuseppe reached a fever pitch, the figure sitting back in the shadows of the far corner of the barn stood up and made his way to the front. Some members murmured, "Look who it is. Look who is here tonight."

Padre Pietro Mancini stepped in front of the group. The barn became totally silent. The priest said, "I have been listening to your discussions tonight. First, let me say that from the day I heard about this *Società*, I envied every one of you. As a group, you came together to achieve something that God would want you to achieve for each other. Not one of you did this for your own goals. It was done for the betterment of this community. You should be praised for this. Take it from one who remained quiet for too long, from one who allowed those more powerful than him to dictate what was worthy to stand up for and what was not. However, one among you forced me to look deep inside of myself. He made me realize it was time to account to myself and to my God. I can remain silent no longer. And it is all because of Giuseppe Sanguinetti."

Giuseppe bowed his head to the priest.

Padre Mancini said, "Some of you are probably wondering what I am doing here tonight. Well, I had heard of your meeting tonight from someone at Church this morning and wanted to be here. I came in during the debate and sat in the back, listening intently. Turiddu, Giacinto and Giacomo all ask what will happen if Giuseppe fails. My answer is there can be no failure.

"If Caruso comes, God be praised. If Caruso does not come, God be blessed because these villagers remained silent no longer. You took a chance to throw down the shackles of oppression. Who knows where it will lead. But you must remember, because of Giuseppe, God has touched Santo Vasaio's heart. Santo will be the key to your freedom. Somewhere down the line, if you fail at the Festival, Santo will always be there working on his father to have his father change his ways."

A few members of the group were nodding their heads in agreement with Padre Mancini's words. Turiddu stood up and said, "Padre, all of us here respect you very much, and I personally am touched that you came here tonight. But if Caruso does not come, take my word for it, Santo Vasaio will either become a puppet for his father or he will be sent elsewhere by his father. No Vasaio would take the chance that their own son would be the reason why their reign came to an end. That is why I told Giuseppe not to make any concessions to Vittelio. Vittelio knows his son must be changed. He must be broken. Giuseppe has befriended Santo. Vittelio knows he has to break this bond to save his son. And with all due respect, Padre, that is why Caruso must come and why we must win this bet. Losing the *Società* and losing the orchestra are terrible things, but the real crux of what will be lost is the chance we have for Santo to lead us down a different path. With failure at the Festival, Santo will be brought back into the fold of his family. If he does not do so under his father's guidance, he will be replaced by a Vasaio relative who Vittelio will train to lead in his own horrible footsteps.

"Padre, you speak of what Giuseppe has done for us. But it took a great deal of courage on the part of all of the villagers not to attend Carlo Vasaio's funeral, particularly the vineyard and olive grove owners who are indebted to Vittelio. They are the ones who will suffer. If Giuseppe fails us and Caruso does not come, we will never be free."

Padre Mancini remained silent. Giuseppe's heart sank as Padre Mancini tried to speak, but had no answer to the comments made by Turiddu. Dondo Spatalanata recognized this and quickly stood up and said, "*Stiamo mettendo il carro davanti ai buoi.*" (*We are putting the cart before the horse.*) Let us see if Caruso comes. Giuseppe said he is going to Palermo to get him. Let him go. We can have this discussion another day if we have to. Right now is not the time."

Luigi said, "I agree. Let's call it a night. Let us see what happens at the Festival."

As everyone began to leave, Giuseppe walked up to Padre Mancini and thanked him for coming. He told the priest, "Turiddu is right. Even Santo knows it. Caruso must come to save us and to save him. Pray for me, Padre."

"I will, Giuseppe."

As Giuseppe made his way back to the village, he felt sick to his stomach. He had to convince Rodolfo to come. There was no question about it. He would go to Palermo Friday night and try to find Caruso. If he couldn't, he wanted

Rodolfo already committed to taking the stage as Enrico Caruso.

How in God's name did he ever get himself in this predicament, he thought. He could have led a simple life, learning the wine business and taking over the store from his father when the time came. Why did he take this responsibility upon himself? Where was Biaggio in all of this? How could Biaggio let him fail?

Well, it was too late now to turn back. Turiddu had nailed it at the meeting. Giuseppe could see it in the eyes of Padre Mancini, Luigi and Dondo, the three men who always tried to protect Giuseppe. For the first time, the full impact of failure hit home in their hearts with the words of Turiddu. They now understood what would happen if the bet was lost. And worst of all, who the villagers would blame.

Giuseppe knew he could not fail. All hope now lay with Caruso, or at least with a singer who resembled him very much.

THE EVE OF THE FESTIVAL BOCCALE

The days leading up to the Festival Boccale were a strange time for Giuseppe around the village of Bellafortuna. As each day passed by, the pressure he was under continued to grow. For the first time in a long while, not one person had asked Giuseppe about Caruso. Apparently, everyone in the village no longer believed that he could get Caruso. They all saw the handwriting on the wall. Their destiny was already written in the stars, and that destiny pointed to failure.

With his father in Italy and Maria in Monreale, he felt very alone. He saw Santo every now and then, but only a quick word was spoken between them. Santo found it very difficult to be seen with his friend the few days before the Festival. Santo knew that if Giuseppe lost the wager to his father, their friendship would come to an end. The villagers would demand it. Vittelio would demand it.

Santo, during one of their infrequent chats, asked

Giuseppe if he had heard any word from Caruso. Giuseppe told him no, but that the Friday before the Festival, it was his intention to go to Palermo and find Caruso and ask him personally to come to Bellafortuna.

Deep down, Giuseppe knew his chances of getting Caruso were slim and that his only real chance to win the wager with Vittelio was with Rodolfo. He and Maria would need to convince Rodolfo to come to his aid. That was the only real option he had left.

The day before the Festival Boccale arrived. Early that Friday morning, shortly after Giuseppe had opened the wine store, Fiorenza came into the store carrying a stunningly beautiful, sequined, all-white clown costume with a huge ruffled collar. Three huge, bright red pompons were situated on the shirt where the buttons would be.

Upon seeing the costume, Giuseppe said, "*Bello*. It's fantastic."

"*Grazie*, Giuseppe. Like I said, I just hope it gets some use."

"I'm leaving shortly to go to Palermo. I still have hope that I can find Caruso and can convince him to come."

"Giuseppe, I want to thank you for all that you have done. I know the pressure you have been under. You know whatever happens tomorrow, these people will still love you."

"You are very kind to say that, Signora."

She came over and kissed Giuseppe on his cheek and left the store. Giuseppe took the costume upstairs to put in his bedroom. He stared at the costume. He tried to imagine Rodolfo wearing it, standing on the stage at the Festival tomorrow. It would be very difficult to look at Rodolfo and not think he was Caruso. At least that is what Giuseppe hoped for.

By 10:00 o'clock that morning, he left Mamma Lucia in charge of the store, hooked up Caruso to his cart, and started his journey to Monreale to meet with Maria and Rodolfo and to try to convince the singer one last time to sing from the stage.

As he departed the village, he noticed that the *Piazza Santa Croce* was already in the process of being decorated for the Festival tomorrow. The stage was being set up in front of the Church, and chairs were being arranged throughout the Piazza. Streamers ran from the statue of Enzo Boccale to the buildings surrounding the Piazza. Giuseppe dreaded tomorrow when the Piazza would be filled with people hoping that Caruso would be there.

When Giuseppe arrived in Monreale, he went directly to the candle shop. Maria's father was hard at work - behind a black pot - forming the hot wax into a candle and inserting a wick into the molten wax. He informed Giuseppe that both Rodolfo and Maria were upstairs.

Giuseppe made his way upstairs and found the two siblings sitting at the dining room table. They were eating a late breakfast.

When Giuseppe came in, Maria asked, "Care for anything to eat?"

"No, thanks. I'm not hungry."

Rodolfo asked, "What brings you here today, Giuseppe?"

"You! I came to see if you would reconsider and come sing one song in Bellafortuna. Just one song."

Rodolfo chuckled and said, "You are persistent. No, I haven't changed my mind."

Giuseppe said to him, "You're my only chance at redemption. I really need you."

"As I said before, I simply can't do it. I really like you, Giuseppe. And you are very good to my sister. I would do almost anything for you. But I cannot do what you ask."

"Then, I will fail."

"Giuseppe, I'm sorry. It's really not my problem."

"Then, it is finished." Giuseppe got up from the table and left the home. The moment he walked out of the room, Maria said to her brother, "But it is your problem, Rodolfo. I'm his for as long as I live. His life is my life. We are one. This is the man I will marry. I cannot see him fail."

Rodolfo said, "I don't want to see him fail either, but I cannot do what he asks. Please understand me."

Maria reached across the table and grabbed Rodolfo's hand. She said, "Come with me to Bellafortuna later today. Giuseppe cannot be alone tomorrow. We will be there for him, offering our support. Will you at least do that for me?"

Rodolfo was silent momentarily and then said, "I will do that. I will go to Bellafortuna with you."

Maria ran downstairs and found Giuseppe seated out in the Piazza. Giuseppe said, "I'm going on to Palermo to try to see Caruso."

Maria said, "Rodolfo and I are coming later today to Bellafortuna to be with you tomorrow. With a good night's sleep in Bellafortuna, perhaps Rodolfo's mind will change. He may do what you ask. For me, he may do it."

Giuseppe said to her, "I love the both of you, you know that. Here is a key to the back door of the wine shop and my home. As you make your way into the village, go directly to *Il Paradiso*. Don't talk to anyone so that Rodolfo can enter the village, arousing no suspicion. People will think the both of you are just making purchases at the store. Park your cart at the stable behind the store. My *zio*, Onofrio, will remember you. He won't say a word. Mamma Lucia will be working in the wine store. Tell her that you are there for the Festival. She will make up a bed for each of you. I'll see you much later tonight, hopefully with good news from Caruso."

Maria said, "We will leave later today, Giuseppe. I'll work on my brother during the whole journey. Hopefully, Biaggio will work on him while he sleeps."

Giuseppe said, "I fear that your brother is the only realistic chance to bring freedom to the villagers. I hope he agrees."

"He will, Giuseppe. He will do it for me. I will ask him tonight. He will do it because I love you with all my heart."

"Maria, you mean the world to me. I thank you for your support."

"I know tomorrow could be a terrible day for you if Caruso won't come, and my brother won't sing. But I will be there for you. I will always be there for you."

"I know, Maria. After this is all over, I will make it up to you."

"Just marry me, Giuseppe. That is all I require."

"Your wish is my command," Giuseppe said with a smile.

She said, "I've never been happier in my life. I hope you find Caruso tonight, and he agrees to come to Bellafortuna tomorrow."

"I know all of my hope lies with your brother. Convince him."

"I will. I promise. *Ti amo*."

"*Ti amo*, Maria."

Giuseppe stayed in Monreale for a light lunch with Maria. A short while later, in mid-afternoon, Giuseppe kissed Maria goodbye, climbed into his cart, and left the city. The little cart traveled along the road from Monreale headed toward Palermo.

Soon Giuseppe reached the junction with the single dirt road that led to Bellafortuna. As he passed it on his way to Palermo, he was startled when a figure jumped from behind a tree. It was Santo Vasaio.

"You scared the hell out of me," Giuseppe said.

"Giuseppe, I wanted to talk with you and thought this a better place than in the village."

"How did you know where I would be?"

Santo climbed up into the wagon and sat next to Giuseppe. He said, "You told me you would be heading to Palermo to find Caruso on Friday. This morning I went to the wine shop to see you. Mamma Lucia told me you had already left for Monreale."

"*Sì.* I went to see Maria."

"Well, I figured you would thereafter be making the journey to Palermo. So I waited for you. My father can't wait till tomorrow to see you fail."

"He may not have that much longer to wait."

"Is there any hope you will find Caruso and convince him to come sing in Bellafortuna?"

"I don't know, Santo. It's worth a try, though."

"My thoughts and prayers will be with you, Giuseppe."

"I need all the prayers I can get."

"Giuseppe, no matter what happens tomorrow, I will always be your friend. You changed my life. You made me see this world and the way life should be lived in a completely different light. If my father wins the bet tomorrow, any chance he will change is over. But I've already been changed. I will leave this village before I ever have to rule it like my father does."

"Santo, even if we fail tomorrow, the villagers need you to stay. You never know what type of aid you could offer us."

"None, Giuseppe. My father will pass on his reign to my cousin, Ennio. He was born with a silver spoon in his mouth and a cold, hard heart. He won't want me around."

"Santo, after losing Biaggio, I never thought I would get close to a friend ever again. You proved me wrong. Over time our friendship has grown. You stuck your neck out for my people and me. I only hope I can repay you by not failing you."

"You already repaid me by changing my life. You cannot fail me."

"I'm glad you came to see me today. But I must be going to Palermo. Wish me luck."

"I do wish you that. In remembrance of your good friend Biaggio, I will say, 'Good fishing'."

Giuseppe smiled at the comment. He said in reply, "I was a better violin player than a fisherman. But I will try to get the big catch. *Addio*, Santo."

"*Addio*, Giuseppe."

With that, Santo climbed down from the cart, after which Giuseppe started traveling down the road. When he had gone a couple of yards, he heard Santo's voice yell out, "*Io riportano*. Giuseppe, just bring him back."

Giuseppe turned in his seat and yelled back, "I will try. I will try my hardest."

Giuseppe turned around and continued on down the

road. He thought of the words he had just yelled back at Santo. He would try but he knew it was for nothing. Giuseppe still believed his best and only chance to win the wager was with Rodolfo. Maria had to convince her brother to sing tomorrow. Absent that, the villagers had no chance for success, which would mean he would have let his father down.

Antonio had not come back from his trip yet. Giuseppe guessed he might come back sometime this evening or tomorrow morning at the latest. He expected to face his father tomorrow and tell him he had failed.

Giuseppe continued down the road. He took that road all the way to Palermo in the hope of finding Enrico Caruso, and in so doing, he would try to convince the greatest tenor in the world to take the journey back with him to the lovely, secluded village of Bellafortuna; a village that still held out hope for a miracle to make it rise to glory and give it's people freedom.

At this late date, Giuseppe didn't care if it was Enrico Caruso or Rodolfo Giulini taking the stage at the Festival tomorrow. He just knew it had to be one of them.

MEANWHILE, back in Bellafortuna, preparations were in full swing around the village of Bellafortuna. The Piazza was beautifully decorated. The stage had been set up for the concert.

Late Friday afternoon, Padre Mancini was practicing with the choir, preparing for the Festival Mass set for 8:00 a.m., Saturday morning. The Church's altar was covered with flowers, picked personally by the all-female altar society.

The Festival Boccale was the event of the year for the villagers. It was a celebration not only of the man who had created their village but a celebration of themselves as a people.

After the sun set that night, the last thing done was the annual blessing of the Piazza, the night before the Festival Boccale. In the presence of the villagers who had been preparing the Piazza for the Festival, the Monsignor stood in front of the Church, raised his hand and made the sign of the cross. The villagers hoped the blessing would help in bringing Caruso to their village.

Then most of the villagers went to their homes and turned in early to get their rest for the Festival tomorrow. Slowly, one by one, the homes went dark as the villagers of Bellafortuna went to sleep.

Around 10:00 p.m. that night, a figure, seated in a cart, illuminated only by the moonlight, drove on the village road leading to the Piazza. The figure was seen by a villager who recognized that it was Giuseppe Sanguinetti who had returned from Palermo.

He was alone.

THE FESTIVAL BOCCALE

On Saturday morning, the day of the Festival Boccale, a bright sun came up over the Eastern Sicilian hills. It augured a day of a beautiful sky and an invigorating climate. The *Piazza Santa Croce* was already decorated for the Festival, which was set to begin at 1:00 p.m. later that day.

Santo Vasaio got up in time that day so that he could attend the special 8:00 a.m. Festival Mass that morning. Giuseppe had asked him for his prayers, and he intended to follow through with meeting that request. He left his home and walked out into the Piazza. The Piazza was fairly crowded with the locals making their way to Church.

The Piazza had streamers hanging above that added a blast of color and gave a very festive feel to the area. Chairs were arranged all over the Piazza, and a few tables were already set up as well. Food was a very important component of the Festival Boccale. The locals would bring their own food and place on the tables the items to be shared by all the villagers.

When Santo got up that morning, he heard his father speaking with a *Scagnozzo*. In the course of their conversation, Santo overheard that Giuseppe Sanguinetti had been seen returning to the village last night, alone. However, so that there would be no surprises at the Festival, Vittelio, since daybreak, had sent a number of the *Scagnozzi* to stand watch at the junction of the road from Palermo. They were under strict orders to watch for any wagon headed to the village and to let him know the names of all passengers. He was specifically looking for one person, namely the great tenor, Enrico Caruso. If Caruso were coming, he would arrive sometime that morning. Vittelio would not be surprised at the Festival. The *Scagnozzi* were reporting every half hour if any movement was seen on the road. So far that morning, none was reported.

As Santo walked through the Piazza, he noticed that no table was set up in front of the Sanguinetti store, which always provided free wine the entire day of the Festival. Perhaps it would be set up later, he thought. The wine store's window was covered from the inside with a curtain, which was not unusual at this time of the morning. However, Santo did notice that the Sanguinetti home's shutters on the second floor were all uncharacteristically closed, which made it look as if no one was there. If Giuseppe indeed had come back alone last night, then that must mean he had no luck in getting Caruso.

As Santo continued walking through the Piazza on his way to Church, he saw Luciano Bonnifonso, a *Scagnozzo*, Luciano, with his black outfit with the Vasaio crest on it, had run into the Piazza and headed directly to the *Palazzo Vasaio,* no doubt making another report to Vittelio.

Santo went to Mass and prayed for Giuseppe's success. He had come to love the boy who had changed his life. He hoped the day would end with a joyous celebration in the village, and with his father's belief that the villagers were worthless, proven wrong.

When the Mass ended that morning, Padre Mancini was standing in the front of Church shaking hands with everyone who had attended the Mass. Santo approached and shook hands with the priest. Padre Mancini asked, "Have you seen or heard from Giuseppe?"

"No, Padre. I saw him yesterday. He was on his way to Palermo to try one last time to get Caruso. I heard he arrived back here last night, alone."

Padre Mancini said, "On my way into Church this morning, I saw your father's employees running from the valley. What are they up to?"

"Watching for Caruso. My father doesn't trust Giuseppe or the villagers. He thinks these people will try anything to win this bet. So, my father wants it reported to him who is coming into the village. They have been watching the road since daybreak."

Padre Mancini said, "The fact that Giuseppe returned alone does not bode well. I fear today is a bleak day for the villagers of Bellafortuna. Today hope dies."

Santo said, "And it is my own father who will extinguish hope, Padre. I hate him."

"Don't hate him, Santo. Pity him. He was raised that way. He never knew any differently. He never had the opportunity to have people like the Sanguinettis make him take stock of what pain his family had caused the villagers. Giuseppe opened your eyes. I just hope, after Giuseppe fails today, your father's eyes somehow get opened too."

"I will try, Padre. But to what end, I know not. I hate to see Giuseppe fail today."

"Me too. But God works in mysterious and wonderful ways. You never know what He has in store. We will have to wait and see. I'll see you later today at the Festival."

"*Addio*, Padre."

Santo left the Church and made his way back to his home. Before entering the home, he looked toward the Sanguinetti home. All of the shutters on the second floor were still closed, and the curtain was shut over the window downstairs.

SLOWLY, the villagers began to go about their day. The Piazza became abuzz with activity as the preparations began in earnest for the Festival. The smells emanating from the different homes in the village were wonderful, as the women cooked the meals that would be served at the Festival.

The Festival Boccale was a real celebration that the villagers enjoyed immensely. Normally, the hours before the Festival were a joyous time of anticipation. Today it was different. Anticipation was replaced with apprehension. Everyone knew what was at stake. There was added apprehension in the fact that the Sanguinetti wine store, which always was open by 9:00 a.m., was closed. With the store's curtain shut and upstairs shutters closed, not a living soul could be seen inside. The villagers started to think that Giuseppe had failed. Caruso would not be coming.

This belief was reinforced when word spread around the village that Giuseppe had been seen returning to the village alone last night. And now, with the Sanguinetti store closed and the home shuttered, they began to wonder if Giuseppe had left the village during the night so that he could stay as far away as possible. They even questioned if Antonio, who still had not returned from his trip from Italy, would also not return in order to avoid the embarrassment of today. After all, Antonio had always returned from his trip to Italy in time for the Festival.

That morning, Turiddu, for the first time, did not yell his remarks to the *Palazzo Vasaio*. How could he? He believed they were defeated because Giuseppe Sanguinetti was unable to fulfill his promise of getting Caruso.

As more and more villagers became aware that morning that the Sanguinetti wine store was dark, all hope was dashed. With the *Scagnozzi* running back and forth, making their reports to Vittelio, the villagers knew their cause was lost.

By 12:30 p.m., the Piazza started filling with the locals. Pots and dishes of food were placed on the tables. It was a beautiful but surprisingly mild summer day. The sun sat high in the sky without a cloud in sight.

The chairs on the stage were being filled with the members of the *Opera Orchestra di Bellafortuna*. They asked among themselves if today would be the last time they could play together as a group in their beloved Piazza. An organization in existence since the 1700s could come to its end today.

Dondo and Victoria Spatalanata and their daughters arrived in the Piazza. Victoria had made a pot of lentil soup, which she placed on one of the tables. The family then found a spot to sit, very near the front of the stage. Dondo looked over at the wine store and saw that it was closed. He shook his head, not in disgust, but because he felt so badly for the young man who had loved his son.

Dondo hated to see Giuseppe fail today. Giuseppe had tried everything in his power to do the right thing. After everything was said and done, Dondo believed that is what the villagers would come to think. Giuseppe had tried to help his fellow villagers by trying to bring freedom to them.

More and more villagers filled the Piazza. Giacomo Terranova and his family came out of their cobbler shop and into the Piazza. His daughters were dressed in new outfits, made especially for them by Fiorenza D'Arcangelo.

The orchestra began warming up. The tables were laden with food. At intermission, usually just after three or four musical selections, the tables would be inundated with the locals, all-vying for food. Turiddu's lasagna was always a hot commodity, as was Mamma Lucia's spizatedda. However, even she had not been seen that morning.

At precisely 12:55 p.m., Vittelio and Ada Vasaio made their way from their home and into the Piazza. They walked directly to two chairs arranged for them in the front of the stage. As Ada sat down, Vittelio turned and surveyed the crowd around the Piazza. His eyes locked on those of Turiddu. Vittelio brought his right hand to directly under his chin, and then with great force, he flicked the back of his hand forward, in a very familiar derogatory Sicilian gesture, effectively telling Turiddu to go to hell.

Turiddu shot the finger back at Vittelio. Vittelio chuckled to himself as he sat down. Santo, who had left his home after his parents, sat down next to his father. Vittelio said to his son, "This is a great day, Santo. This is the day we will finally achieve respect. These people put their trust in the Sanguinettis and have gotten burned. The *Scagnozzi* tell me that since this morning, no one has come on the road to Bellafortuna. Caruso is not coming. These villagers will realize that I am the provider for them like you will be when I step down."

Santo said not a word. He turned one last time to look at the wine store. There was no sign of life. Right at that moment, Luigi walked onto the stage to begin the festivities. The crowd clapped as Luigi did so.

Luigi shook hands with the first violinist, Dino Mantovanisti, and then turned to the crowd and said, "*Signore. Signori*. Thank you for coming to the Festival Boccale. We have great selections for you today. However, first it is my pleasure to introduce Monsignor Montarsolo who will lead us in prayer."

Seated next to the Monsignor out in the Piazza was Padre Mancini. He helped the Monsignor to his feet, and the older man made his way to the stage. The Monsignor said a quick incantation and made some very brief remarks about Enzo Boccale and what his life had meant to the village and why they were so thankful for him.

After the Monsignor finished, he left the stage, and Luigi walked in front of the orchestra once again. There was a touch of sadness in Luigi's voice as he spoke. After saying a few words about the importance of the Festival Boccale, he introduced the first musical selection, the *Intermezzo* from *Cavalleria Rusticana* by Mascagni. The crowd clapped. Luigi turned and conducted.

As the beautiful strains of Mascagni's melancholy melody filled the Piazza, almost every villager thought of their chance of freedom and how close they had come. But it was for naught. Caruso had not come.

Vittelio sat beaming in the front. His head turned as if on a swivel, looking at the faces of the villagers. As he did so, he smirked at the villagers seated throughout the Piazza. As the orchestra continued to play, a few villagers began to weep, knowing that the control of Vittelio Vasaio would not come to an end today, but would only grow stronger.

The audience clapped when the first selection came to an end. Luigi turned to the crowd and then back to the orchestra and asked them to stand. All of the members rose up as one and bowed to accept the applause. Luigi thought to himself how much he would miss this; the gift of music played in the Piazza in his beloved village of Bellafortuna to his fellow villagers, for without Caruso this would indeed be the last concert.

After the crowd quieted down, the orchestra members began to sit down before playing the next selection. As they sat down, the first violinist, Dino Mantovanisti, stood in place, looking over the heads of the seated audience toward the wine store directly across the Piazza. He stared without moving a muscle. The other members of the orchestra noticed this, and after looking at Dino, they looked out into the Piazza to see what he was staring at. Luigi became aware of this, and he too turned his back to the orchestra and looked across the Piazza. As he did this, the audience members did the same. All eyes were on the Sanguinetti wine store.

The door had been opened, and out walked a man dressed

as a clown. His outfit was all-white, sequined, and with a huge ruffled collar. Three huge, bright red pompons were situated on the shirt. The man had a white cone hat, with another red pompon at the very top. His face was painted white with makeup, and his lips made into a frown. Dark tears were drawn below his eyes to make it seem like he was crying.

The crowd in the Piazza sat in silence. Vittelio Vasaio rocked back and forth in his seat, trying to get a view over the heads of everyone seated in the Piazza.

The clown stood in the doorway and then stepped to his right, allowing Giuseppe Sanguinetti to walk out of the front door of the wine store. He had his usual smile on his face. In his left hand, he held his violin and bow. The villagers murmured to themselves when they saw Giuseppe walk out of the store.

The two men made their way to the stage, amid virtual silence. They walked near the *Palazzo Vasaio*, and entered the stage from that side.

Giuseppe walked over to Luigi and whispered into his ear. The crowd stared the entire time at the man dressed as a clown. Was this Caruso? Was this person dressed as a clown, the greatest tenor in the world? If not, who was he? What was Giuseppe up to? All of these thoughts ran through the minds of the villagers.

Luigi motioned to Dino Mantovanisti to move his chair to allow Giuseppe to stand. Dino acquiesced in the request, and Giuseppe made his way to his place.

Meanwhile, the man dressed as a clown walked over to where Luigi was standing. Luigi grabbed the man's hand with both of his, bowed slightly while shaking his hand profusely. Luigi then turned to the crowd and said, "*Signore. Signori.* Enrico Caruso sings."

The man dressed as a clown bowed deeply. Even though his face was made up to look like he was frowning, a smile was visible. Vittelio Vasaio looked on with disgust. He turned to his wife and said, "*Questi farabutti mi prendono per un buffone. (These scoundrels take me for a fool.)* They send out this person in a clown suit and say here is Caruso." He then turned to Santo and said, "Giuseppe not only has failed today. He has shown his true colors. These people are disgusting liars."

Santo sat quietly in his seat. What was Giuseppe up to, he thought. Was he trying to pull a fast one on his father?

Right at that moment, from out of the wine store, walked Antonio, Mamma Lucia, Maria, and Rodolfo Giulini, as well as another man who was very tall with a full beard. They stood out front of *Il Paradiso* next to each other.

Luigi turned to the orchestra, brought his hand up, and began the music to the aria "Vesti la giubba" from *Pagliacci*. The man dressed as a clown stood on the front of the stage. The drum beat, and he began to sing.

> *Recitar! Mentre preso dal delirio,*
> *To act! While in the grip of delirium,*
>
> *non so più quel che dico e quel che faccio!*
> *I don't know what I'm saying or what I'm doing!*

The moment his voice came forth, it vibrated around the Piazza, making it seem as though the walls of the buildings would come tumbling down. From the first few notes, everyone knew this was no ordinary voice. People sat astonished at the full timbre of the voice, the tremendous breath span, the combination of sweetness and power, and the highly dramatic baritonal personality of the voice. Without question, this was the voice of the greatest singer who had ever lived. This was the voice of the one and only Enrico Caruso.

Eppur è d'uopo sforzati!
Still I have to try!

Bah! Sei tu forse un uom?
Bah! Are you a man?

Tu se Pagliaccio!
You are a clown!

Vittelio Vasaio slumped in his chair. Santo sat in awe. Giuseppe had gotten Caruso. He wondered how Giuseppe could have pulled it off?

HOW CARUSO HAD COME to the village is a story in and of itself and, thus, an *intermezzo* is needed.

The best way to describe it is to say that the village of Bellafortuna was touched by grace that day. It is a story of a father's love and a broken-hearted man's sense of fulfillment through kindness.

THE INTERMEZZO

*a*fter Giuseppe had left Santo the Friday afternoon before the Festival Boccale, he made his way to Palermo arriving in the capital city around 4:00 p.m. He traveled along the *Corso Vittorio Emanuele*, which led directly into the heart of the city. He made his way to the Piazza Verdi, located centrally in the city and which is dominated by the *Teatro Massimo* Opera House.

He parked his cart and made his way to the Opera House. As he did so, he thought of all the times he and his fellow villagers had come to the huge building to see the glorious opera stories told from its stage.

Giuseppe entered the building and came into a small entrance foyer. He immediately noticed a counter with a man seated behind it. A nameplate on the counter gave the seated man's name as Vincenzo Cassinelli, the head usher for the *Teatro Massimo*.

The man was writing with his head down, so he did not

see Giuseppe enter the building. Giuseppe walked over to the counter and said, *"Mi scusi, Signor Cassinelli. Il mio nome è Giuseppe Sanguinetti da Bellafortuna.* I was wondering if I may have a word with you?"

The man stood up and extended his hand, saying, *"Si, Signor* Sanguinetti. How may I be of assistance to you?"

"I will take only a moment of your time, *Signor.* I have a small token of appreciation to give to *Signor* Caruso from the people of my village. I thought you might be able to tell me where he is staying while he is in Palermo this weekend."

"Signor Caruso is staying at the *Grand Hotel et des Palmes."*

"Where is that, *Signor*?"

"Just a few blocks from here on the *Via Roma.* Do you know where the *Via Roma* is?"

"Si."

"Then just go to the *Via Roma,* and someone on the street can point the hotel out to you. You can't miss it. It's a beautiful hotel. One of the city's oldest. All of the city's famous visitors have stayed there. Even Wagner stayed there. And it was at that same hotel he completed his last opera, *Parsifal.* That is the place where Caruso is staying. I don't know how you will get to see him, though. You know on Sunday, he is receiving the Golden Palm of Persephone."

"I know. I wish he was singing while he was in town."

"Me too. What a voice. But with everything that's going on in his life right now, we are very lucky that he still came to our city. I think he used the opportunity to get away from everything for a while."

"Grazie, Signor Cassinelli. I believed the opera house was the best place to come to find where Caruso was staying."

"Prego. Take care."

"I will."

Giuseppe left and made his way back to the entrance, then left the opera house and made the short trip to the hotel, located on the *Via Roma*, where the greatest tenor in the world was staying.

GIUSEPPE FOUND the hotel and entered the lobby. The lobby of the *Grand Hotel et des Palmes* was exquisite. It was a mixture of gold, marble and mirrors. Windows illuminated the entire interior. Ornate columns lined the room. The lobby was filled with people seated in chairs, reading, talking, playing cards, or drinking wine and coffee.

Off to Giuseppe's right was an armchair roped off. Giuseppe read the sign next to the chair. It pointed out that, as Richard Wagner sat in that exact chair, he was inspired to complete his opera, *Parsifal*, while he was a guest at the hotel. The elder composer would sit in the lobby for hours, writing the orchestration for his epic opera.

Giuseppe looked over to his left and saw the concierge desk. He realized at that point that he had no idea how he would go about trying to find Caruso. He could wait in the lobby and see if the great tenor came into it, which would allow Giuseppe the opportunity to speak to him. But Caruso might use a back entrance. He finally decided to take a chance. He walked over to the concierge desk and asked the man behind the desk, "Could you tell me where I could find Signor Caruso?"

The man looked at Giuseppe for a moment before responding. He said, "I think they left to take a tour of the city. Last place I saw him and his entourage were up on the terrace having drinks. But like I said, I think they have left already."

"Where is the terrace? I'll go see if they are still there."

After receiving directions, Giuseppe took a flight of stairs and then walked out onto a beautiful terrace, which afforded a panoramic view of the ancient city of Palermo. A bar sat on one side. Tables, with umbrellas, were arranged all over the terrace.

Giuseppe's heart sank as he saw that all of the tables were empty except for one table with a man whose back was to Giuseppe. Caruso indeed had left.

Now what, thought Giuseppe. He had no plan to find Caruso. He would have to wait in the lobby and try to see Caruso if he came in. That was his only chance. If that failed, then his only hope would be Rodolfo.

Before leaving the terrace, Giuseppe walked over to the bar. He asked the bartender for a glass of Chianti.

As the bartender poured the wine, Giuseppe asked the man, "Was Enrico Caruso just up here?"

"*Si.* His party just left a short while ago. Here is your wine."

"*Grazie.*"

Giuseppe turned and began to walk to one of the tables. As he turned, he now could see, seated at a table, the man whose back was to him when he had entered the terrace. Giuseppe's eyes grew wide. His jaw dropped. He stood dumbfounded. The man seated at the table grinned. Giuseppe finally said, "Papa. What are you doing here?"

Antonio said with great emotion, "*Verrà a Bellafortuna, Giuseppe.*" (*He is coming to Bellafortuna, Giuseppe.*)

Giuseppe's knees buckled from the surge of tension being released from his body. His father stood up from the table and grabbed his son to hold him up. Father and son stood on the terrace, holding each other for a long time. Finally, Giuseppe asked, "How do you know he is coming? What's going on?"

"Come, Giuseppe, sit with me, and I will tell you everything. It all began with my trip to Italy."

They sat down at the table. Sipping wine, with the glorious views of Palermo in a setting sun, Antonio told Giuseppe the story of how he had gotten Caruso to agree to come to Bellafortuna.

WHEN ANTONIO LEFT Bellafortuna to go on his annual trip to Italy, he knew that his trip this year would not be solely for the purpose of purchasing wine. Instead, he would travel immediately to Florence. It was his intention to go to Caruso's villa to try to see the great tenor personally and to convince him to come to Bellafortuna.

Sitting on the terrace, Antonio momentarily stopped his story and said, "I could not bear to see you fail, Giuseppe."

Antonio traveled to Florence and immediately went to Caruso's villa at Le Panche. When he arrived at the villa, he found himself in front of a very large wall that surrounded the property. Antonio did not know how he could get to see the great tenor, but he was desperate to save his son and his village.

He rang the bell, which dangled near the iron-gate that led one onto the property. After a few moments, a nice looking middle-aged man, dressed in overalls covered with mud as if he were working in the garden, came walking along the dirt path that led from the villa to the gate. The man came up to the gate and asked Antonio, in a very strong Neapolitan accent, what he needed.

"I would like to see *Signor* Caruso."

"He is not seeing anyone at this time."

"*Signor*, please help me. Please, I beg you. Tell him it is urgent."

"I'm sorry, *Signor*. He wishes not to be disturbed."

The man turned his back and began to walk back to the villa.

Antonio reached into his pocket and pulled out a piece of cloth. He stuck his hand through the gate, extending the cloth to the man. Antonio said, "*Signor*. At least do me this favor. Give this to Caruso. Tell him the boy's father is at the gate."

The man turned and walked back to the gate. He grabbed the cloth and looked at it. It was the napkin with the drawing of Caruso dressed as a clown.

Giuseppe cut into his father's story and asked, "You took the drawing with you?"

Antonio responded, "My visit to the villa was the main purpose for my trip. I thought the napkin might come in handy." Antonio continued with his story.

The man lifted his eyes from the napkin and looked into the eyes of Antonio. He then said, "*Aspetta*. Stay here. I'll be back." The man, with the napkin in his hand, walked back to the villa.

After what seemed like an eternity, the man returned to the gate. He no longer had the napkin with him. He reached up to the lock and opened the gate. "He will see you," the man said.

Antonio entered the grounds and walked with the man toward the villa. As they did so, the man said, "My name is Mario de Palma. I'm the head gardener for the property here."

"You're not from around here, are you? I can tell by your accent."

"I'm from Naples. I went to grammar school with Enrico. Most of his employees are cronies of his from Naples. He likes to have us around to reminisce about simpler times. Fame does have its downside."

They reached the front door of the villa. Upon entering the home, Antonio walked into a beautiful front parlor. The main piece of furniture in the room was a grand piano. Mario said, "Enrico is in the garden."

As they walked through the villa, the beauty of the place astonished Antonio. Mario said, "Enrico renovated the entire home. I thought it would never be finished. During the summer, the workers would stop work for hours, mesmerized by the voice of Caruso as he practiced every day."

Down a long hallway, Antonio noticed the walls covered with drawings done by the Maestro himself. As they walked, Mario said, "Excuse me for earlier. The press, as of late, has hounded Enrico. I'm sure you are aware about his present situation with his wife. The poor man is devastated."

"I am aware, *Signor* de Palma."

They reached a pair of French doors that led to the gardens. Through the glass panes of the doors, Antonio could see Caruso seated at a table, alone. Mario opened the door and showed Antonio out into the garden. Antonio walked toward the table.

Caruso has an open book in front of him. It was filled with his precious stamp collections. On top of the open page was the napkin Antonio had brought with him. Caruso stood up and extended his hand to Antonio.

"*Signor* Sanguinetti. You have brought my mind back to wonderful times. Those days seem so long ago now."

"*Commendatore* Caruso, thank you for seeing me."

"Please, call me Enrico. What brings you here today?"

"My son. The person you drew that picture for those many years ago. He has written to you. I don't know if you ever received his letters. But I brought one for you to read. If you will allow me." Antonio reached into his pocket and pulled out the letter. He handed it to Caruso, and as both sat down, Caruso began to read it.

Antonio could tell that the letter moved Caruso. When Caruso had finished reading it, he neatly folded the letter and shook his head as though he was trying to hold back his emotions. Antonio said, "Since February, he mailed this letter to you every month, praying that you would receive it and respond."

Caruso said, "I never got it. If I had, I would have at least responded to him. After all, a promise is a promise." Caruso rang a small bell that was located on the table. Quickly, a very tall gentleman, with a full beard, came out of the villa. Caruso introduced the man to Antonio as one of his assistants, Marcello Panzeca. "Marcello, have you seen this letter before?"

Marcello took the letter from Caruso and perused it. He

handed it back to Caruso, saying, "*Si.* I recall receiving at least two or three of the same letter."

Caruso asked, "Why didn't you ever show it to me?"

"Enrico, you get hundreds of letters like these asking you to make an appearance. We can't bother you with everyone you receive. Besides, you haven't performed publicly in Italy for what, five years now."

Caruso said sternly, "But this was different. This one quoted me as making a promise. You should have shown it to me."

"Sorry, Enrico."

"*Va bene.*" (*It's all right.*)

Marcello returned to the villa. Caruso sat quietly for a moment. He then stood up and said to Antonio, "Walk with me."

Caruso led Antonio away from the table toward the gardens. The flowers in the gardens were in full bloom. As they walked, Antonio could see, far off in the distance, the tower and dome of the *Duomo*, the Cathedral of Florence. It was a magnificent sight.

Caruso spoke not at all. Antonio walked beside him, afraid to speak to the great tenor who seemed to be lost in his thoughts. Suddenly, Caruso stopped and said, "Tell me about your village. Tell me about Bellafortuna."

Antonio said, "It's a magical place, beautifully set among the Sicilian hills. The entire village glows with the setting sun. But the heart of the place is its people. They are good people, Enrico. Good people who are ruled by the evil of greed. Poverty has been forced down their throat. And yet, the village remains a place of decency and grace."

Caruso sighed and said, "Does decency still have a place in this world, Antonio?"

"I hope so, Enrico."

"That is but a dream, *amico*. Decency is hard to find. Everything you believe in, everything you trust in, can all come crashing down within minutes. Your entire world can be turned upside down just by the action of another. And yet, we are expected to go on."

"We have to, Enrico. My son's best friend died, and he did not falter. He used that death to try to bring freedom to my village. My son took a chance. And now, it is up to you to help my people become free. You must believe that by doing good, life becomes better. You see, down in the valley of my village, the residents live by three simple rules. After a storm, check your crops, thank God it wasn't worse, and move on. And I like to add one more thing to that saying, and that is when we move on, do so in such a way to make life better for yourself and for others. Grow and learn from your experience. Bring decency to the world by the way we live our lives."

Caruso said, "I'm a singer, Antonio. I use my God-given talent to provide entertainment for people. In return, I am blessed with fabulous wealth. And yet the riches mean nothing to me. My life is destroyed. The woman I loved, the woman whom I cared for, the woman who brought my children into this world, has run off, and not with someone above my station. No. She runs off with my driver. Do you realize the embarrassment and humiliation she has brought upon me? The press hounds me everywhere I go. They don't want to speak of my career; all they want to discuss is my personal life. I'm sorry for speaking so candidly to you. I have no one I can speak to. To my friends, I am the great tenor. When, in reality, I am nothing more than a failed man. I don't know where to turn."

Antonio, putting his right hand on the great tenor's shoulder, said, almost in a whisper, "*Vieni*. Come to Bellafortuna. Come sing one song in my village. Bring freedom to us. And through your actions, you may find freedom for yourself, freedom from your problems."

Caruso was silent for a moment, deep in thought. He then repeated the words, "Come to Bellafortuna," before becoming silent once again.

After a few more moments of silence, Caruso said, "You know, I cancelled my entire schedule of events this summer, save one. My friends thought I should still go to Palermo to get my honor. Then from Palermo, we are traveling to Tunis, to spend a week there to get away from everything, especially the press. So I kept my trip to Palermo scheduled. Perhaps destiny has played its hand. Your son's letter and your words have deeply moved me. I have never forgotten your son. When I met him that night in *Milano*, I knew there was something special about him. I want to see him again.

"*Verrò a Bellafortuna. (I will come to Bellafortuna.)* Transact whatever business you have in the mainland and then meet me back here in a week. You shall travel with me by boat back to Palermo. Late the night before the Festival in your village, I will travel from Palermo with you and my assistant, Marcello. I will sing in your village. But you must promise, as long as I am alive, no one will ever find out that I did this."

"I promise, Enrico."

"I hope by singing in your village, my fortune changes."

"It will, Enrico. It will."

"So, Giuseppe, that is why you found me here. I was having a few drinks with Caruso and his entourage before they left. He is meeting me much later tonight to come with me to Bellafortuna. I will go to *Signor* Bertocchi's stable to get my horse and cart to bring Caruso to the village. Only a very small contingent of his party knows what he is doing. Everyone believes that tomorrow he will be resting in his hotel room all day when in reality, he will be with us."

Giuseppe sat quietly at the table. He finally said, "Papa, I can't believe you did this. He is actually coming. Vittelio Vasaio will die tomorrow."

"Turiddu will be happy about that," Antonio said with a laugh. "There is one thing, Giuseppe. On the boat ride to Palermo, I told Caruso about your plan with Rodolfo and the clown costume. Caruso is adamant that he wants to wear the costume at the concert. He will even bring his makeup kit with him. He wants to have his face made up when he takes the stage. He is fully aware of the drama of the occasion and wants to enjoy it to the fullest. After all he has been through, I think he is using this opportunity to have a good time and forget about his troubles for a while."

"Papa, I love you."

"I love you too, Giuseppe. Tomorrow we make amends for the actions of Salvatore. Tomorrow at the Festival, we bring freedom to our friends. Now, come with me to get a bite to eat. After that, I want you to go home to prepare our house for our visitor later tonight. I'll see you later when I bring him."

"Papa, Rodolfo and Maria are going to be shocked when they find out."

"Let's not tell them. Let them and Mamma Lucia find out when Caruso and I get there much later tonight."

Giuseppe laughed and said, "They are going to kill me for not telling them."

"It will be worth it to see their reaction. Come, let's go eat."

"Papa, thank you."

"No, Giuseppe. Thank you."

AT THE VERY moment that Antonio and Giuseppe were having their conversation on the terrace in Palermo, Maria and Rodolfo arrived in Bellafortuna. The villagers paid little attention to the small cart that made its way to the stable behind the wine store.

Maria and Rodolfo went inside the store from the back door and were shown to the living quarters on the second floor by Mamma Lucia.

Later that night, Giuseppe returned alone. He sat down with Maria and Rodolfo in the living room. He said not a word to them about the events of earlier in the day. Mamma Lucia had already retired to bed.

After some small talk, Rodolfo said, "Maria has spoken to me all the way here. Giuseppe, I love you like a brother, but I cannot do what you ask. I'm sorry."

Maria's face showed total dejection. She couldn't raise her head to look at Giuseppe.

Giuseppe said, "It's all right, Rodolfo. I understand."

The three continued talking for quite some time about tomorrow but were interrupted by the sounds of heavy footsteps heard on the stairway leading from the wine store. Then the door to the Sanguinetti home was opened. Into the living room came Antonio, followed by two gentlemen, Caruso and his much taller assistant, Marcello. Giuseppe smiled. Maria looked at the shorter man and said, "*Gran Dio*." At the same moment, Rodolfo said, "*Ecco Caruso*." They all stood up.

Antonio said, "Enrico, may I introduce to you my son, Giuseppe Sanguinetti, a very special young lady, Maria, and your double, Rodolfo."

Everyone laughed as they all shook hands with the great tenor. Caruso looked at Giuseppe and said, "For you, tomorrow, I will sing 'Vesti la giubba'. This has become my signature song."

Giuseppe smiled and said in reply, "An excellent choice. Thank you so much for coming."

"I'm glad I'm here."

For a couple of hours thereafter, they sat up, drinking wine, listening to the stories related by Caruso about different singers, conductors and composers whom he had worked with over the years. Mamma Lucia, who had risen from her bed when she heard the commotion going on, served everyone *cassata alla siciliana*, a light cake filled with ricotta and candied fruits.

Giuseppe sat in disbelief. Here in his front room was the greatest tenor in the world, brought to his village by the man who meant the world to him, his father.

Later, while everyone prepared for bed, Mamma Lucia, at the request of Caruso, closed the shutters outside the windows, making sure no one could see any sign of life from outside.

For some time after everyone else had retired for the night, Caruso and Giuseppe continued talking about opera as well as Giuseppe's dream of bringing an opera house to the village of Bellafortuna. Afterward, they both retired to enjoy a well-earned peaceful sleep.

———————

THAT IS the story of how Enrico Caruso came to the village of Bellafortuna. It is now easy to understand the absolute shock felt by the villagers when Caruso took the stage at the Festival. It was a moment that no one believed would happen. And yet it did.

As Caruso continued singing the aria, the villagers sat in amazement at both the resonance and beauty of that voice as well as the fact that indeed Caruso had come. Vittelio Vasaio, on the other hand, buried his head into his hands.

Come back now to the Festival Boccale and the singing by Enrico Caruso of "Vesti la giubba" from Leoncavallo's *Pagliacci*.

VESTI LA GIUBBA AND THE SILENT OVATION

*T*he storyline for *Pagliacci* was based upon the composer Leoncavallo's personal remembrances when, as a young boy, he attended a murder trial presided over by his father as the trial judge. It was the trial of a jealous husband – a member of a traveling troupe – who was tried for killing his wife and her lover. Leoncavallo took that experience and created this opera of an interrelated story within a story by the use of the artistic and dramatic format of the *Commedia del Arte*, an unscripted and improvised Italian comedy but with standardized situations and set characters, and which was very popular during the 16th through the 18th centuries.

In the opera, a strolling group of players come to a small Italian village to perform a play. The lead tenor character, Canio, the clown, has just found out that his real-life wife, Nedda, has been cheating on him. In the aria, "Vesti la Giubba", Canio is preparing for the performance by putting on his clown makeup and costume, all the while trying to tell himself to go forward and put on a happy face. What makes matters even worse is that in the play, his wife assumes the role of Columbine, who is trying to run off with an admirer, Harlequin. Canio is distraught at having to go on with such a play while his own heart is breaking.

Enrico Caruso reached the apex of the magnificent aria. For Caruso, the words must have been haunting. On the stage in Bellafortuna that day, he sang with great emotion.

> *Vesti la giubba e la faccia in farina.*
> *Put on your costume and whiten your face.*

> *La gente paga, e rider vuole qua.*
> *The public is paying, and they want to laugh.*

> *E se Arlecchin t'invola Columbina,*
> *And if Harlequin steals your Columbine,*

> *ridi, Pagliaccio, e ognun applaudirà!*
> *laugh, clown, and they will applaud!*

> *Tramuta in lazzi lo spasmo ed io pianto;*
> *Change your tears and sorrows into jokes;*

> *in una smorfia il singhiozzo il dolor.*
> *change your sobbing into a laugh.*

Tears were visible running down Caruso's whitened face as he reached the climax of the aria. His entire body shook with emotion as his voice thundered forth.

Ridi, Pagliaccio, sul tuo amore infranto.
Laugh, clown, at your broken love.

Ridi del duol che t'avvelena il cor!
Laugh at the grief, that is poisoning your heart!

At the last note, Caruso's voice faded into tears as he grabbed his head with both hands and looked down at the stage. The villagers, sitting out in the Piazza, sat quietly at the end of the aria, stunned, before finally standing and erupting into applause.

Luigi, moved by the voice he had just heard, stood in front of the orchestra, his eyes blurred by tears.

Rodolfo Giulini looked over at Antonio and mouthed the words, "Incredible."

Antonio turned to Marcello Panzeca and said, "That is the greatest voice God has ever put on this earth."

Marcello nodded his head in agreement and replied, "I have never heard him sing with such emotion before. I'm sure the words to the aria renewed thoughts of his wife."

Vittelio Vasaio and Ada were the only people not clapping in the Piazza. They sat in their seats, staring blankly at the stage and at the figure of Caruso, who by now had extended his hands outward, accepting the warm applause of the audience. Next to Vittelio, Santo was standing, cheering wildly for the Neapolitan tenor. As Santo did so, he caught Giuseppe's eye. Giuseppe smiled broadly at his good friend.

To every villager in the audience that day, and particularly the members of the *Società della Libertà per Bellafortuna*, their feelings of joy at hearing the great tenor in person were surpassed by the realization that the grip of Vittelio Vasaio would now be lessened. For the first time, in the long history of the village since the arrival of the Vasaios, the villagers would be able to recapture some element of control over their lives.

Giuseppe looked out toward the wine store and saw Maria. She brought her hands up to her lips and, with a big smile, blew him a kiss from across the Piazza. Giuseppe then turned his head slightly and noticed Padre Mancini. The priest had tears in his eyes. Padre Mancini brought his hands up in front of him as if in prayer and nodded his head and hands toward Giuseppe. As he did this, Giuseppe thought how much he had come to love the priest. He also thought back to his very short tenure as an acolyte, and that first day when he met Biaggio. How he wished his good friend could have lived to see this day. Thinking of Biaggio made Giuseppe survey the crowd to find Dondo. When he found him, Dondo raised a finger toward heaven to let Giuseppe know that Dondo knew well that Biaggio was smiling today on the events down in the Piazza. Victoria was smiling at Giuseppe through tears streaming down her face; she knew what this day meant to Dondo and Biaggio.

As Giuseppe looked around the rest of the Piazza, his eyes locked onto Vittelio Vasaio's eyes. Vittelio was still seated near the front of the stage. The superiority and swagger that was always perceivable in Vittelio's face and body were now gone. He looked like a beaten, disgusted old man. Giuseppe bore his stare deeply into Vittelio's mind and soul. The old man stared back intently. Finally, Vittelio closed his eyes and solemnly bowed his head toward Giuseppe. At that moment, Giuseppe became overwhelmed with the full realization that he had won the wager.

As the clapping continued throughout the Piazza, Caruso raised his hands in an attempt to quiet the crowd. Luigi aided him in trying to quiet the crowd. However, the excitement among the crowd was too great to make this an easy task.

Finally, the crowd quieted down. Caruso stood at the very front of the stage. Luigi spoke and said, "*Commendatore* Caruso would like to say a few words to us."

Caruso said, "I have sung in front of hundreds of thousands of people in all of the greatest opera houses all over the world, yet today has been the best reception I have ever received."

The villagers of Bellafortuna cheered again. Caruso continued, "I would like to thank the Sanguinettis for providing me with this opportunity."

"Bravo Antonio. Bravo Giuseppe," the crowd chanted.

Caruso continued, "I would ask that Antonio come join me on the stage." As Antonio made his way to the stage, Caruso said, "I was asked to sing one song at the Festival. And so I have. However, as a tenor in opera, there is one song I never have the opportunity to sing. It's a choral song by the great composer, Giuseppe Verdi. In talking with the Sanguinettis, I know how important this song is to all of you. So as a token of appreciation to all of you, I will sing it for you, and I would ask that you join in as well."

Antonio reached the stage and shook hands with Caruso. Caruso then turned to Giuseppe and made him come stand next to him and his father on the stage. Luigi brought his baton up and began the music to "Va, pensiero."

Dating all the way back to 1842, when Verdi's opera first appeared, the choral anthem probably had never been sung better or with more emotion than that day at the Festival

Boccale. With Caruso leading the way, the entire village sang the song. Midway through, Vittelio and Ada got up out of their seats and returned to their home, followed by the *Scagnozzi dei Vasaios*.

When the song was completed, people wept openly as they yelled their bravos. Antonio turned to Caruso and extended his hand. The tenor pushed the hand aside and hugged the elder Sanguinetti. Caruso then turned to Giuseppe.

Giuseppe said, "*Grazie*. I thank you for coming."

"A promise is a promise, amico. And in return, I have found a place of decency and grace left in the world."

Giuseppe hugged Caruso. He then went over to his father and hugged him. Antonio whispered into his ear, "Now the sins of your grandfather are truly repented for. We have made it up to our villagers."

"We have, Papa. Indeed we have."

AFTER COMPLETING THE SONG, Caruso was led through the adoring crowd to the wine store so that he could change his clothes and take off the clown makeup. A short time later, when he reappeared, he was seated at a table as food was placed in front of him, with the women of the village all vying to have the great tenor taste one of their dishes.

Seated at the table with Caruso were Antonio, Mamma Lucia, Giuseppe, Maria, Rodolfo, the Monsignor and Padre Mancini, as well as Luigi and Marcello, Caruso's assistant. There was an open spot next to Giuseppe for Santo to sit, but he was nowhere to be seen. Giuseppe stood up and looked around the Piazza to see if he could find him.

Off near the statue of Enzo Boccale, Santo was standing next to Giacomo Terranova, who was introducing young Vasaio to his seventeen year-old daughter, Mirella. She was dressed in her new outfit by Fiorenza.

When Santo finally made his way over to the table, he was a nervous wreck. He asked Giuseppe if Mirella was seeing anyone. Giuseppe, without hesitation, said she was not. Santo confessed to Giuseppe that he was attracted to the girl and would like to see her again. Giuseppe had to smile to himself as he thought how many times poor Giacomo had paraded his daughters through the Piazza and that it might finally result in a match, with none other than the son of Vittelio Vasaio.

Meanwhile, Mamma Lucia was busy serving her spizatedda. She quickly put a bowl of it in front of Caruso. As he partook, he said he envied the men who were fed daily by such a cook. Mamma Lucia was in love.

As Caruso ate, more and more villagers came over to say a word of thanks to the tenor. He was very gracious in his responses. Turiddu brought over a plate of lasagna for the great tenor to taste. Caruso savored every bite. Turiddu was very pleased.

Turiddu then turned and came over to Giuseppe. He patted him on his back and said, "Young Sanguinetti, I owe you an apology. You and your father came through for us. What both of you have done will never be forgotten. What a day!" Giuseppe stood up and hugged Turiddu, letting him know there were no hard feelings for all that had transpired before.

Shortly, Luigi made his way back to the stage to continue with the concert. At the request of Giuseppe, Rodolfo followed Luigi to the stage. Rodolfo sang aria after aria from the stage, as people continued eating. The villagers were very impressed with his voice. Even the great tenor took notice. During the next intermission, when Rodolfo returned to the table, Caruso gave Rodolfo the name of a prominent teacher in Palermo.

Caruso said, "I will see him tomorrow. I will tell him you will be calling and that I liked your voice. You will have a career, young man." Caruso leaned forward and whispered into his ear, "And not a career impersonating me."

Rodolfo laughed. Maria came over and hugged her brother, whose dream had finally been given hope.

Caruso sat at the table, listening to the music and telling everyone seated around him stories from behind the scenes of the opera world. By this time, many villagers had pulled seats near the table so that they could listen to the stories.

As the Festival began to come to a close hours later, everyone approached Caruso and thanked him for coming. Giuseppe and Santo left the festivities to go retrieve the cart in which they would bring Caruso back to Palermo.

When they returned, they parked the cart close to the table where Caruso was seated. As Caruso and Marcello made their way to the cart, Giuseppe stole a few minutes to speak to Maria.

She said, "I can't believe he came. I'm so happy for you."

"Thanks for being there for me. You mean everything to me."

"I'm glad to hear that, Giuseppe. You mean everything to me. When we get married, I want to live in Bellafortuna."

"We will, Maria. *Giuro*! I swear! *Sei tutta la mia vita.*" (*You are my whole life.*)

As Caruso and Marcello reached the cart, Giacinto Bordelli approached Caruso and said, "For your remembrance of your visit to our village, I present to you this painting."

The painting was of a view from the valley looking up toward the village of Bellafortuna.

Caruso replied, "I thank you for this gift. It will always allow me to remember this day and this place. It will have a place of honor in my home."

Caruso and Marcello climbed into the cart along with Giuseppe and Santo. Caruso, while standing, said to everyone who had circled around it, "Coming here today has meant a lot to me, more than you will ever know. Antonio Sanguinetti told me that his village of Bellafortuna was a magical place. And the reason is due to its people. That is a sentiment with which I agree completely. *Addio*."

The cart began to leave the village. Without any planning or prior discussions, the villagers spontaneously formed lines on both sides of the road leading out of the Piazza to the *Via Valle*. As Caruso passed by in the cart, every villager bowed to him. Not a word was spoken nor a sound made, except for the rolling of the cartwheels and the click-clack of the pony's hoofs striking the ground.

Standing by a window in the *Palazzo*, with his hands behind his back, Vittelio Vasaio watched the moving spectacle down in the Piazza. He was surprised by the solemnity of what was occurring. The villagers were not gloating in their victory. Instead, they were showing respect for Caruso and the occasion. Perhaps, Vittelio thought, there was more substance to these people than he and his ancestors believed.

The cart carrying Caruso made its way out of the Piazza. Throughout his life, Caruso was generous with his voice. Little did people know how generous he was with his heart. His generosity was always a very private thing for him. That day, the villagers of Bellafortuna were made aware of it.

Caruso left the village with tears in his eyes. For the remainder of his life, whenever asked, he said that the greatest and most moving "ovation" and moment he ever experienced as a singer occurred many years ago when he departed a Sicilian Village, a village he never would name. To his closest friends, he always referred to it as "the silent ovation."

When the cart reached the *Via Boccale*, Caruso asked Giuseppe to stop the cart. Marcello and Caruso got out of the cart. Santo and Giuseppe got out as well.

The sun was setting in the west, just over the last line of hills. Sitting on top of the plateau, in all of its majesty, was the village of Bellafortuna, glistening in its golden glow from the setting sun. Looking at the village, Caruso said, "It is a magical place. Giuseppe, I have something here for you. A little token of my esteem. This trip has done wonders for me."

Caruso reached into his pocket and pulled out a piece of paper. As he handed it to Giuseppe, Caruso's face had a wry, whimsical smile upon it. On the paper, Caruso had drawn a picture of Rodolfo Giulini, dressed in the clown costume. Above Rodolfo's head, Caruso had written the words, " 'Va, pensiero', Bellafortuna, July 28, 1908." Below the drawing, he had written, "*Ecco Caruso!*" (*Here is Caruso!*)

Giuseppe looked at the drawing and laughed. Caruso was

laughing too. However, he grew serious and said, "Giuseppe, my little drawing is a tribute to your courage and your father's decency."

Touched, Giuseppe said, "*Commendatore* Caruso, you have no idea what your coming here today means to me and to all of my fellow villagers. We all owe you a debt which we will never be able to repay."

Caruso said in reply, "You don't owe me a thing. This was a much-needed trip for me. I will never forget your beautiful village."

Giuseppe replied, "And we will never forget the day Caruso came to sing in Bellafortuna."

They climbed back into the cart and continued down the road on their way to Palermo.

AFTER LEAVING Caruso at the *Grand Hotel et des Palmes*, Santo and Giuseppe made the return trip to Bellafortuna. It was dark as they traveled along the road. They spoke about the events of the day during the entire journey.

While on the road to Bellafortuna, they passed the dilapidated home of Ettore Fizzarotti. Pointing to the home, Santo said to Giuseppe, "That is where it all began. My visit to that home changed my life forever. I wonder what old man Fizzarotti is thinking tonight. A new day begins for him tomorrow. And it's all because of you and your father."

Giuseppe replied, "And you, Santo. Soon our village will once again have a winery and olive presses, and we will once again produce *Vino e Olio di Bellafortuna* and sell it outside of our community. The villagers of Bellafortuna will see the rewards for their hard work. And they will work hand in hand with the Vasaios in making this village rise in prominence."

Santo smiled and said, "And then, in turn, the amphitheater will be turned into an opera house. Your dream will be fulfilled."

Giuseppe said in reply, "*Si.* And at the start of every performance, the orchestra will play 'Va, pensiero', as the entire crowd sings along."

"I can't wait to see it, Giuseppe."

"Neither can I."

They reached the junction with the road leading to *Antica Campanèlla* and stopped momentarily. Santo said, "One day, the villagers will speak of you and your father as they do of Enzo Boccale. Biaggio would be very proud of you."

"I merely followed through with a last request of a dying friend."

Santo put his hand on Giuseppe's shoulder and said, "You did good. You did really good."

The two friends traveled to the Pandolfini stable to put the cart away for the night. After doing so, they entered the wine store from the back door.

The Sanguinetti wine store was all lit up. Seated around the store were Antonio, Turiddu, Giorgio, Giacomo, Dondo, Salvatore, Fiorenza, Giacinto and Luigi as well as a few other members of the *Società della Libertà per Bellafortuna.*

Upon Giuseppe and Santo entering the store, everyone inside erupted in applause. Giuseppe asked what everyone was doing over so late.

"Making plans for the winery and olive presses," replied Turiddu.

Giuseppe said with a laugh, "Without question, this is the hardest working *Società* in the world. They don't even take a break to celebrate."

Giacomo said, "No time, Giuseppe. You gave us freedom, and we will not let our chance slip by."

Turiddu meanwhile walked over to Santo and extended his hand. He said, "*Grazie*, Santo. What you did for us took courage. Little did we know it, but our years of oppression finally came to an end through the actions of the sons of the two most powerful people in the village, Vittelio Vasaio and Antonio Sanguinetti. What you have done for us will never be forgotten."

Choked by tears, Santo could only reply with, "*Prego, Signor.*"

Giuseppe smiled. Tomorrow would beckon a new day for the village of Bellafortuna. A village that knew it had finally been blessed by grace.

EPILOGUE

VINO AND OLIO BELLAFORTUNA

*V*ittelio Vasaio, the man whom every villager long despised, showed in the end that he was a changed man. He abided by the terms of the wager and immediately reduced the interest charges, thus allowing the villagers to sell their product to the cooperative wineries and olive oil companies that Vittelio had dealt with in the past. With the profit this generated, the villagers were able to turn funds over to Antonio to help in the rebuilding of the Boccale Winery and olive presses.

In 1910, the Boccale Winery and olive presses were rebuilt, and production began in earnest. Both facilities were built on the location of the old Boccale Winery near *Antica Campanèlla*. Once again, *Vino e Olio di Bellafortuna* were on the market. Antonio and Giuseppe ran the winery and olive presses as well as the wine store. They paid full value for the villagers' harvests.

Even after the Boccale Winery and olive presses had been

rebuilt and production began with significant profits for the villagers, the people of Bellafortuna retained their traditions and remained good, decent people, caring for their village, their community and for one another. After all, that is at the heart of what it is to be human.

Giuseppe married Maria Giulini in 1910, and the two lived with Antonio and Mamma Lucia above the wine store. Within two years of their marriage, in 1912, they were blessed with a son-Biaggio Antonio Sanguinetti.

With the Boccale Winery and olive presses in full production, the residents of Bellafortuna thrived. Once again, harvest time became a celebration of life. Within several years, all the debts owed Vittelio were paid off, and thereafter the harvests' profits came directly to the villagers.

It took a long time for the mutual feelings of dislike to entirely disappear between the villagers and Vittelio. But over time, these feelings were replaced with respect. It helped that Santo ended up marrying Giacomo Terranova's daughter, which marriage produced a son, Matteo Vasaio.

Vittelio Vasaio died in 1916. The villagers paid their respects; they attended the funeral Mass. Santo took over from his father. He did whatever he could to help the villagers make a good life for themselves.

With the substantial profits from the wine and olive oil businesses, the amphitheater in *Antica Campanèlla* - around the year 1920 - was cleaned up and converted into a viable facility to hold opera performances. Giuseppe Sanguinetti was named the General Director of the Opera, and Luigi, the head conductor of the *Opera Orchestra di Bellafortuna*. The amphitheater was duly christened the *Anfiteatro di Bellafortuna*.

The first performance at the *Anfiteatro* occurred on June 14, 1921. Giuseppe had kept up a correspondence with Enrico Caruso over the years and hoped that he would be available to sing at the opening of the house. But Caruso's health was in decline. Just two months after the opening performance, Caruso returned to Naples at the age of 48 to eat pasta and die.

Nabucco, of course, was the first opera performed at the *Anfiteatro di Bellafortuna*. Rodolfo Giulini, after a successful season at La Scala, sang the tenor lead, and through friendship, got the great baritone, Luigi Montesanto, to sing the title role. Rodolfo Giulini would be a regular at the *Anfiteatro* every year thereafter, until his retirement from the stage in the 1930s after a hugely successful singing career.

At the first performance, before the start of the opera, Luigi entered the pit. The orchestra stood up and played the chorus, "Va, pensiero". The audience members sang along. This would be the custom at the beginning of every performance. It was the villagers' way of remembering their past.

As the years passed, the *Anfiteatro di Bellafortuna* did very well. The *Opera Orchestra di Bellafortuna* was supplemented with twenty-five off-season musicians from the orchestra of the *Teatro Massimo* in Palermo. Soon, people from all over Italy made the journey to Bellafortuna to see the opera performances during the summer festival. Giuseppe kept very busy trying to organize the season every year. As such, Santo Vasaio began to help Antonio and Giuseppe with the running of the Boccale Winery and olive presses.

ANTONIO SANGUINETTI DIED IN 1931. Monsignor Pietro Mancini said the funeral Mass. Mancini had remained in his beloved village all these years, caring for the people whom he had grown to love over the course of his ministry. He never wore French cuffs.

Antonio was buried next to Biaggio's final resting spot, near the *Stagno Azzuro,* across from the *Anfiteatro di Bellafortuna,* so that even during their final, peaceful rest, they could both hear the music during the summer opera festival.

After Antonio's death, Santo Vasaio was named as the head of the Boccale Winery and olive presses. Giuseppe gladly relinquished control to Santo, since he was so busy with the opera company and the wine store.

Santo continued the same management style as Antonio, and the winery and olive presses continued to bring prosperity and prestige to the villagers of Bellafortuna.

AUTHOR NOTE

When writing a novel, the initial creative flash of an idea and the first few tentative steps of the writing process are all performed singularly by the author. Yet, by the time the novel is presented to the public, many people have had a part to play in seeing it come to fruition. This novel was no different, and I, therefore, have many people to thank, and a few in particular, who I would like to mention here.

I first must thank Allison Cohen, a literary agent at the Gersh Agency, who championed this book and really worked closely with me on making it a better story. I also owe a great deal of debt to my two dear friends, Stephanie Quinlan and Kathy Schott, who helped me immensely, working out many details in the novel.

I also thank my children, Matthew and Ellie, for providing me the inspiration. I also thank my parents, Vincent and Lynda LoCoco, and my sisters, Pam Montz and Beth Doody, for all of their input. And lastly, I thank my wife, Wendy, who always believed in this story. Instead of embarrassing her by saying how I feel about her, I will just quote an Errol Flynn movie: "Walking through life with you Ma'am, has been a very gracious thing."

I must also thank three individuals who really made this book sing – and which also has provided an international flair to the novel. Signora Giuseppina "Pinuccia" Cellini, the wife of the late Italian opera conductor, Renato Cellini, provided all of the English translations of the opera arias and choruses used in the novel. Signorina Federica Carbotti, of Martina Franca, Italy, helped me with the Italian phrases used throughout the novel. And lastly, I am indebted to Ana Grigoriu, of Stuggart, Germany, who designed the fabulous cover.

A vital ingredient in this story has been my personal experience of living my life in the midst of the Sicilian-American community of New Orleans. They have lived with a dedication to their faith, their families, their culture, the community in which they live, good food, good wine, and opera.

Grazie.

Vincent B. "Chip" LoCoco
New Orleans, Louisiana

LISTEN TO TO THE MUSIC OF A SONG FOR BELLAFORTUNA

We have put together a Spotify Playlist with music from the novel along with some traditional songs from Sicily to give the reader a flavor of this magical region in the world. Be sure to follow it to get updates.

The Spotify Playlist can be found as:

THE MUSIC OF A SONG FOR BELLAFORTUNA

ABOUT THE AUTHOR

Vincent B. "Chip" LoCoco, lives in New Orleans with his wife and two children. His novels, *Tempesta's Dream – A Story of Love, Friendship and Opera* and *A Song For Bellafortuna* have became Amazon bestselling novels and both have been named as a Top Rated Novels in Italian Historical Fiction. He is currently at work on his next novel, *Saving the Music,* which is book 2 in his Bellafortuna Series. It is set to be released in Spring 2020.

facebook.com / Authorchiplococo
twitter.com / VincentBLoCoco
amazon.com / author / vincentlococo

MORE INFORMATION

THE STORY OF BELLAFORTUNA CONTINUES

Be sure to check out

SAVING THE MUSIC

Book 2 of Vincent LoCoco's Bellafortuna Series

If you would like to let others know about this novel, please consider leaving a review on Amazon.

If your group or book club is interested in inviting Mr. LoCoco to discuss his novels or the writing process in person or by Skype, please use the contact form on his website at www.vincentlococo.com.

Lightning Source UK Ltd.
Milton Keynes UK
UKHW010640020620
364265UK00002B/314